THE BOOK OF DANIEL

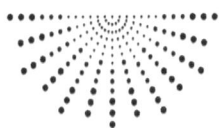

Z.A. MAXFIELD

For everyone who needs a little St. Nacho's in their life.

CHAPTER ONE

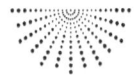

I grinned when the waiter brought me a clean ashtray. It was
a Monday kind of grin.

It was an I-got-drunk-and-stoned-and-screwed-around-all-
weekend, barely-crawled-out-of-bed lift of the muscles that
parenthesized my lips. On a dog, you'd call it fair warning.

I'd been having a lot of Mondays like that. I'd even hit the
trifecta of fucked-up Monday mornings the week before when
I'd woken up in a stranger's home in Santa Monica with no
memory and a really kickass kanji tattoo on my right shoulder.

Really kickass.

I had no idea what it meant, but it looked good.

And maybe my brother Jake would have had a thing or two
to say about that sort of shit if I let him in on it, like...maybe
he'd have said I'm not a shallow guy and I'm just having a
midlife crisis, but I am and I'm not, respectively. I was on the
trail of tears to forty, newly divorced, newly out and proud, and
I didn't give a damn.

It wasn't like I hadn't tried to do everything right, because I
had tried. Hard. I'd made my mother happy when she was alive.
I'd treated my wife well even though she left me for some other

asshole, thank fuck. I'd let her get away with the house, her car, and an income because I was not a monster. My father was a monster, and I knew what one of those was like.

So really, I was not a monster.

I was just a guy who finally, finally had the chance to get it right. And it was my turn to pick and choose.

My second vodka Mary had appeared on the table next to my good elbow while I'd been sitting there, eyes closed, drifting. Enjoying the buzz from my first drink and the warm flush of nicotine.

The sound of the waves hitting the sand behind me was soothing. It interspersed with children playing, the sound of two or three portable radios, and seabirds. As grim as the morning had started out, the day promised high temperatures. People had come early, prepared to stake out their territory and wait for the sun to burn off the clouds. I could feel its radiant warmth on my face and shoulders even though the light breeze off the water was chilly.

I ate my olive slowly, savoring its salty, bitter aftertaste. The chair was comfortable. I found if I crossed my feet at the ankles and slunk down a bit, it supported my head and shoulders, and I could avoid that sprawled, knees-splayed appearance while I relaxed...

"Dan?"

"Hm?"

"Dan, are you asleep?"

I shook my head. Hell no I wasn't asleep. I was just resting my eyes. *Wasn't I?* A quick scan of my surroundings revealed my cigarette had burned to ash and my drink had a thick layer of water at the top.

"Shoot. Sorry, yeah, I think I was." I pushed up in my chair to shake the cobwebs out of my brain. "Wild weekend."

Jake sat down and shot me a smile I think he might have invented just for me. There was never any disappointment in that shy half-moon of perfect white teeth and lips. It had begun to appear on his face long before he'd even had those incisors that were evident now when what his mouth revealed had been like the tiny white Chiclets in gimme-sized boxes of gum people handed out on Halloween.

"Where'd you go?"

"Santa Barbara. Up in the hills. Nice place. You'd have liked it. We went to a place for brunch yesterday that was out of this world."

"Yeah? Who'd you go with?"

I shrugged. "Some guy I met at Sandpiper. Stunning course. Really beautiful. First-rate golf. I want to go back sometime. Want to come?"

Jakey shook his head. "*Golf.* As if."

"You mock now, but someday the golf bug will get you."

"Hardly. Golf has to be the most effete, boring fucking game...Bunch of guys hunting for a little white ball. Oh, woe is me. The ball is in the sand. Call me when that sand explodes."

"Do you actually *want* the sand to explode?"

He frowned. "No. But there has to be a happy medium between almost getting killed and I'm going to drive this little cart off a cliff just to make something happen. Anyway, how are you golfing with that?" He indicated my hand.

Yeah. My hand was still in a brace, still showing the effects of a brutal crush injury and several surgeries. The bones of my wrist were barely mended, the radius and ulna held together with titanium strips and pins and screws.

My bionic arm. Except—unlike Steve Austin's—it was weak and pale and scarred and useless.

"I can't hit the long-range balls because my grip is fucked-up, but I can still putt. I found someone who"—heaven help me, the memory of the three days I'd spent with Julio made me blush and shift in my seat like an adolescent boy—"likes to drive."

"You went and just picked some guy up? Again?" Jake didn't want me to think he was on board with me fucking around. To be fair, he probably wasn't done reeling from the revelation that I was gay. I kicked his foot with mine, looking down at our hairy ankles. We wore nearly identical leather boat shoes, and our legs were tanned.

What is it about living in a beach town that makes a guy go without socks? Before I'd come to St. Nacho's, I could count on the fingers of one hand the number of times I had worn shoes without socks. Each time there'd been a reason, like I had fallen into a pool, or I was on a Caribbean island vacation.

This...this new boat-shoe-and-no-sock thing was just me not bothering anymore.

"So how'd you meet this...driver?"

"Oh, that's a funny story, actually. I met him at Nordstrom's. I had to go shopping. BreeAnna, the little woman, finally sent my clothes."

"Yeah? It's about damn time."

Originally my housekeeper was supposed to pack up what little I was taking away from my twelve-year marriage to Bree-Anna. I'd been buying things—like a pair of jeans or a pack of tightie whities at a time, as needed, thinking my clothes would arrive any day. But Bree fired the housekeeper when she realized I cared about the woman, and there followed negotiations through lawyers and a great deal of obfuscation. I'd waited for most of my clothes for four long months.

"It didn't go quite as well as I expected."

Jake's face fell. "What happened?"

"She ran everything I owned through an industrial shredder first."

"What the hell?" He motioned the waiter over and asked for a beer. I indicated I wanted another Mary.

"Well, I may be exaggerating a little, but nothing was wearable. She shredded my business clothes, poured paint on my

4

casual stuff. Cut the toes off my socks and drew targets on my underwear. You have to admire her determination. If we'd put half that effort into the marriage it might have worked out."

"You know that's not true. You tried."

Jake always believed the best of me. He *needed* to believe I'd treated BreeAnna with compassion and caring—to see me as basically good. But I'd picked a fragile girl and married her, knowing ahead of time that I could never, ever love her like she deserved to be loved.

Jake saw me as a man who did what was right and suffered for it. Except that's not who I was, and I didn't have the stones to tell him.

"I deserve nothing but contempt from her, and we both know it. I'll buy a new wardrobe for each of us if that's what it takes to get through this." I reached for my cigarettes and lit one up. I couldn't help it any more than I could help avoiding the sadness I knew I'd find in his eyes.

Smoke screen in the truest sense of the word.

The waiter brought our drinks and set them down on cocktail napkins. Afterward, he took my empties and replaced my ashtray with a clean one.

I nodded to him. "Thanks."

"You're welcome." He winked before he left, and I wondered if he was one of the many, many young men I'd danced with here at Nacho's when I first got to town. He might even be someone I'd taken back to the hotel Jake and I had lived in until we found our place. Fuck if I knew. I was newly single and ready to belly up to the Y-chromosome buffet at that point, and my hunger apparently hadn't abated just yet, or I wouldn't have noticed how those tight black pants highlighted our waiter's fine, firm ass.

"You're such a hound."

"Guilty as charged. And it's working for me."

Jake relaxed back into his chair with his beer. "I knew you'd cut a swath through all the gay men in this place, but I thought that arm would slow you down a little."

I lifted my hand and looked at it. My fingers had been crushed and bore the alarming tracery of thin white scars. My wrist and arm were thin and pale, obviously cut open and closed over a number of surgeries. There had been skin grafts. I knew he didn't mean it that way, but it was a source of irritation to me—that wretched, noticeable imperfection. I'm hardly perfect, but I'd traded on the gift of above average—some people had called them extraordinary—good looks and wads of cash for a long time.

"It's not so bad. It's a miracle they saved it. For a few days after the accident I thought I'd become some kind of campfire story, the guy with the claw for a hand who—"

"Don't joke about that." Jake pressed his lips together.

Chastened, I said, "All right."

"I swear I'd have traded places with you in a second."

I shook my head. "I wouldn't want that. You know I wouldn't." No way in hell.

"I know."

"So…" I glanced around. "Are we gonna eat or what?"

He shifted in his seat, glancing at the patio door toward the restaurant where even now Cooper, the violinist who played during the dinner hour, was tuning up. I realized something was up.

"What's going on?"

Jake smiled. "I'm expecting JT."

"Yeah?" *What a surprise.* Jake and JT had been inseparable since the accident where I'd hurt my hand. It was kind of sweet really if you liked that sort of thing. "His idea or yours?"

"His."

It was hard to even look at him, he was so gone in love. If I'd cherished any notion that someday Jake and I would play the field together, share bachelor digs, drink too much and party and wind up owning a brothel in Cabo, JT had effectively disabused me of it. He was a decent, hardworking, and fairly sober family man. Jake idolized him. There was no downside to this except the obvious one: I wasn't ready to relinquish my brother to JT because I had all this newfound freedom—at last —and I wanted Jake to share it with me.

I took a drag off my cigarette and looked away. I know I'm a prick. Sometimes I shame myself. But even that might not stop me.

"So, why Nacho's on a Monday night?"

"We both had the day off, and we thought it might be fun. Dinner with the family."

I nodded. In that he was right. He and I were the only family we had.

My ears picked up the strains of some pretty tune. Cooper was playing the hell out of whatever it was as usual. I'd once read a news story about a famous concert violinist who played in the subway as an experiment, but I'd never been privileged to hear anyone of his caliber up close, playing whatever I wanted. For a few bucks and a smile, Cooper gave you a musical experience you could never get anywhere else. It was like an immense, unexpected gift, and the people of St. Nacho's were smart enough to cherish it.

Cooper's violin was part of the magic of St. Nacho's. Part of the sticky satisfaction Jake found here, what kept him grounded and caused him to open his bakery a couple of streets over. I was always glad to listen, glad to put my money into the hat and grateful for the experience, but St. Nacho's didn't suck me in the way it had Jake.

I liked the vibe of the place. I liked Nacho's Bar. I liked the beach and the bakery, but whenever I had the chance, I headed north to San Francisco or south to LA. I made stops in Santa Barbara for the music and the art. I went to Santa Monica for sex.

I wasn't Jake. With the end of my marriage, I'd proved something important to myself about the kind of man I was, and I had my freedom to look forward to.

I'd told the last lie I was ever going to tell.

Jake stood up when JT appeared at the door.

CHAPTER TWO

"H ere he is." Jake's smile went critical and flooded the area around us with happiness. "Hi, babe."

"Hey." JT embraced my brother warmly and gave him a kiss.

"Dan." JT turned to me and offered his hand. I took it with my bionic dexter and noticed he was gentle when he held it in his. He'd been the EMT to triage and treat me when they pulled me from the car after the accident, and while he'd seen a thousand injuries like mine—and far worse—he'd taken his time and been genuinely compassionate. I'd always be grateful for that. "Good to see you."

"You too," I answered. *Gzzzzzzt*. The lie detector in my head mocked me only minutes after I'd declared myself prevarication-free.

I looked behind JT and saw Cam Rooney walk in. I glanced up at him in some surprise. Both JT and Cam? To what did we owe the pleasure?

Cam raised a supercilious eyebrow—something you don't expect from a brute like him—and stayed silent. It was no secret that Cam and I hadn't exactly become BFFs. That was odd, really, and I'm sure he attributed it to sour grapes, since he was on the crew that cut my Lexus in half with the Jaws of Life, and I'd teased him about it. Not so. My gratitude for the men of the St. Nacho's fire department was genuine. It was only Cam who chapped my ass. I had the feeling he didn't think too much of me either.

The thing is, I was on constant alert around the man because he did something to my gut—something that made me go all boneless and vulnerable—and I knew if I didn't protect myself, I'd fall into his blue eyes and drown. I might have let myself do just that if it weren't for the fact that once I sank to the bottom, I'd only be one of hundreds, thousands maybe who'd done the very same thing.

"Well, if it isn't the abominable fireman."

Cam's smile didn't fool me for a second. "That just never gets old."

"Cut it out, you two." Jake buffeted me with his shoulder. "You're like toddlers."

"But he cut my car in half." I am not above making a bad situation worse. "I want it back."

"I suppose you'd like the use of your hand back too." Cam pulled out his chair and sat down, startling me. "Must get pretty lonely without it."

"You would know." Jake always invited me, and JT always invited Cam. I assumed they'd given up any matchmaking aspirations because it seemed clear we couldn't thaw out, but maybe they just did it because it added a weird kind of tension, like sweet and sour. Like every party needed contrast, and we were it.

I finally opened up the menu and glanced at the selections, although it was perfectly obvious what I would order. I always ordered the same thing when the four of us went to Nacho's together—anything with shrimp in it—because Cam was allergic to shellfish. Why I did that, I don't know, except he looked at my shrimp with longing, and I liked to get his goat.

St. Nacho's was a small town, and there wasn't a lot to do. Certainly nothing much more fun than finding myself the object of Cam Rooney's undivided attention, even if it wasn't the good kind. Jake argued that I spent too much time on things like that, but from the moment we'd met, and even after he'd saved my life, I'd had an unholy jones for the big blond fireman. Maybe the thing I liked was his corny fresh-faced charm. Maybe it was the fact that we were the two biggest players in St. Nacho's.

Maybe it was because he looked at me like he knew exactly who I was, and he found it disappointing. Even so, I shivered whenever he caught my gaze across the table.

The waiter brought appetizers and with them beer for all of us. I shoved a lime into the neck of my bottle and sipped it slowly because I was already enjoying a really good buzz. Once JT and Cam arrived, smoking was out, but that was okay. Once the platter of nachos, taquitos, and chips with homemade guacamole came, there wasn't much need for the emotional camouflage of tobacco.

JT and Jake lived in a happy world all their own. Cam and I might as well be furniture for all we mattered.

Big platters of fajitas arrived, steaming and sizzling on flat cast-iron skillets. Grilled chicken and beef for them and shrimp for me, along with soft, chewy homemade tortillas, caramelized vegetables, and fresh salsa. Nobody talks much while they're eating at Nacho's. The food is too damn good. But after we'd put away the better part of our meal, JT seemed on edge—more so than I'd seen in a while.

"How's work? Everything okay?"

He blushed. "It's fine. We had a long weekend. Couple of bad wrecks on the highway."

"You seem a little tense."

"I'm just hungry I guess." JT's gaze fell to his food.

I glanced at Jake, but he didn't look up from his plate. I

watched him nervously shovel beans into a tortilla. One thing you learn when you live in an unhappy home—and I had lived in those all my life—was when things have gone from sugar to shit, you have to find out why fast. Bad things happen when you don't pay attention to subtext.

"What's going on?" I put down my fork.

Cam and JT exchanged glances. All three pairs of eyes turned to me.

Great. Everyone knew whatever it was except me.

JT took Jake's hand in his. "We were going to wait for dessert, but I guess we can say this now. I've asked Yasha to marry me, and he's accepted."

Whatever I was expecting, it wasn't that, and I didn't have time to school my face. I wish I could take that back because whatever Jake—Yasha as people called him in St. Nacho's—saw caused his eyes to cloud with sadness. I smoothed my napkin in my lap with both hands to stall for time, but when that ran out, I went after the conversational ball I'd dropped.

"Congratulations. That's great. I thought it wasn't legal."

Jake swallowed hard, and JT answered for both of them. "It isn't legal under the California constitution, but we'll be having a commitment ceremony with our rabbi, and that's…"

"It will be legal someday." Cam spoke quietly. "But a commitment belongs to the people who make it."

I sat back in my chair and told my second lie of the night. "That's…that's just great, then. I'm happy for you. Have you decided when?"

"June."

"That soon?"

"Danilo. I need to know…will you be my best man?"

There was an awkward, awful pause until JT said, "Cam's going to be mine. You're still on board, right?"

Cam's smile was genuine. "Yeah." Cam clasped JT's hand and pulled him in for a big bear hug. "You got it. Whatever you need.

I don't suppose you'll let me throw you a huge, nasty bachelor party, 'cause that could—"

"I don't think that will be necessary. We're going to have an engagement party. Maybe you could help with that?"

"You can count on me." Cam's grin was wide and guileless.

I finally found my voice. "Me too."

Three gazes leveled at me, and they all communicated an appalling lack of faith.

"Really." I fiddled with the label on my beer and finally took a big swig. "Anything you need. It's on me."

A muscle jumped in JT's jaw, and Cam frowned.

"I need to talk to my brother alone if that's okay," Jake told them. "I'll see you guys later, all right?"

"Sure." JT leaned over and kissed him. They smiled for one another, and then he turned to me. His chin shot up, and he said, "See you."

"Yeah," I tried to keep a pleasant smile plastered on my face. "See you."

Cam left with JT. I think he must have winked or given Jake a wave, but he didn't say anything.

"What is it with that big—"

"What the fuck is your problem?" Jake throttled his beer like he wanted to break it.

"I don't have a problem."

"I'm not even going to talk about how you treat Cam, but can't you find it in your heart to be happy that I've found someone?"

"Of course I'm happy, but—"

"But what? You think I can't see your sarcasm? You think I'm too blind to see what you really think? It was written all over your face."

"What do I think?" I threw my napkin down. "If you know so much, tell me what I think."

"It's obvious you were surprised. You have misgivings, and

you probably don't approve, but instead of talking to me about it, your response is to paste on a fake smile and throw money around. 'It's on me.' Fuck you, Dan. If that's all you have to offer anyone anymore, take care of our tab."

Jake pushed his chair back and left me sitting there alone.

After he stalked away, our waiter came back, tentatively offering to-go boxes and asking if I wanted anything else in such a way that I figured I was right; I had taken him home at one point.

"I see your arm is healing," he offered, along with a really nice smile. I doubted he'd smile at me like that if I told him I couldn't remember exactly who he was.

"Yeah. I've been doing some physical therapy."

He hugged his tray to himself and rocked back on his heels. "How's that going?"

"Tough." I shrugged. "But you do what you gotta do, right?"

He nodded. "Listen, I'll be getting off my shift at seven…Do you want to go somewhere? Or…"

I looked him over. He was cute. A young Latino with a smile that held a spark of mischief. Ordinarily I'd have taken him up on it, whoever he was, because he was hot. But the look on Jake's face when he left bothered me. It wasn't there, what I'd grown to expect from him. What I'd grown to depend on. If I didn't figure out why, the hole that seemed to be gnawing at my gut more and more lately would only get bigger.

"That's a great offer, but my hand hurts like fuck, and I think I need to ice it down, take some pain pills, and sleep. Maybe some other time."

Worried brown eyes surveyed the table. "Watch what you take. You did a lot of drinking, and mixing shit is bad."

I nodded. "Yeah. Thank you. Good point." I took out my wallet. "Look, if you could just get me the bill, then I'll—"

"Oh, no. Cam, you know? The firefighter? He paid already."

14

"Cam paid? Well, shit." I stared at my wallet, wondering what to do next. "We weren't even done."

"He took care of everything though, so it's fine."

Maybe my head wasn't as clear as I thought, because I pulled a twenty from my wallet and tried to give it to him. "I'm sure he did, but here you go. Thanks for everything. See you next time, all right?"

He backed away from me, frowning, and when I was smart enough to look into his eyes, there was pain there. "*No.* I said Cam paid. He took care of everything. You can just go."

I'd hurt him, damn it. I hadn't meant anything by the offer. The idea of leaving nothing felt wrong, since I had started the tab before anyone else came along. But then Jake and his friends came and left. And fuck, was that how it was going to be? Like I was the table and people came over and sat down and got up and left without even leaving the bill for me to pay so I felt like I was part of it?

"Dan? Are you okay?"

Marius. That was his name. "Marius."

Marius smiled. "That's me. I thought for a minute maybe you didn't remember me."

"How could I forget?" Third lie of the night. Was that commission, omission, or platitude? I should know that.

I still had the twenty clutched in my good hand. "I meant no disrespect. Just wanted to tip my waiter."

Almost reluctantly, Marius held his hand out, palm up. "As long as it's on account of the job. You have my number."

Did I? I nodded. "Next time."

CHAPTER THREE

My physical therapist, Jordan, always looked away while he iced down my arm. I think it was because those first few times I fought a losing battle against crying or being sick. He's a compassionate guy. He doesn't share much, but I get the feeling he *needs* to take away my pain. It's as if he's atoning for something, so it's rough on both of us.

I'd spent nearly forty-five minutes working my hand that day. He warmed me with compresses and gradual movement, and we'd progressed to pronation. My range of movement—just turning my hand over at the wrist is gone for the most part. My bones had to be stabilized in such a way that the muscles don't flex like they used to. Lifting my wrist, squeezing a soft rubber ball, picking up marbles, and using my fingers to grip a flexible web were all innocent-seeming tortures for me day in and day out.

Inevitably pale and sweating, exhausted and depressed, I left Jordan and the Day-Use Ex Machina gym where he worked. I did that twice a week still, sometimes three times, and followed up with homework. Exercises with equipment and little finger-tapping routines—thumb, forefinger, and each other finger after —counting off twenty reps before bed.

I didn't toss my cookies anymore after our sessions, something for which I'm sure we were both grateful.

The pain was manageable, and even though I'd told more than one person I was on pain medication to get out of awkward situations, I hadn't taken narcotics since the very beginning. I was killing my liver with alcohol and NSAIDs, but you wouldn't find me in line to get hooked on narcoanalgesics. I'd seen one too many colleagues—bright, clever people—go down that road, and I for damn sure wasn't going to let that be my destination.

"I got you something." Jordan was opening a UPS parcel. "I think you can probably start using this now. It's one-and-a-half pounds in strength, the lowest this manufacturer makes, so the pressure shouldn't hurt you, but as with anything, start slow."

What he pulled from the box was a yellow plastic and spring contraption that looked like part of a trumpet, with buttons for each of my fingers. Just looking at it hurt. When I finally accepted it, I felt my eyes burn, and it was a sign of how tired I was that I didn't hide it. He demonstrated with a red one, pushing the little spring bar with his index, then his middle finger, his ring finger, and pinkie. He casually rippled them over the buttons, back and forth like a child would wave with little wiggly fingers.

My heart sank when I realized I would never, ever have that kind of dexterity, the kind he took for granted, the kind that allowed him to move his fingers independently, that let him push buttons without the gut-clenching fear I felt just looking at my new toy.

"I don't expect you to do this with each of your fingers just yet. It's simply another weapon in our arsenal."

I swallowed down the nausea that it made me feel. "Sure."

"This..." Jordan frowned. His optimism seldom wavered, but

I could see how watching me suffer was taking its toll. "This isn't easy, I know. I think you have a realistic outlook and you're working really hard. If I could make this better, if I had a way to make it easier—"

"It is what it is," I said, and at the time I meant it. It's amazing how far I'll go out of my way to cheer someone up when they're upset about my pain. "A couple of Advil, a blowjob. I'll get my mind off it somehow."

Jordan was never shocked by what I said, but sometimes it made him color a little. "Whatever it takes. It is going to get easier. You'll see."

"I know. Besides I have the hottest PT in town." This is an old joke. Not only was he the only certified sports medicine PT in town, he was the son of my brother's business partner, and she was a friend. "I'll see you."

He nodded, then opened the door for me. When I looked back it was to see him unguarded. He was worried about me, maybe, and a little depressed that he couldn't make things better. I'd seen that look on his face before.

"You make it a lot easier to take, Jordan."

He nodded again but put his hand on my shoulder. "I wish I could make it go away."

Would there have been any sense in my saying *Me too*? I didn't think so. I just left to make my way across the gym, which as usual was chock-full of healthy athletes, first-rate bodies working like finely tuned machines, gripping, lifting, squeezing, and pumping iron with perfect hands and arms while I…

It didn't bear thinking about, so I put my head down and started walking. I held my new yellow torture device in my good hand, manipulating it with ridiculous ease while my injured arm rested in its special sling, when someone getting up from a weight bench tripped over his towel and hurtled into me on the right side, a mass of muscle and bone that smashed and flailed against my just-iced hand and caused such pain to explode inside my skin that fireworks of color burst behind my eyelids.

"*Fuck.*" I doubled over to protect my hand even as my knees buckled from the pain. "Fuckity, fuck, fuck, *fuck.*"

"*Watch it!*" a voice behind me barked. Warm hands drew me away from the collision and into another solid mass of muscle, this one tall, hot, and damp—I guessed from working out—but oh, so gentle and fuck almighty, I turned into whoever's touch that was and nearly passed out, savoring the warm embrace and the smell of a clean man's honest sweat.

"Are you all right?"

I couldn't open my eyes and still squeeze back tears, so I nodded.

The man who tripped into me said, "It was an accident, man. I'm so sorry."

I nodded again. "'S'okay. Shit happens."

Jordan had apparently seen the collision, because soon he was standing right at my elbow. I recognized his distinctive, fresh cologne, and he and whoever had caught me were leading me back to the therapy room where I could sit down. A big hand stayed where it had landed on my shoulder, soothing me while I learned to breathe again.

"I'll get more ice." Jordan hurried to the door. "I won't be long."

That left me with my Good Samaritan, so I opened my eyes, prepared to thank him and tell him I would be fine.

It was Cameron Rooney, and I had no words.

"Don't worry. I've got you, Daniel."

I hadn't recognized his voice because it was different, as unlike the voice of the firefighter who'd cut me out of my car as it was unlike the man who'd verbally sparred with me the night before at Nacho's. Maybe that was the first time I realized that Cam Rooney had lots of different voices. That he suited what he said and did to the moment more perfectly than anyone I'd ever known. In a way, he was the ultimate chameleon. Later, when I thought about it, I realized that when we were alone, he called me *Daniel*.

"Thanks."

"You're welcome." He got up and moved to the wall on the other side of the room and struck a cowboy pose, hunched over with arms crossed, his leg bent at the knee and his foot braced against the wall. He was so beautiful I just stared at him.

A long silence stretched out between us, and I figured that was because we usually took potshots at one another, and he didn't want to fire at me when I was already down.

He surprised me again by saying, "I don't get you."

I glanced up at his face. "What's to get?"

He shook his sweaty blond head, which had for some reason at one point resembled a buffalo head to me, and I never got tired of telling him that. "I figure we can agree that sometimes I see people at the worst moments of their lives. People are hard-wired for survival, and a firefighter gets a front-row seat to the best and worst, you know?"

"I never thought about it that way."

"I've seen nice people run from burning buildings and leave their kids and pets behind. I've seen men and women die trying to save someone they don't even know. When I pulled you and Yasha out of that wreck, he didn't want to leave without you. I thought I'd have to knock him out. I would have too."

I had to smile at that. I had no doubt. My hand had been crushed between the seat and the door, and Jake refused to leave me, even though it was a massive pileup in the fog with impact after impact. The worst night of my fucking life, and there was Cam to save the day.

I'd tried to get my brother to go to safety, but he was stubborn as hell. In those awful, endless moments before rescue I thought we'd both die right there. Then Cam's face appeared in the window on the driver's side. His gauntleted hand shone a flashlight into the crushed passenger compartment of my once-beautiful Lexus, and he'd grinned at us like a blond angel.

Did he think I *wanted* Jake to stay with me?

"I tried to make him leave."

"I know you did," Cam said in that quiet, soothing voice I'd never heard before. "It was obvious you were hiding how badly you were injured. You weren't about to let him see the pain, so you joked it away. Lied like a damn rug. After he left, I saw what you didn't have to hide anymore. Excruciating pain. Terror."

I had to clear my throat to talk above a whisper. "He's my kid brother. I look after him. I always have."

"Then why'd you treat him like you did last night? Can't you be happy for him? Can't you hide your feelings when his happiness is at stake and not just his life?"

I had no answer. I still didn't know why I'd reacted the way I did. Part of me understood I'd become an accomplished liar. Why couldn't I lie about that?

I nodded again to let him know I'd heard him, and we both jumped a little when Jordan came back. I felt Cam's eyes on me while Jordan iced me down again, and then I heard him leave.

For a beat or two I was inexpressibly bereft. I wanted him to say my name again because it felt so damn good.

"You're swelling." Jordan sounded concerned.

"I'll be all right. I'll elevate it, and in the morning it will be fine."

"Are you sure you shouldn't see a doctor?"

"It's okay, really."

Jordan's boss, Izzie, poked her head in. "You okay, Dan? I heard you got hurt."

"It's fine," I told her.

She peered at me. "You don't look so good."

"I never look good when I leave this place. I'm going to go home and rest up. I promise if it swells up more or if there are any other problems, I'll go see the doctor, all right?"

"Okay."

"What do you think?" Jordan asked Izzie. I thought that was odd at the time, because while Izzie is a lovely woman, as far as I knew she wasn't a doctor.

"Why are you asking her?"

"Izzie's a perceptive," Jordan said before turning to her again. "What do you see?"

"Zip." She shrugged. "Which is really weird. I can count on one hand the times this has happened to me."

I looked up from where I'd been studying my hand. "I'm sorry. What are you talking about?"

"Izzie sees auras." Jordan announced that like he was observing the weather. Like, *the sun is out.*

"Auras?" My face probably betrayed my disbelief.

"As it turns out, I can't read Dan at all."

"Really?" Jordan asked.

She shrugged. "Dan is a blank wall."

Maybe that wasn't a bad thing to be. I imagined if she actually could read my "aura" the news of what she saw there—my undeniable, foolhardy attraction to Cam—would circulate around the gym faster than athlete's foot. I was only too happy to be her *blank wall.*

"Okay."

Her lips quirked up in a tight smile, and I wondered if she knew what I was thinking. A second later, she left me without a doubt.

"I wouldn't be too happy about that, Mr. Livingston. What happens to a blank wall is anyone can write anything they want on it."

CHAPTER FOUR

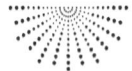

I woke up at just about three in the afternoon. For a minute I couldn't remember why I'd been sleeping during the day in the first place, and then I remembered lying down to close my eyes after the collision at the gym. What a waste of the fat part of the day. It was unavoidable, especially on physical-therapy days. I would travel home half-sick and exhausted, ready to settle onto the couch and read the paper for a few minutes, only to wake up hours later. The disorientation got to me at first, but I'd grown used to it.

Three o'clock in the afternoon is just about the best time of day to have a word with Jake, so I headed over to his fledgling bakery, Café Bêtise. When I got there it was jumping, even though he and his business partner, Mary Catherine, had only opened the shop a couple of months before. I was gratified—but not very surprised—to see my faith in them was shared by the community. It stood to reason though; my brother's an awesome pastry chef.

My brother's pal, Muse, waited tables—and held court—while other employees took orders at the counter. At this time of day Bêtise would be besieged by the hordes of hipster kids

23

who liked to study there. I walked in, and there Muse stood, all five feet nothing of her, garbed as a traditional *garçon de café*—black trousers and vest, crisp white shirt, with a white apron wrapped twice around her tiny waist. I knew exactly why the boys and about half the girls hung out at Bêtise. I had kind of a crush on her myself.

"Is my brother here?" This week, her hair was black again, but I'd known her to wear it purple or blue. It fell from either side of straight severe bangs, sleek as an otter, over sharply chiseled cheekbones and curved under her jaw where it cupped her chin.

"Who wants to know?" Muse prickled with piercings and attitude. At nineteen, she'd somehow become one of my brother's best friends. She was competent, clever. Putting herself through school. I admired her a lot, but she scared me too. She had a frank, piercing gaze that saw uncomfortably beyond the obvious.

"What did I do now?"

Muse shot me a glare to let me know she might have heard about how I'd responded to Jake's announcement the night before. "Way to support your brother, dude."

"Is this about them announcing their engagement? I was surprised is all. I'm happy for them. I just…That's something I never expected."

Jake spoke from behind me. "So naturally, you handled it like everything unexpected. Glue some money over it and hope it holds."

I hadn't realized that he was beneath the counter, restocking the refrigerated cases. "I said I was sorry. I came to apologize some more. If you like, I'll grovel. The sooner we get this done, the quicker you can tell me what you need from me, and I'll get right on it."

"We have more fruit tarts in the back, Muse." He rose,

holding an empty sheet pan covered with sticky parchment paper. "What I need is for my brother to be happy for me."

"Okay, sure. But I'm in the middle of a divorce. Our parents are divorced. Everyone I know has been married and blown it, and frankly that's what my first thought was. Oh, *no*. Here we go again."

He blinked at me. "That's honest, at least."

"I don't want to be honest. I want to say what you need to hear. But I don't know what it is. You guys might make it. People do. No one *I* know, but—"

"Okay, now it's time for you to stop talking," said Muse

"All right." I almost raked my bad hand through my hair. More than once I'd forgotten and been sorry. "Maybe we could go for a walk and talk, all right? I know I'm not saying the right thing. I don't know if I'm even capable of that. But I've got your back, you know that, right?"

"I know." He put the tray down and started to unbutton his chef's coat. "I'll go change, and then you can drive me over to the high school."

"What's there?"

"I've been unofficially helping out the soccer team, and they need a ref."

"Are you serious? Aren't you just finishing up a full day's work?"

"I ref a couple times a week. I like it. It feels good to run around a little." He took the tray and started through the door to the kitchen in back.

"It's your legs." I turned to Muse. "Can I get a coffee to go?"

"I guess." She eyed me archly. I resisted the urge to rub my nose or check my fly.

Jake stopped. "Want me to make you a sandwich or something to go?"

"No thanks." I hadn't eaten lunch, but truth be told, I wasn't often hungry after therapy. It's amazing what chronic pain will do to your appetite.

"Therapy day, huh?"

I nodded.

"I've got a little something, and I'll throw it in a bag. If you get hungry, it will be there."

I nodded.

Muse gave me a coffee. She'd drawn something on one of the little sleeves. Since she didn't like me much, I imagined it probably wasn't the ancient sigil for *Have a nice day*. If I were feeling more energetic, I would have gotten out my phone and looked it up on the Internet. Someone, somewhere probably had a list of "stuff to draw on the coffee sleeves of people you don't like."

Muse went off to wait on a table full of trendy boys with laptops and long eyelashes that fluttered like laundry on a line as she refilled their coffee. Was I ever that young? I couldn't help noticing they were beautiful, the lot of them. Lean and strong with long, elegant hands and big feet they hadn't quite grown into yet. Their leader, made obvious by the way he slouched in his chair with his arms spread over the backs of his friends' chairs and his legs splayed wide in a perfectly primal display of his sex, jerked a chin in Muse's direction.

I wondered what she wrote on his coffee sleeve. If it wasn't at least the ancient runic symbol for *fucking horndog*, I'd feel singled out. It wasn't a secret that Muse spent most of her free time with Minerva, the owner of a little bookstore called Rune Nation, and Izzie, who owned my gym. Whatever Muse was getting up to in her occult studies, I figured it was mostly benign. I'd been calling the three of them the Witches of Westwick since I'd moved to town.

Sometimes the interconnected nature of the people who lived in St. Nacho's made my skin actually *itch*, and it was usually then that I got in my car and left.

"What are you looking at?" The curiosity of the alpha of Muse's little pack of admirers had turned to me.

Apparently I'd spaced out while watching Muse pour coffee, and his little tribe figured I was checking her out or something.

I couldn't help but laugh. Jake originally described Muse to me as a "feisty marmoset" and we both felt absurdly protective of her. Maybe I was bristling because all that lean young flesh was sizing her up. One of them knocked a fork off the table, and when she bent to pick it up, they leered at her ass and nudged one another.

I actually sputtered like some enraged father. "Knock that off, you—"

"Back down. I can handle these monkeys." Muse nudged me with her shoulder as she passed me. "I put something in their coffee. They won't be able to get it up for a week."

This was met by a classic spit take by a boy in a white T-shirt with some bloodied video game zombie on it. While he was gathering napkins to wipe himself down, she grinned back over her shoulder at me.

"Or I would if I only knew of such a thing."

Jake witnessed the last bit of that exchange and growled a warning. "*Muse.*"

"All right, all right. I promise I won't render the customers impotent."

"That's all we ask." He handed me a huge, doubled shopping bag that felt awfully heavy for a quick sandwich.

"What have you got in here?"

"Just some sandwiches and salads I made up earlier. Some bread and pastries. A piece of *dulce de leche* cheesecake and some bottles of iced tea."

"Enough for an army. I can't possibly eat this much."

"That's good, because it's not just for you. You can share with me and the other refs, and we eat like the athletes we are." He grinned. "It won't go to waste."

"Thank you." I hefted the bag and pushed through the front door. "Car's this way."

Jake nodded and followed me. To get to the car, *of course* we had to pass by the firehouse. I noticed some of the crew out cleaning the truck, stretching and sweating in the midafternoon sun. I didn't see Cam among them, but even as I walked by—trying not to search for him—I realized I could still hear him say *Daniel* in that velvety dulcet voice he'd used on me that morning and even the memory made me shiver.

Who would have thought such an immense and vibrant boy-man could be so tender?

A vaguely disquieting yearning was building inside me to investigate that further. Maybe I would, later—or maybe I wouldn't.

Things could get complicated quickly between me and a man like Cam.

When Jake and I got to the car, he insisted that he should drive. I think he just liked to drive my car, so I flipped him the plastic electronic key.

"Are you getting used to driving an automatic now?" he asked once we got in.

"I miss the IS F and its racing transmission. I miss zero to sixty in less than five seconds."

"That wasn't a car. That was a gasoline-powered penis."

"I *know*. That accident emasculated me."

"Not from what I've heard."

"I was speaking metaphorically. Physically, not so much." Recent memories made me own up to the truth. *Not so much* was an understatement. I admitted—if only to myself—I'd been enjoying a true free-for-all of casual sex.

Jake started my new GS. It really was a gorgeous car. Deep-sea mica blue with gray leather seats and bird's-eye maple accents. It had all the bells and whistles. No one in their right mind would put on the pity-party hat while riding around in a machine like that, but I was so fucked-up I couldn't get attached to it.

"I think you may just be confused, Dan. You're unhappy about your car because you think you have to be glad you kept your hand. And maybe what you really miss is—"

"Thank you, Dr. Freud."

"Freud would have called your old car your compensatory *penis* and left it at that. You know I'm right. It's okay to be angry, but you've chosen your battle unwisely here. Don't take it out on this sweet honey of a car. It kills me. You don't deserve her at all."

"And you do?"

"I cherish her." He teased. "She's my precioussssss."

"You can wash her next time then."

"Oh, yeah. I'll wash her." He leered at the steering wheel and started stroking it like a lover. "I'll get her all soaped up and slippery and use my big, fluffy microfiber towel on her. That's what I'll do."

"You're starting to creep me out." I knew he was right. Well, not to anthropomorphize a car like that, but that I should be glad I had both my hand *and* a new car. My doctor thought someday I'd be able to drive a manual again. Maybe. It shouldn't have mattered, but it did. Everything mattered. What I'd lost, how long it was taking me to recover. Everything.

Simple, *stupid* skills I had never given a single thought to until it became necessary to use them, only to find that I no longer had them—like eating with chopsticks.

"It's taking a while to adjust, Jake. Sometimes it feels like I lose something new every day."

"The adjustments will bottom out. You'll find yourself on an upswing soon. You'll gain new skills and regain old ones. In the meantime, I'm here for you if you need me to drive you anywhere. We could try looking for a doctor in New York if you aren't entirely satisfied with the docs at Cedars in LA. I could drive you in your car."

I could always count on Jake to lighten a mood. "Thanks. We're doing okay. Me and my Frankenstein hand. Still scaring the faint of heart with its patchwork appearance but doing all right."

"It's not that bad, you know?"

"Sure," I said, looking out the passenger window. I found it ugly. There were times I couldn't even look at it. I flexed my fingers where I could see them and felt a familiar, sickening lurch in my gut. "I know. I'm grateful I still have my hand."

As we passed the intersection behind the gym, we heard the first wails of sirens behind us and pulled over to let fire trucks and the EMTs pull past.

"That your man?"

"Yeah." Jake squinted after them. "He's on shift. Cam too. I wonder what's up. Something on the highway probably."

"Probably." As we pulled into the parking lot next to the high-school field, we could still hear the sirens. "Do you ever give any thought to what they might be going into?"

My brother flashed me such a look of contempt it surprised me. *Of course he did.* I was stupid to even ask. The man he loved was in that paramedic unit, and they could be rolling into anything. I have to admit, I'm a seriously self-absorbed fuck sometimes. If I loved someone like that, I'd be holding my breath every time I heard the trucks pull out.

"Of course you do. That's JT out there. I wasn't thinking of it like that."

"It's time you did think of it like that. *That's* what I'm asking of you. Fuck the ceremony, fuck the party, *fuck* whatever it's going to cost. I'm committing to the man I love, and I need you to treat my feelings like they deserve to be treated. Like they're real. Like they're significant. If not...Don't bother showing up."

He got out of the car and started marching to the field, leaving me to extricate myself.

"Aw, Jakey." I ran after him carrying the bag of food. "*Yasha.* Don't be like that. I'm always the last person to arrive at these things. You *know* that. But I get there eventually. I get it. I do. I'm sorry."

"I know," he said before he left me to join the team holding practice. He turned back around with a wry grin on his face. "Eat your dinner. Later I'll explain emotions to you again, you sorry bastard."

I sat down on the bleachers and wondered what I was doing there. I'd originally gone to mend fences. Had I done that or made things worse? I peered into Jake's bag with some notion of grabbing a bottle of iced tea, but as soon as I did, I saw he'd carefully packed everything he knew I love to eat.

There were containers of his special chicken salad, which he made with grapes and celery and I don't know what all— crunchy bits of candied nuts and some elusive middle-eastern spice that elevated it to gourmet fare. He had some sort of sand- wiches wrapped in parchment paper that I discovered were full of grilled vegetables and herbed goat cheese. I found a container of peppers and one of pickles. Each course was beautifully prepared, each thing wrapped perfectly so that it stayed that way.

"Jeez, Jakey." When I got out a fork and lifted that first fresh bit of chicken to my mouth, I realized he must have forgiven me before I'd even arrived.

I looked up and found him watching me from the sidelines while the players did a dribbling drill.

I waved, and he waved back, smiling.

Fuck my hand. I was lucky I got to keep my *brother*. I had a feeling that if I focused on the most important outcome of our accident, I'd be just fine.

My phone rang, so I got the earpiece from my pocket and answered it that way. "Livingston."

"Daniel, it's Bree."

I hesitated before talking because she wasn't supposed to call me. Ever. She was supposed to call her lawyer, Jim Anderson, who had the spectacularly bad judgment to also be her lover, and he was supposed to call mine. "Yeah?"

"It's probably nothing, but I found a letter in the mailbox for you today. I wondered why it didn't get forwarded, and then I realized it doesn't have a stamp on it. Why the hell would someone drop it off?"

"I don't know. Who is it from?"

"Anybody could have dropped this off, right at my door. Does this mean that one of your—"

"I asked, *who is it from*, BreeAnna?"

"There's no name. It just says it's private. Personal for you only. They obviously aren't aware you don't live here anymore. The only reason I haven't turned it over to Jim is because you've been pretty fair. But if it's something from a woman…or a-a man…and it proves you fooled around on me, I wanted to give you a chance to come clean."

More like you want another shot at controlling me. "Go ahead and open it."

"What?"

"Open it. Or throw it out. Whatever it is, it probably doesn't matter. I couldn't care less. You won't find anything sensational enough in some hand-delivered letter to break our prenuptial agreement, and I think you know that."

I almost hung up, but I heard paper rustling. At last she said, "It's from your father."

CHAPTER FIVE

"Wait. What?" I asked. "My father?"

"It's a letter from your father. And there's a post-script from someone named Joyce."

Shit. "That's my father's daughter's name," I replied slowly. "She's about…nineteen?"

"How should I know? I only corresponded with him. It seems he's still living in the Long Beach area, and he'd like you to contact him. It says he's sick, or he'd come to you. Oh. Apparently Joyce is the one who left it in my mailbox."

I can't think about this now. I rubbed my eye with the heel of my hand. "Can you overnight that to me?"

"Is it urgent?" Bree asked.

For a moment I forgot we were supposed to be at daggers drawn and I confided in her. "It might be. Jake's getting married, and I don't want him to be blindsided by this. He doesn't really know—"

"Jacob is getting married? I thought he was gay?"

"He is. He wants to commit to his lover, JT."

"That is the most repulsive—"

"We don't need your opinion, Bree."

"Fine," Bree said shrilly. "Then how about I just throw this letter into the backyard barbecue while I'm cooking Jim some steaks?"

"You won't do that."

"Oh, won't I?"

"No." I sighed. *Damn.* Was this the woman I'd considered my partner for twelve *long* years? "You won't do that, because it's in your best interest to play ball at this point. Things can get uglier."

"Oh, all right." BreeAnna's voice was tiny. Fragile. "I'll overnight it."

"Thank you very much, BreeAnna."

She hung up before I could wish her a pleasant evening. I was so absorbed in my thoughts I didn't hear Jake jog over.

"Something wrong?" He peered at my face. "You don't look so good."

"I'm fine. Bree called." I put my phone back into my pocket. "Something stupid."

"When will that woman let go?" Jake frowned. "Isn't she supposed to do everything through your lawyers?"

"Yes. It's fine. It was just a quick question, but anger can boil up over nothing. I honestly don't know how it gets this way. We used to be friends if nothing else."

"Did you like the food?" Jake's expression was closed, and I realized—too late—that he might be sensitive to hearing about other people's shipwrecks as he prepared to embark on his own voyage.

"It was great. Thanks." I shot him a sincere smile. "You made all my favorites. I guess you weren't so mad at me after all, huh, Yash?"

"Maybe not, *Danilo*. The game's about to start, so I've got to go. You going to be okay here?"

"I'm good. I like soccer." I wouldn't have minded refereeing a game myself sometime, but the mere thought of jogging and jarring my arm with each step caused me to break into a cold sweat. "Who's playing?"

"Orange jerseys are the Crush, and in the black we have the Bandits."

"Should I have a preference?"

"Ken Ashton's kid brother is playing for the Bandits."

"Go Bandits." My PT was Ken's partner, so Ken's kid brother was therefore part of my new and very convoluted St. Nacho's family. That would make him my brother's business partner's son's brother-in-law...whatever. Everyone in Nacho's was interconnected somehow. That's how it is in a small town.

At halftime I passed around salad, sandwiches, pickles, and peppers. The boys ate frozen grapes and chugged water and sports drinks. I listened to parents talk about how the season was shaping up while we watched the boys gambol around on the field. We could all see a worrisome plume of black smoke billowing toward a fairly clear sky. As the boys played, it changed color and stretched and flattened, pushed toward the east by the breeze from the ocean.

The acrid scent—smoke and sulfur—that perfumed the air was particularly bad around the time the game finished up. I had to admit, the game was exciting—a come-from-behind squeaker decided when the Bandits scored on a goal kicked in by the one Jake had identified as the Ashton boy. Despite that, by the end of the game, we were all looking nervously at the sky.

I stood when Jake came toward me. Very real worry clouded his features. "It's probably nothing," he said.

"Yeah."

Jake nodded and pulled his black-and-white shirt over his head. Underneath, his own T-shirt was soaked through with sweat. "That's exhausting, huh?"

"They keep me hopping."

"There are some awesome players. That Ashton kid is really something."

"I think he'll make baseball his sport. He might like soccer better, but I think he feels like he has to play baseball because his brother never got his chance." All this and Jake still kept his eyes on the sky.

"Let's go by the firehouse and see if JT is there before we go home. He can tell us what happened."

Jake grinned at me. "Thanks. I know I'm being paranoid, but—"

"But people you care about put it on the line every day. And it will make you feel better. I'm not an insensitive asshole, Jake. Maybe I just lost my faith. That doesn't mean you have to lose yours."

"Thanks, man." Jake very nearly brushed my shoulder with his, but I saw it coming and couldn't help flinching out of the way.

"Oh, sorry." His brows drew together. "I didn't think."

"It's fine. I forget all the time. Especially just for a few seconds when I wake up in the morning. Just long enough to try to slap the Snooze button on the alarm clock or get a grip on my dick. I realize what I've done when—" I stopped abruptly, realizing that I'd made a promise to myself that I'd stop sharing shit like that. When would I learn?

There's no point in discussing chronic pain. It doesn't make the pain go away, and people just get more uncomfortable being around you. The last thing I wanted was to be *that guy*, the one people avoid because they can't stand to hear him chirp along brightly about what it's like to live with pain.

I was not only *in* pain. I was becoming a fucking pain in the ass. From what I could see the only remedy was solitude, and when forced into the company of friends, the judicious use of alcohol and lies.

We got to my car, and Jake drove back. When we arrived—

when Jake finally parked in the Bêtise parking lot—the guys were still out on the call.

Jake put on coffee, and we shared small talk and some sweet rolls. It was another hour before the big trucks rolled back into the station, and we gave the firefighters time to get their gear off and clean up before we went over. When we did, it was obvious that all was not well.

I'd had the chance to observe the local firefighters firsthand since Bêtise had opened. I secretly believe that was one of the reasons Jake had picked that particular location. From the tables by the front window, patrons could watch the firefighters work to maintain their equipment, toss around a football, or—since a number of them smoked—spy on them while they fed their habit. They laughed and joked among themselves—often engaged in some inevitable roughhousing. Firehouses are homes, and the crew is family. That night, that's how I could tell that something had gone spectacularly wrong.

Three firefighters stood silent and separate in the area they usually used to smoke and play. They stood hunched over, eyes downcast, so still their motion-sensing security lights had shut off, surrounding them with darkness. All three focused on their feet. They looked tired, but worse than that, they looked beaten. Jake stepped into the shadows with them, and the lights once again flared to life. "Is JT here?"

One of the men, I think his name was Chad, shook his head.

"Is he...? Are you guys okay?"

"We're fine." He stubbed his cigarette out on the ground, then picked up the butt. "It was just a tough call is all."

Jake nodded.

"JT's rig transported a victim. He'll be back after he's done at the hospital."

Silence closed in on us again. The image of Cam came to me as he'd been that morning: solid, reassuring, unashamedly gentle.

My heart tightened inside my chest. "Where's Cam?"

Chad tilted his head toward the firehouse, and before I even knew what I was doing, I'd taken several steps in that direction. I stopped and turned, meeting my brother's surprise.

"I'll be back." I didn't think he'd go anywhere without seeing JT in the flesh first, anyway. He nodded that I should go on.

I went in through the garage, past the trucks, past the rec room and the card table where most evenings you'd find a lively poker game. I turned right at the kitchen where some men sat drinking coffee because I could hear the rhythmic *clink clank* of free weights, and instinctively I knew I'd find Cam in the weight room.

I got to the door and took in the sight. Cam was shirtless—wearing a pair of those breakaway workout pants with a stripe down the side. His bare feet looked oddly vulnerable. Gloved hands gripped the barbell as he bench-pressed what seemed to be enormous iron wheels of weight. With each push—*clink*—his muscles stood out, straining and sweaty, bulging, stretching... reaching the limit of their ability before Cam grunted and brought the bar back to the cradle. *Clank.*

I didn't have to be a personal trainer to know that what he was doing wasn't advisable or safe to do alone.

"Whoa there," I said, and instead of spotting him—because how could I?—I placed my left hand over his and said, "Stop."

When he stilled, I let him go and looked for something to sit on. The only thing I found was a massive exercise ball, so I rolled it over. When I sat down, it squeaked like a fart, and I thought again that the day could surely have gone better than it had. The barest lift of his mouth in a half-smile told its own story.

"What happened?"

"Bad call." His tone was clipped.

I hardly knew him, and I knew he didn't want to tell me what happened. Because I didn't know what else to do, I put my hand on his again. My feelings about St. Nacho's, about small towns, about my divorce, my brother, and my life in general were complicated. Taking Cam's hand was nothing of the kind. He was basically good, a mischievous boy-man with a tough job, and he was hurting. A broken Cam was an awful, *awful* thing.

"Will you tell me?" I asked.

His eyes opened, and I realized I'd never really looked into them before. Cam's irises reflected the blue of alpine skies, brilliant and clear with a smudgy charcoal circle around the outer edges. The pupils were surrounded by what appeared—in that light—to be silver starbursts. The whites of his eyes were red, and his lashes damp from crying.

"Kids and fireworks."

Ah, *shit.* I wondered if I really wanted to hear the rest.

"We were called to a single-family home containing a cache of illegal fireworks. Kids found them and lit them in an enclosed space. Things got out of control before they could stop it. The rest of the house went up in just minutes. Four boys. Two brothers and two neighborhood kids. The house was fully involved when we got there. JT transported one of them."

Oh…that meant…

"Some days I can't do my job worth a fucking damn." He sat up and discreetly wiped his eyes with his thumb and forefinger.

I had to open my mouth to breathe without making a noise, but maybe even that was a kind of embarrassed sob.

"Daniel?" he glanced up at me. How wrong was that? To be so glad to hear him say my name when his heart was breaking.

"Yeah?"

"Do you think kids die for a reason? Like…does God really need them for something?"

I shook my head. "I don't know."

"What reason could there be for three kids losing their lives like that? It can't be a lesson. That's too cruel. But it can't be random."

"Ah, *Cam*. Please don't. Don't do this to yourself."

Why was I even there? What could I say to help Cam with whom I normally lived in a state of friendly détente and unrequited lust? I had followed my feet and my instincts, but now he needed something, and I was absolutely out of my depth.

I leaned over and wrapped my arms around his neck, and it was like grabbing on to a bull. Muscles rippled as his arms slipped under mine and banded tight around me, crushing me. He held on to me as though I was the only solid thing left on earth. He pressed his face into my neck, and I felt the wetness of tears there.

"It's going to be all right," I said stupidly.

He shook his head. He was openly crying, and I was acutely aware that there were probably ten people, most of whom were only meters away, who understood what he was going through better than I ever could. I felt his grief like a hot wind all along the place I stuff my inconvenient emotions, and it blew away anything trivial I had ever stored there.

"I'm so sorry, Cam. You did your best, right? You guys...you always do your best. And you have to face that you can't...that sometimes there are no miracles. Sometimes the fight is over before you get there."

Cam's big head nodded against my skin, and I wanted more. I wanted to pull his body into mine, maybe even kiss away his pain. I'd have done anything to make it better, but he asked nothing further of me than to be held.

"I'm sorry." My own eyes burned. "It takes guys like you to bear that, and I know it's hard. But only you can. None of the rest of us could shoulder a burden like that."

I heard footsteps approach the door behind me, but I didn't turn. After a second, whoever it was walked away.

I SLEPT POORLY THE NIGHT OF THE FIRE. AT ABOUT FIVE A.M., I gave up and started coffee because there was no hope that I would go back to sleep. If I did by that time, I'd just waste the day, and I had things to do.

I went outside for the paper before the sun had even cracked the horizon and sat down with coffee and a leftover roll from the bag Jake had given me the night before.

The fire story had made the front page of the newspaper. There were pictures of the brothers who died, interviews with the parents. They reported the current condition of the boy JT had transported, who held on to life by an ever-thinning thread. Someone had snapped a picture of Cam and the rest of the crew as they packed up their equipment after putting out the fire.

Cam stood in the foreground, grimy and wet with sweat as he pulled off his helmet. The photographer caught him looking back at the house with naked regret.

Seeing that picture brought home to me how painful Cam's job could be and what an extraordinary thing it was that any firefighter could roll out on each new call with fresh determination in his heart. It was no wonder they had all come home silent and exhausted.

I'd interrupted Cam in his private grief and seen the man he hid from the world. And I'd discovered I had much more than a passing attraction to him. I wanted to take away his pain, even if it meant bearing it myself.

Since I had nothing better to do that early, the beach beckoned. I changed and took off for a walk to the pier. There was no one out yet, just some seabirds and a light mist of fog. It was time to consider my own dilemma.

My father, Elton Livingston, was trying to get in touch with me.

This was no surprise to me, but it would shock the hell out of Jake. I'd never told him our father had written to me. I'd never found a good way to work it into a conversation. Now I worried how he would feel if he knew.

Jake probably only remembered our father as an abusive man who came home disappointed every night—only to get drunk and take it out on us. My mom stood up to him on our behalf and got the worst of it, but I took more than one beating to protect Jake, who was so much younger.

It all ended the day I was finally big enough to put a stop to it. That physical confrontation left my father lying on the ground with a broken nose, looking up at me with fear in his eyes. The image of his frightened face was burned into my memory as the single most conflicted moment of my life.

I hadn't wanted to win, but I couldn't bear to lose anymore either.

The next day, our mother's father took us to the beach, and when we came home, all the mementos, the photographs, the letters and postcards—every last trace of my father—had disappeared. For the rest of my childhood, it was as if he'd never existed at all. For my part, I'd always thought good riddance.

By the time I heard from him again, I was in graduate school and Jake was in Israel with our grandfather—our *zeyde*—doing his mandatory service in the Israeli army.

Our father wrote me to tell me he had a new family, and all I could think was…good luck with that.

Fuck my father anyway.

He should have been the one to tell Jake about them because I could never do it. And now Jake would think I'd kept it from him for some private, selfish reason of my own. Maybe I had. Maybe I didn't want to see him hurt again.

Our father had burdened me over the ensuing years with apologies, requests for financial assistance, and news I'd rather not have gotten. Photos I wish I'd never seen of a boy who looked like me and a girl who looked a little bit like Jake around the eyes.

I had siblings I didn't know. Siblings I didn't *want* to know. And they were trying to find me to tell me that a man I had hated for most of my life was sick.

I didn't want to know that either.

It was while I was on the boardwalk that I happened to spot Jake and JT along the seam of the sea—where the rush and foam of water met a line of damp brown sand. They'd taken off their shoes and carried them while they walked with their arms wrapped around each other. Jake wore his white chef's coat and apron as though he'd left the shop midbake, and JT wore his uniform under a navy-blue windbreaker with SIFD on the back.

If Cam's reaction to the fire and its aftermath hadn't warned me that a serious tragedy had occurred, all it would have taken was seeing JT's body language and the careful way my brother watched his face and listened to what he had to say.

At some point, JT crumpled, and Jake caught him and held him. I turned around and headed back the way I'd come, leaving my brother and his lover to have one of the most emotionally intimate moments I'd ever seen, alone.

Instead of going home, I headed straight for the firehouse, to Cam.

CHAPTER SIX

I found Cam on the lawn outside the station, walking his cat.
I could tell that whatever had passed between us the night before embarrassed him. He wouldn't look directly into my eyes for one thing. But maybe a grown man walking a cat in a little sparkly collar on an equally shiny leash had more things to worry about than a perfectly justified emotional outburst.

"That, sir, is a cat." I pointed out the obvious.

"What's your point?" A light flood of pink colored his cheeks beneath a day or two of golden stubble. "It's a special day for her. Spot is the firehouse mascot and an elementary school is coming in to visit and take pictures with us."

She certainly was spotted. She looked like a tiny leopard. Cam gathered her up and held her between the palms of his enormous hands. Her triangular face reminded me in some absurd way of Muse.

"But she's a cat."

"Spot is not just *any* cat. She's an ocicat. They're an especially outgoing, friendly breed, and they like interacting with humans. They're highly intelligent and"—at this, he whispered so she wouldn't hear him—"doglike in temperament. I rescued her

44

when she was a kitten. And…you know. She likes dog stuff. I don't want to treat her like an ordinary cat or anything when she clearly wants to be a—"

"So she thinks she's a dog?"

Even though he didn't look up at me, I saw his lips twitch at that. He covered her ears. "Shh. She'll hear you."

Since I'd seen her on a leash prancing proudly along in perfect heel, no, I did not want to ruin things for her. Delusional cats were outside my area of expertise.

"Are you all right?" I asked.

He brought Spot to his face and rubbed his chin along her fur. "The fourth boy, the one JT transported, died early this morning."

"*Shit.*" I put my hand on his arm, but he pulled it back. Today he didn't want my comfort.

"It's the job." He turned as though he was planning to walk back into the station, but I called out to him.

"JT's taking it hard, isn't he?'

Cam turned back. "We're all taking it hard."

"Is…Do you suppose there's something I can do for the families? Is there a fund, or—"

Cam's irritation plainly showed on his face. "JT is right about you. You can't help yourself. You just have to respond to everything by offering cash, like money is a panacea—"

"Wait just a damn minute." I stepped toward him. I had to look up a good six inches—which seemed crazy because I'm not a small man at all—but I was willing to go toe-to-toe over this. "I don't know these people. I've lived here like…two minutes. But I do know how crippling funeral expenses can be, and I also know that grief has got to be ten times worse when you're scrambling for money to give your child a decent burial. I know it means something when you realize your neighbors care, even if the only way they can show it is with their *filthy money.*"

Cam unhooked Spot's leash and said, "Truck," and damned if

that little slip of skin and bones and spotted fur didn't rush to the fire engine and climb till she was perched on the top, looking down at us like a vulture.

"I'm sorry I said that, Daniel."

There it was again, that thrilling little rasp, that purr when he said my name. It went straight to my cock. Did he fucking do that on purpose?

I tried to tamp down my attraction to him, at least enough so it didn't show on my face while I vented my irritation. "I worked two jobs all through college and graduate school and even then, I had a hundred thousand dollars' worth of student loans to pay off after I got my MBA." Why did I need to defend myself? It was probably about Bree—about how it hadn't taken me long to realize money was *all* she thought I had to offer. Maybe that's why it stung. For the first time in a long time, I'd actually tried to offer friendship, compassion, companionship, and Cam had rejected it. "Money is everything when you don't have any. There are plenty of people who believe I have nothing more to offer than that."

His head shot up, and his gaze was fierce. *Angry.* "I'm not one of them. And maybe other people will take a hint when you stop leading with your wallet."

He took off, and I didn't pursue him, because...maybe he was right.

AT THREE THAT AFTERNOON I GOT CAUGHT DAYDREAMING BY Alvin Benchley, one of my business partners at Livingston Properties, my second-in-command. He tapped on the table. "Focus, Dan. I think you've only listened to about half of what I've said so far."

I shook my head. "I'm sorry."

"I didn't drive all the way down here so you could fall asleep while I'm trying to talk to you."

"I apologize. Go on."

"BreeAnna's lawyer is giving us an indication the settlement is less than they would like. I wouldn't worry about that because they're motivated to get this over with. So that's good news anyway. On a slightly less positive note, it looks like the homeowners' association at Orchard Homes is planning a class action suit against the builders, and they're naming Livingston Properties in the lawsuit."

I frowned. "I told the board that going with the cheapest bid on that recreational facility would cost them a boatload in the long run. They went against my advice. What do they want me to do about it now?"

"I don't think they have a prayer of prevailing against LP, but we're going to have to defend it, and it's going to cost money."

"Everything does," I said. The light from the afternoon sun slanted in from the blinds. It made long strips of light and dark on the floor that reminded me of fingers, reaching into the room.

"The purchase of the Shelby office building in San Jose is complete. Only four of the tenants have exhibited any concerns about the change in ownership at all, and since I told them you planned on maintaining the status quo, they're satisfied."

"Good." I wondered if I could get a cat like Spot.

"*Dan.*" Al was clearly irritated with me. "I hope I'm not boring you."

I tried to snap out of it. "I'm sorry. I don't suppose you heard about what happened here yesterday."

"The fire that killed those kids? Yeah. Helluva thing. Devastating."

"I didn't sleep very well last night. My brother's EMT boyfriend transported one of the kids, the only one to make it, but he died this morning, and—"

Al held up his hand. "Say no more. I get it. If you want to set up a meeting another time…"

"You drove all the way down here, and I'm trying not to waste your time. What else?"

"I think I went over everything. Orchard Homes is the only big problem I see on the horizon, but even that is more of a minor annoyance. You covered your ass perfectly there. So… You have anything else?"

"Not currently."

"Have you thought about looking for opportunities around here?"

"Besides the loans I made to Jake and Mary Catherine for Bêtise? No."

"There's some spectacular undeveloped coastal land around here. I've done some research. I'd like you to consider a resort property."

"I…" I frowned. I had given that some thought. "I'm not sure I'm interested in staying in St. Nacho's. When I've recovered as much as I can, I plan to look for a place in San Francisco."

"What does that have to do with anything? You bought an office building in San Jose, and you don't live there."

"I guess I wasn't ready to think about it." Which was odd, since I always thought about things like that: the next project, the next big deal. "I barely got here before we had the accident. Yeah. Maybe. Look into things here then. I'm thinking I'd like to do something here without changing the place too much."

"I'm not sure what you mean by that."

"St. Nacho's is a small town. It doesn't aspire to draw much in the way of a tourist market."

"That doesn't mean it couldn't. A first-rate hotel with a spa, something that would pull some upscale vacation trade. Fine dining."

I thought about Nacho's Bar and how people came from up and down the coast for both its evenings as a gay hangout and its family Sunday brunches. "I don't think it would be easy to change the nature of the place."

His eyebrows rose. "It's going to happen. St. Nacho's is surrounded by as yet unmolested coastline. Bored tourists are always looking for new places to go. People are willing to travel farther than ever to get to jobs. Politics changes in the state capital all the time, and in a down economy, suddenly it's okay to drill offshore or plunder the wetlands. I say despite the recent elections, it might still prove fruitful to look into something here."

Absurdly, my skin felt tight when he said that. "I don't know."

"I've been looking into something new." Al seemed to hesitate.

"What?"

"Gaming." He dropped that word between us and waited.

"What? Like...gambling?" I'd always balked at the idea of gambling. "Most gambling is illegal in California, and—"

"I'm not proposing a casino. Gambling here is the purview of the local Native American tribe and demand won't support the competition. That's their schtick. I'm talking about a resort with tournament video gaming and card rooms. Maybe something with its own cachet, like the World Series of Poker Tournament. We create new high-stakes tournament play. Given the surging popularity of Texas Hold'em on television, I've been thinking a mid-California mecca for the gamer, the geek, and the twentysomething demographic that plays hard, drinks hard, and spends hard."

"A resort with card rooms?" I'd never been much interested in video games. I couldn't even remember playing any. "I think the good citizens of St. Nacho's would run you out on a rail."

"Yes, card rooms. And high-tech video gaming. Sophisticated laser tag. That's...Look, I've been doing some checking around since you landed here. The area just north of St. Nacho's is unincorporated. Let's say you take a long-term conservative approach. You buy the land and start pitching plans for a resort. It won't be hard to find capital for the property even in this economy. Once we do that, we put together a prospectus and start building support for the resort. Think luxury poker destination for folks who want a reasonable drive from commercial centers all up and down the coast. It's only a matter of time before someone comes along and develops here, because change is inevitable. You could be on the ground floor of something huge, a once-in-a-lifetime opportunity. You can build green, pitch it as responsible land management and an increase in jobs for the denizens of St. Nacho's and other local communities. At this point we both know the state isn't going to stand in the way of tax revenue."

While he talked, something snakelike deep within me came to life and unwound. I didn't like it, but he was right. It was a matter of time.

"We need to do a lot of serious research, but the more I look into it, the more promising it sounds. There's a lot of money to be had for a project like this if we frame it right." Al watched me, gauging my reaction.

That new, living something slithered through my limbs. A flood of adrenaline caused a landslide of doubt to spark a small flame of righteous indignation—an emotional disaster film à la Irwin Allen. "I can't say I'm feeling the love right now."

"I've been working on this for a couple of months. I'm almost ready with a proposal. I'll pitch it formally in a couple of weeks. You'll see when I have the numbers. There are still really tough times ahead, Dan. I don't have to tell you it's a wounded economy and the pain isn't over yet. But there are places where growth is not only possible; it's inevitable."

I couldn't put my finger on *why* exactly, but I started to feel sick. "I don't know. Native American tribal gaming is—"

"This isn't *gaming*. It's card rooms. The money ventured

belongs to the players, not the house. It's focused on tournament play. We put together televised tournaments, get in some of the big players. There's advertising money to be found, sponsorship money. There are entertainment companies, beverage companies, tobacco, the makers of high-end toys."

"Wait. Toys?"

Al grinned. "Like your motorcycle."

This was probably going to come between us. He was committed, and I was digging in my heels. But we were adults and professionals. We'd weathered disagreements before. "No. I'm not...I really don't want to be involved in gambling on any level."

"What? Never? I need you to at least consider this."

That was the most he'd ever asked of me, and he'd given me everything he had for years, damn it. His loyalty had never been in question. It paid to reward it. Yet my heart had started to hammer and not in a good way. I didn't have any emotional investment in leaving St. Nacho's intact, but as Al talked, what he said just seemed more and more...wrong. Not just wrong but dangerous.

All my senses called for him to stop.

Instead I sighed. "I'm not saying I'm interested in this particular project, but you've done a lot of work here. It seems to me that there's a lot to be said in favor of purchasing the land on speculation. Find out everything you can. Be discreet. Stealth is key if we don't want to alert anyone to our interest and drive up the price."

"I'll do that."

What would I do with land around here if I had it? Not a gambling center, that was for damned sure. "I'll think seriously about your recommendations. You've always been spot-on, but I don't mind telling you this one makes me feel...apprehensive."

"Thank you for at least considering it. I can work with that."

"I think that's all for today."

"Fine." He straightened the papers he'd had me sign—with my new *official* left-handed signature—and placed them in his stainless-steel briefcase. "Great, I'll get back home in time for dinner."

"Give Ellie and the kids my love."

"Will do." He stood, and I stood, ready to see him to the door. "Can I say something? Frankly?"

"Sure." I trusted Al more than anyone except my brother. We'd been through a lot together. "Shoot."

"Maybe you need to see someone. A counselor or something."

"Yeah? What makes you say that?"

"Things are going to be different from now on. Nothing can change that. And it's not just the arm. Of course, that's an awful loss, but...You're forging a whole new life. Your marriage is finished, and now you've gone over to the *dark side*." He used air quotes. I knew he believed I was going through a phase. Like it was only natural for me to want diversity and quantity—to go on some bisexual kink odyssey—after a rather lackluster sex life with my wife. "Whether you wind up here or somewhere else, nothing is ever going to be the same. Ellie said she thinks you should find someone to talk to. I promised her I'd tell you."

"Tell her you delivered the message, and thank her for me, will you?"

"Yeah."

"Why don't you and Ellie meet me down in Pismo sometime and bring the kids. I found a place where you can rent horses to ride on the beach."

He grinned, glad to be on safer ground. His wife and girls loved horses. "We would love that."

"Then that's a plan. Have Ellie call—"

I still had an executive assistant in my office up north, but since I'd slowed way down, I made my own appointments. I grinned. "Have her call *me*, and I'll make all the arrangements."

"Will do."

I watched him head out the door and climb into his car. Since Livingston Properties had gone from a voracious real estate investment consortium with a focus on acquisitions to one that mostly oversaw the management of a number of properties, I'd shuffled and shifted and downsized. Due to the current financial climate and after that, my accident, Alvin and I had put a plan in place so LP could run with only the barest necessary day-to-day input from me. Six hours, maybe eight, three to four times a week—not the fourteen-hour days I'd been used to putting in.

I headed for the porch where I could light up a cigarette without hearing about it from Jake later on.

When I checked the mailbox, the overnight delivery from Bree was tucked inside. I didn't really want to read what my father had to say. Surely, it was more of the same. He'd been young and unhappy, and he'd handled it poorly. He'd learned from his mistakes and was trying to do better. He might say he had done better with his new family as though my mother, Jake, and I were his practice pancake and that was perfectly all right.

"Not today." I put the mailer, unopened, beneath the stack of bills and junk mail I always found in our mailbox.

A flutter of movement among the trees that surrounded our rented house caught my attention. It wasn't the first time I'd seen it, the flutter of a hand-dyed peasant dress, a colorful ripple of fabric as whoever was wearing it darted for cover. In fact, a number of similar incidents had happened over the weeks and months I'd lived in St. Nacho's, and I had a pretty good idea who was behind them.

Well, I guessed.

It seemed I'd picked myself up a stalker or three. Sure enough, when I headed toward the street and looked around, the pavement was covered with chalk symbols in pastel colors, and they looked an awful lot like the one Muse had scrawled on my coffee sleeve. I wasn't imagining things.

I sat down on my padded chaise lounge and lit up a cigarette while I gazed thoughtfully around me. From where I sat, I could hear the slight susurration of waves on the shore. There was a salty crispness in the air. Seabirds wheeled overhead.

Whoever had covered our sidewalk with seals and signs apparently had an ax to grind, but I wasn't worried. Whatever they wanted, I wasn't about to let it get to me.

Nothing could feel quite so benign as a warm spring day in St. Nacho's.

So, for some unknown—and probably unknowable—reason, the Witches of Westwick were trying to freak me out. I blew out a long, thin stream of smoke and grinned.

Cool.

CHAPTER SEVEN

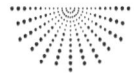

In mockery of everyone's sadness, the day of the funeral turned out to be brilliant. Perfectly beautiful. The sky was a vast and clear cerulean blue, and the sun radiated down to bake the pale golden-brown adobe facade of Iglesia Santo Ignacio. Not only did the crowds fill the church itself, the attendees overflowed into the social hall next door to watch on video monitors. Some folks milled around outside, having found no seat in either place but unwilling to go home without a chance to show their support to the families.

I watched the funeral from the banquet hall, but when the video panned the crowd, I saw Cam and JT in their dress uniforms. They sat with several members of the SIFD, somber and serious.

At the center of everyone's attention, four closed caskets sat covered with sprays of beautiful white lilies and gladioli.

After mass, Cam and JT were among the many men who bore the caskets from the church to the cars waiting to take them to their final resting places. The receiving line was endless. After spending some time with their neighbors and friends, each family left to bury its dead.

The death of kids that young was unbearable. Unthinkable. Their deaths left behind too many broken hearts, and eventually people would start asking hard questions about blame and restitution. The families, united now in grief, would splinter under guilt and the exhausting process of starting over.

Everyone was already asking themselves what they might have done differently, and whether they could have averted the tragedy in the first place if only they had been a little more careful.

I cornered Cam after he talked with the families and told him to come with me. The look on his face was priceless—like I'd grown another head—but I'd done odder things since coming to St. Nacho's. He blinked at me but didn't argue. I imagined he was so surprised he followed me because he couldn't think of a reason not to.

"Where are we going?" he asked when we got to my car.

"My place." I caught him giving me a nervous sideways glance, and I laughed. "Don't worry. I'm not coming on to you or anything."

He was wary, and I didn't blame him. I'd given him enough shit—stupid teasing like calling him the abominable fireman—that it made sense to look twice at an overture of friendship from me.

I wanted to tell him to relax—to prove that I could be a good friend. I wanted to tell him he'd given me a lot of food for thought with that crack about leading with my wallet. There weren't a lot of people in my life who'd have the nerve to say such a thing to me. Then again, there weren't a lot of people in my life, period.

"I've been thinking about what you said," I told him. "About money."

Cam shifted uncomfortably. "Maybe that wasn't the most—"

"You were right. It probably does seem like I use that to keep from connecting. I admit I was blindsided by Jake and JT. It seemed sudden to me, and I handled their announcement badly. But regarding the boys who died…What was I supposed to do? Offer to resurrect them? I don't know them. I don't know their parents. But I wanted to help. So the first thing I thought of was funeral expenses. I'm not proud that I didn't think of establishing an educational trust or a burn foundation in their name, I just…I didn't think of those things, and I did think of funeral costs."

"That was a practical suggestion. I felt bad about saying that after. I didn't have the right to tell you how to respond."

"You had a point though. With Jake anyway. I used to lead with my heart. I can't always remember how anymore."

Cam shrugged. "He really looks up to you."

"I know he does." I recalled Jake's face, hopeful, then crumbling to hurt when I admitted my inability to be optimistic for him. "I want him to be happy."

"It's what you do from now on that counts, Daniel."

"I guess." I pulled into my driveway and used my remote to open the garage door. "I'll let you be my conscience from now on."

"Don't do that." Cam looked down. "I'm the last person who should be telling anyone what to do about family."

I wanted to pursue that, wanted to know more about where Cam came from and what kind of family he'd left behind to come to St. Nacho's, but we'd arrived at my place, and I had some other things on my mind.

"I couldn't stop thinking about you the last few days."

"Yeah?" Cam still wasn't looking me directly in the eye. He rarely looked right at me, but that was the first time I considered how odd that was, since he was direct with everyone else.

"I discovered…" I swallowed. "I realized I wanted to do something for you. Maybe prove I don't always think with my checkbook."

"Jeez." Cam shoved both hands through his short hair. "I regret ever saying that."

"You were being honest. I appreciate that more than you know. You've always been really good to me. I haven't made it easy."

He chuckled. "No. You most certainly have not."

"Come with me." I got out of the car and came around to his side. "I have something I thought…" Suddenly I was afraid to show him.

"What?" He got out of the car and stood there, waiting.

"I wanted to show you something. To share it with you if you'd like it. But it seems really dumb now."

Cam gazed at me thoughtfully. He was still in his uniform, and I couldn't help but notice how good he looked. At the same time, he was distant. Maybe it was that—the air of command his uniform gave him that made me doubtful. Maybe I was afraid he'd see this as just another time when I threw money around to make a problem go away. But maybe he'd realize I'd been thinking about him, and I wanted to see him happy.

Cam grew impatient. "How will I know if you don't just spit it out?"

I took him into the garage and pulled the tarp off my motorcycle with a sigh I couldn't keep from escaping.

I fucking *loved* that bike.

I'd had it brought to St. Nacho's and paid a mechanic to come down and maintain it regularly, knowing I couldn't ride it. Knowing I might never ride again. Part of me wanted to sell it and part of me couldn't let go, so there it sat in my garage under a sheet like a piece of furniture.

Cam's eyes grew round. "Ducati?"

"It's…yeah." A Multistrada. I'd heard some of the firefighters rode when they were off duty, and I couldn't think of a better way to blow off steam than to take out a bike or a better bike to take out. I sure the hell would have if I could. "Do you ride?"

"Yes…but…" He ran the flat of his hand over the seat as if he were afraid to touch it. "Nothing like this."

"I used to ride all the time. I got this bike because it's comfortable for touring. I thought maybe if we got away once in a while, Bree and I could bridge the gap growing between us. It wasn't like we even talked anymore, and I had some crazy notion that we could get some matching leathers and ride up and down the coast or head out into the wine country on weekends. That it might help. I admit it was a pretty stupid idea."

"It's not that stupid."

"You'd think it was ridiculous if you'd ever met Bree. Taking Bree for a ride on a motorcycle would be like putting a leash on a tropical fish and dragging it for a walk through town. There's never been anything more incompatible than the people Bree and I turned out to be."

"Maybe that's what brought you together."

"Like opposites attract?" I shook my head. "When we met, we weren't that different."

Cam's eyes narrowed. "Actually, I meant that you knew you'd never have to love her or even *like* her. You probably thought if you didn't care about her, it wouldn't bother your conscience to use her like you did."

Where the hell had that come from? "You need to choose between the muscle-bound party slut or the marriage counselor, because it's really fucked-up when you try to do both."

Cam turned a dull shade of red. "I should probably just go." Despite his words, he didn't remove his hand from the Ducati's saddle. *Ah, hell.* Cam couldn't help himself; he had to tell the truth even if it was going to cost him something he wanted badly.

"Take the bike, Cam." He lifted his gaze to mine even as his brows drew together. I pulled the keys out of my pocket and handed them over. "Let the wind blow some of the pain of this god-awful week from your soul. Get out of here."

He took my keys and looked at them for a while before saying anything. "You could come with me."

I shook my head and turned. If he looked too closely, he'd see I was paralyzed by fear. With only one arm, I doubted I could hold on properly, and the idea of more pain—more trauma to an arm that already hurt almost all day, *every* day was unbearable.

"I've only got the one helmet." I called over my shoulder before I opened the door into the house.

"I have a helmet."

That made me smile. "Good thing, since you have a head like a buffalo. You probably couldn't fit mine over your left nut. Take the bike for as long as you like. As long as you need it. Do something for yourself for a change, Cam. I really want to see your smile again."

"I...Thank you."

"Take it and go." My voice grew hoarse. "Ride it for both of us."

I didn't watch to see if Cam used my helmet or whether he knew what he was doing. The Multistrada was entirely electronically controlled. It had four different riding modes with endless permutations on those—all available to him at the touch of a button. Whatever he chose, I heard the bike start up and idle on the drive for a bit. I'd had a Harley once, and the Ducati purred like a sewing machine next to that bike. I imagined he was going through all the screens to see what she had on offer until he got the hang of things enough to take her out. He was a grown man. He didn't need me peering out the window and worrying about whether he was doing it right.

I listened for a minute, waiting, and when I heard Cam ride away, I breathed a sigh of relief. After that I pulled a bottle of Zyr from the freezer and prepared to do vodka shots and watch *Headline News* until I escaped the tight bands of self-pity compressing my chest or I was no longer conscious, whichever came first.

I slouched into Bêtise that Sunday morning, praying for a quick and painless death. Muse was probably delighted to see me so miserable.

"Love the shades. Did we do a little drinking last night, Dan?"

"That." I pointed to the huge copper cappuccino machine behind the counter. "Triple shots. Extra large. Whatever. Just lots."

"Sit down before you fall. I'll bring it out to you."

I didn't even question her kindness. I just flopped into a chair at a table as far away from the windows as possible. A few minutes later Jake sat down across from me.

"You look like hell. What happened?"

"Vodka," I growled. "*Vodka* happened. And no matter how many times I go through this, I never fucking learn."

Jake laughed. "I see. Well how about a nice *baveuse* omelet? Or maybe some greasy chicken sausages."

My stomach roiled.

"I know. I could fix you up some lightly fried eel?"

I ran to the bathroom with Jake's laughter ringing in my ears. By the time I returned to the table from getting sick, then cleaning up and splashing cold water on my face, Muse had delivered my coffee. I put my shades back on.

"You'll never guess what I saw last night," said Jake. "I saw a crotch rocket just like yours on the on-ramp to the 101 South with a man that looked like Cameron Rooney riding it."

"In no way can that bike be described as a *crotch rocket*."

"You loaned your bike to Cam?"

This was a tricky subject since I'd never allowed Jake to ride it. I could already tell he was building up a good head of right-eous indignation. "Yeah."

His tone turned frosty. "Yet you never let me ride it."

"I'm sorry." I came clean. "I've been having a hard time letting it go."

"Just because you can't ride it now doesn't mean you never will ag—"

"I can't think that far ahead anymore. I really can't." I swallowed hard.

"So, what? Cam happened to admire it and you thought, what the hell? Even though I've never let anyone touch my bike, ever, I'll give him the keys?"

"Yeah." I took a sip of coffee even though it was hotter than molten rock. "That's about it."

To my very great surprise, Jake flashed me a huge grin. "Yeah right."

"What?"

"He came in here this morning, and for the first time in days, he didn't look like he was carrying the weight of the world on his shoulders. You did good, brother mine. Good call."

"Yeah, yeah." I waved his compliment off, but it secretly delighted me to hear that Cam might be feeling better. "Like I care what the abominable fireman is feeling."

Jake got up and flipped me off. "Kippered herring." He headed back toward the kitchen, turning every so often to call out some repulsive breakfast food. "Cheese grits…biscuits and gravy…black pudding…" He went through the kitchen door. All eyes seemed to be on me. Had no one ever seen a hungover man before?

CHAPTER EIGHT

The cryptic note I'd gotten from Muse that morning bore the same mark she put on my coffee sleeve. She asked me to meet her outside Nacho's Bar at nine p.m. I have to admit, I worried I was being set up, in Stephen King's *Carrie* fashion, to expiate the sins of all the voracious capitalists of the world. It turned out being the person who put a smile on Cam Rooney's face—I guess my brother told her I loaned him the Ducati— went a long way toward elevating my status in her eyes.

"You wanted to see me?" I waved the little note.

"Yeah. I wanted to tell you how sorry I am that I've been giving you such a hard time. Yasha told me what you did for Cam. I guess I just wanted to say how nice I thought that was."

I tried to think of something to say to that. *You're welcome* didn't seem appropriate, and I wasn't exactly bursting with small talk. "All right. You couldn't say that this morning?"

Muse's small face always bore a hint of something slightly impish, and it positively glowed with mischief now. In the light of the mercury-vapor streetlamps, her hair had a blue cast and her heavily lined eyes looked like bruises. "I want to show you something."

"Okay." I went along.

"It's a tree."

I nodded. "Ah…Okay. Cool."

She indicated I should follow her, and so I did, even as I prepared myself for an elaborate practical joke. She walked about fifty yards and stopped at the base of a really big, really healthy-looking tree whose branches were so thick and low that even though Muse wore a short dress and a pair of lug-soled boots with towering heels, she easily climbed to my eye level in no time.

"What are you doing?"

"Climb up here," she urged, and I froze where I stood.

"I can't climb up there. Are you kidding? With only one arm?"

"You can. I tried it out this afternoon. You can mostly do it with your feet. This is the best climbing tree in all of St. Nacho's."

I took my first step up onto a low branch. "Did my brother put you up to this?"

"Nobody put me up to this. I just want you to see something."

"Can't I see it from down here?"

"You have to come up. It's the best way."

Maybe because she was a mere slip of a girl in a dress and high heels, and maybe because I was a man and I didn't want her to think I was a fucking coward, even though I was, I took one step up, then another, and it turned out she was right. It was easy. I held my injured hand close to my chest, protecting it against possible bumps and scrapes, but getting up into that tree was really a nearly effortless combination of gripping with my good hand and stepping from branch to branch. By the time I got to where Muse sat up in the loftier branches, her eyes sparkling with happiness, I was probably doing a little sparkling myself. I'd always loved climbing trees.

"This is actually fun," I said breathlessly. "What am I supposed to see from here?"

"Well. For one thing, the clouds are moving fast, and you can see the moon," she pointed out.

"Nice. Too bad you can't see many stars."

"Some nights you can."

"I'll bet. I'm going to keep this in mind for when I can't sleep."

"Do that." Her nose wrinkled when she laughed. She started to swing down.

"Hey, where are you going?"

"Home. It's getting late."

"All right." I started to move too, but she put her hand up to stop me.

"Just because I'm leaving doesn't mean you should. Being in a tree is spiritual. It helps you get in touch with nature. Izzie may not be able to see your aura, and Minerva might think you pose a threat to St. Nacho's, but I've been wondering if maybe you just need a little nudge in a more organic direction."

"Don't *nudge* me. I'm in a tree," I teased. "I'll fall."

She grinned at me. "I know, but don't worry. It's perfectly safe up here."

She scampered down and took off, and once again I was left wondering if everyone in town was batshit crazy.

The problem was I liked it there up in that tree. The branches were thick, and the bark soft. Nothing dug into my back or my ass. The leaves were green and moist, and they felt cool and soft when the wind blew them against my skin.

I could hear the ocean and the strains of dance music from Nacho's Bar. I could watch as clouds whispered across the circle of light cast by a nearly full moon. There was no downside to being up in that tree until the thick limb I sat on shuddered.

Something had hurtled up against my tree.

What kind of a place was St. Nacho's that a man couldn't

hide in a tree without somebody coming along and ruining the moment?

I glanced through the thick branches and tried not to make a sound when I realized it was Cam resting against the trunk of my tree—shoved there by some man I'd never seen before.

That figured.

It would take slamming something the size of Cam to nearly shake me loose from where I sat among the highest branches that would hold my weight. I had to stay perfectly silent and still and pray neither man looked up until they were through with whatever they planned.

And wasn't that just peachy.

It's not like it's unprecedented for a guy to find a quiet spot to contemplate a difficult problem or make plans for the future, but most people wouldn't expect to see me doing my thinking in the branches of a tree.

A moan escaped from someone, and I realized that my new favorite haven was about to get awkward. Cameron Rooney was getting a blowjob—and it looked to be a really good one—not fifteen feet below where I was sitting.

Any one of a number of men I'd met at Nacho's Bar or in town could be braced against the tree below me, legs spread wide—pants open and belt dangling—making needy little moaning noises as the man on his knees took him to the back of his throat and gagged a little from the size.

Why did it have to be Cam?

My theory that bodybuilders had to lose something in order to gain all that muscle was being blown all to hell right there too. I was perched directly above them, and I could see the whole, choking length of Cameron Rooney's cock. It sprang from a bush of pubic hair that in the moonlight looked dark, but I thought might just be red, because if he wasn't a Viking fucking god, I didn't know who would be. I could just imagine it, a vast ripped expanse of tan belly, gleaming Adonis belt defined by a heady ridge of muscle, a fiery red treasure trail, and a thatch of rusty pubic hair.

The guy who was blowing Cam took his time, and since there was nothing I could do at that point to reveal myself that wouldn't be asinine and embarrass the hell out of everyone, I stayed frozen in stunned silence—all the while getting turned the fuck on. Because yeah. That was hot.

Somewhere in my head there was a voice that said, "This is wrong. You must alert them to your presence." But there was a much louder voice saying, "*Fuck yeah*. Take that, you bad, bad boy. Let me see you come. Let me have it, Cam. I want to watch your face when you lose yourself down somebody's throat."

I'm conflicted like that.

On the one hand, I always know what's right.

On the other hand, I don't always do it.

Cam grunted and shifted as his knees got weak, and I felt and heard him brace against the tree again. His big meaty hands clamped onto his lover's head, and his hips started to pop. The guy whose face he was fucking made motorboat sounds in his throat like a purring cat, and Cam...he was panting now, no doubt thinking they were alone and he could let the happy fuck noises rip. His was the sexiest voice I'd ever heard anyway, and now it slid over my spine like hot cream. Silken and smooth. Deep and rich and perfectly musical. I'd have bet my car he could sing.

His cries grew deep, rough with anticipation and vibrating with need. It made the fine hairs stand up all over my body, and my cock throbbed in response.

What a man. I knew how gorgeous he could be, but I never even imagined him like this.

Oh fuck, who am I kidding? Of course I had. I had imagined him exactly like this—but with my mouth wrapped around his cock. The reality was so much better. He was the picture of masculine perfection—all power and sinew and sweat. I couldn't take my eyes away as he signaled his lover he was ready. He suddenly jerked wordlessly, soundlessly, and froze. He tilted his buffalo head back and that big, chiseled jaw of his tipped up and up...It was only a matter of time before he—

"*Fuck!*" He shoved his partner back, knocking him to his ass on the ground below. "Fuck, *fuck*, sorry, man. Jeez."

"What the hell?" The man wiped his mouth with the back of his hand, and I could see he was shaking with adrenaline and nerves.

"I think something landed on me. Like"—Cameron glanced up at me and back down at his friend and continued—"a bug or something."

"What?"

"Look. I'm kind of...I gotta go." Cam took off running.

"Are you kidding me? *Motherfucker!*" screamed the man on the ground. He watched Cam lope off toward the beach on unsteady legs. "Pretty is as pretty does, you bastard."

I couldn't blame him for giving his dick a few quick, perfunctory pumps. He shuddered as it spit cum on the ground beneath where I sat, still unnoticed.

By him anyway.

I was going to kill Muse. She had to have known this would happen. Something like this. That little *monster...*

What a doll.

Cam's friend stuffed himself back into his pants and stomped off, and I found I could breathe normally again.

I'D BEEN TO CAM'S PLACE ONCE BRIEFLY WITH JAKE AND JT TO drop something off, but a lot of the fifties-style apartment buildings right on the beach looked alike. Still, I saw my bike parked on the street, so I headed up the stairs of the one I believed was Cam's. There were only three apartments, and I knew he didn't live on the end, so I tapped lightly on the middle door.

A sisal mat beneath my feet invited me to "Wipe Your Paws."

I heard footsteps on the other side of the door, and when they stopped, I imagined Cam standing on the other side of the peephole looking out and wondering if he should open the door. That's what I'd be doing. I'd be paralyzed with indecision and hoping I could get away with pretending I wasn't home.

"I can hear you." I headed for the shortcut. "Failure to answer the door won't persuade me to leave."

I heard the dead bolt turn, and then the door opened a crack. One blue eye peered out.

"I came to apologize to you." The door opened farther, and I saw Cam's face, awash with the pink tinge of a blush. "I should have let you know I was there. I'm sorry it seemed like I was spying."

"Weren't you?"

"I was actually there"—why *had* I been there?—"being *nudged* in a more organic direction."

Cam blinked at me. "I beg your pardon?"

"At the time, I thought it had to do with St. Nacho's own unholy triumvirate. Muse, Izzie, and Minerva. They've been stalking me, and—"

"Wait, what?" He frowned.

I glanced back up at him. In this light, his unshaven whiskers gave off little glints of copper and I knew, *I just knew*, I was right. His treasure trail and the thatch of pubic hair I'd seen would be a burnished, coppery red.

"Everyone in this town is insane, aren't they? Can I come in?"

"I guess it could seem like we're crazy, but we're pretty harmless." Cam relaxed a bit and stood back.

I crossed the threshold but only just enough so he could close the door. "Those three, Muse, Izzie, and Minerva, have been drawing chalk symbols on the sidewalk outside my house and on my coffee sleeves. I see them sometimes, diving behind the trees when I get the paper in the morning or running away when I go out to smoke in the afternoon."

"But why?"

I shook my head. "That's not important right now. Muse seems to have softened toward me since I loaned you my bike."

"Since you loaned—"

"Like I said, what's important is I wasn't up that tree to spy on you. I should have let you know I was there, and I'm very, very sorry if I embarrassed you."

I relaxed, happy to have the reason for my call out of the way.

"Wait, okay. You were up that tree because…" He waited for me to answer.

"Muse told me to climb it."

"You climbed a tree—*with your arm*—because a nineteen-year-old girl told you to do it?"

"Well, she said it was easy, and it was. She climbed up first even though she was in a skirt and heels. I stayed there to think. I'll bet she guessed you'd show up, and along you came, right on cue. Are you some tree-hugging horndog? Or is that tree your particular favorite? I guess I can ask around at Nacho's if you don't want to answer that. Anyway, she must have wanted me to see you, although I can't think why…except…"

Cam flushed a dull red, and I thought he might be angry. "Except *what*?"

"She might have tumbled to the fact that I like to see you smile," I admitted. "Although I think she might have taken that a little further than—"

"Wait…You like to see me smile?"

I shrugged. "But maybe not—preferably—because of a public sex act."

Cam closed his eyes when I said that.

"I'm just sayin'. You know. Against a tree and all."

He waved that off. "Everyone does that."

"I don't." Well, I hadn't done *exactly* that. That didn't mean if Cam invited me I wouldn't. I guess Cam realized how hypocritical that was at about the same time I did, because he was quick to comment on it. "That's because you don't want to get caught."

"And you do?"

"I guess you don't have to worry about your *wife* anymore. Or the financial repercussions of cheating on her."

I knew he was probably talking about the prenup Bree and I had—which only she'd been *caught* breaking. We'd both violated it. My brother Jake had an awfully big mouth.

Cam dragged his fingers through his short hair and walked toward the kitchen. "You want a cup of coffee or something?"

"Is this an *over coffee* thing?" I asked, following him. His place was damn nice. It looked professionally decorated—like it came straight out of *Everyday Living* magazine. *Who knew?* His loopy fire cat/dog rubbed up against my leg along the way.

While Cam added water to the reservoir of his coffee pot, he said, "I talked to your brother a lot when he first came to town. He was getting together with JT, you know? I guess I have one of those faces. Or maybe I was the one person who wasn't afraid to tell him what I thought about men who go out publicly with girls and then get off with guys in private. The subject of your marriage might have come up."

So. Jake really *had* told Cam all about me. I'd given Jake a ration about JT being in the closet too. I'd just come out to him and—at the time—JT's behavior seemed duplicitous. I recognized it pretty easily since I was guilty of the same thing.

"You warned Jake off JT?"

"Yes. A few times actually." Cam grimaced at some memory or other.

"Yet now you're JT's best man. What happened?'

"I didn't blame JT for being afraid. But he still could just as easily have thrown everything Yasha had to offer away because he was worried what people might think. I didn't want Yasha to get hurt. JT is on the level, now anyway."

If I condemned JT, I condemned myself by extrapolation. "No one can know what he was thinking, though," I hedged.

"Uh, yeah, we can." Cam put the pot beneath the grounds with a *clank*. "A guy like that"—he looked pointedly at me—"is only thinking about how he can get what he wants without having to live with the consequences. He's thinking, *I can lie, cheat, screw around, and deceive everyone, and as long as I don't get caught, I'm golden.*"

"That's a little harsh."

"The truth hurts sometimes." He watched steam puff up from his coffeemaker.

It was pretty obvious the truth had hurt me in Cam's eyes. I wasn't proud of what I'd done. I'd married a woman although I identify as gay, and I'd cheated on my wife more than once. I'd gone the route of paying for men or tricking anonymously so I would never get emotionally involved, and I'd convinced myself it was perfectly all right, even legitimately kind, to do it that way.

What a crock of shit.

I didn't have to examine that through Cam's filter to know how wrong it was.

The way Cam flip-flopped on me reflected some pretty conflicted emotions. But one thing he'd never pulled any punches about was a man who used a woman as a beard.

"Maybe I should just go."

"That's probably for the best," he said quietly.

I started making my way to the door. "I just came by to say I'm sorry. It wasn't personal—with the tree. I just happened to be up there and—"

"*Daniel?*"

Fuck it all, there it was again, that damned voice of his, and by then I could absolutely swear he did it *only* for me, covering me with it like thick honey and cream when we were alone and no one else could hear him use it.

I froze.

He hesitated. "Do you really like to see me smile?"

"Yeah." I turned to find him gazing down at me. "I really do."

I barely breathed. We'd been dancing around that compelling *something* between us ever since he'd pulled me out of my wreck—maybe even before that, back when we met the first night I landed in town and got drunk with Jake at Nacho's.

Cam hooked me by the back of my neck and pulled me to him, palming my head like a basketball. His hand was so warm it heated my scalp through my hair. He gripped my head hard as he slanted his mouth over mine.

For a second it felt exactly like free fall—a sudden shocking surge of fear along with a tremendous rush of excitement—and then I just caught fire.

Cam had softer lips than any man his size had a right to, but the brush of his beard stubble was scratchy and electric. His tongue twined around mine and tickled, exploring my teeth and palate, and licking my lips as he opened up and let me do the same. He touched, tasted, and teased me while all my blood rushed south to pulse uncomfortably behind my zipper, and I kissed him back so hard my lips went numb.

He both seduced and devoured me until my head swam and my good arm went around his neck to cling to him. I let my other arm hang limp. I really longed for it. I missed using both hands to touch and manhandle, to grip a lover's ass and squeeze. He gently insinuated his arm around me underneath mine to get a better hold, and again, his hand—that unexpected plate-sized circle of warm flesh—explored until it pushed its way beneath the waistband of my jeans to touch my naked flesh.

Our cocks pressed together, hard and insistent, and right

then I knew—I thought I knew—exactly how good it could be between us.

Just like that, I'd have been willing to ditch my clothes and offer myself up to him. He was everything I wanted, but then I think we both remembered what brought me there in the first place.

"Oh, fuck." Cam pushed me back just a bit. "I…um…accept your apology."

"I guess *so*," was all I could think to say.

My lips felt puffy from being crushed and kissed like that. I might have liked the rest of me to feel that way too—only not when I'd seen him getting blown by someone else an hour before. Or when we had that whole, *lying liars that lie* thing between us.

"There are a lot of reasons this isn't a great idea," Cam whispered.

I nodded. "I need to leave while I can still remember what they are." Damn it, I couldn't make myself let him go. "Look. Will you meet me for dinner at Nacho's sometime?"

"I don't know…" Cam had already drawn back, but he stood indecisively for a few seconds. He pried my arm from around his neck and walked me to the door. "I wish—" He bit his lip against the words.

"Me too. *Fuck yeah. Me too.*" I went for broke. "Are we going to keep pushing each other away?"

One side of his sensuous mouth lifted. "Are you going to keep being a lying sack of shit?"

Jeez. I might still be a sack of shit because I had lied—either plainly or by omission—for over a decade. And after fucking up everything else I'd ever done by trying to grease it and make it easier with white lies or harmless bendings of the truth, or outright whoppers, I could unequivocally say that hadn't worked out so well. So *no*. I didn't plan to lie anymore. Especially if Cam could consider giving me a fresh start given what he knew about me.

The Machiavellian genius who wore my skin said, I'm not going to lie *even if I make everyone miserable by telling the truth*. He said, *fuck 'em*, and there was a part of me that liked that too.

I was still working out the particulars of my new, honest existence.

Cam sent a thorough, assessing glance my way.

"Have dinner with me, Cam. Just a casual dinner at Nacho's. No pressure."

"I'm free the day after tomorrow for an early dinner."

"All right." I felt happier than he looked. "Yeah. Okay. I'll meet you, all right?"

He nodded. When I was once again on his silly sisal mat, I turned to him, but he was closed to me, as distant as he'd ever been.

"You're a good brother." I think he said that as a way of softening things between us. The door closed and clicked shut, but I put my hand on the wood as if by doing that I could keep us connected somehow.

I wanted to be more than a good brother. I wanted to be a good man...

It's odd how you never know what form a karmic correction will take. I headed for home and the rest of the bottle of vodka in my freezer. After that, I slept fitfully and woke several times in the darkness, sick and confused.

CHAPTER NINE

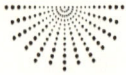

When I met Cam for dinner at Nacho's Bar, I tried not to *look* like I'd spent all of the previous day obsessing about how I looked. I'd ended up wearing a soft black sweater and jeans, with an expensive leather jacket, which made me look more like a member of Mossad than a guy who buys and sells apartment buildings. From the way Cam's eyes widened when he caught sight of me, it was worth it. A tiny bubble of nervous laughter escaped me to ruin the moment, and he shrugged.

After I found us a table in the corner where we could still hear ourselves talk over the sound of Cooper's violin, I saw Izzie and her police officer boyfriend, Andy. That night Izzie was a fashion plate in a sweater and microscopically short, slim skirt that hugged her bodybuilder figure and revealed legs any runway model would kill for. A halo of pale blonde hair stood in stark contrast against her spray-tanned skin as she tottered toward us on towering stiletto heels, pulling the stalwart Andy across the bar. I couldn't help remembering what she'd said about me being a blank slate. Next to her, a lot of people probably seemed blank.

"Evening, Cam." Andy stuck his hand out. Cam rose and pulled him in for a hug.

"Evening." Cam nodded. Something passed between them—two guys on the job acknowledging the aftermath of tragedy rather than a simple greeting—the taciturn but sincere connection I'd gotten glimpses of from hanging around JT and Cam at the firehouse.

There was no help for it; I invited them to join us.

"Just for a minute," Izzie said, glancing at Andy. "I want my guy all to myself for dinner."

Izzie was such a big, powerful woman, those words conjured the image of her devouring him. He gazed at her with rapt adoration, and despite my snobbery, I had to like them.

Izzie got right to the point. "You need to see Minerva."

"I've seen her. She writes things on the sidewalk of my house when she thinks I'm not looking, then hides behind the trees."

"So she tells me." Izzie grinned. "She can take a little getting used to."

Andy nudged her.

I said, "I think she hates me."

"She doesn't hate you." Izzie picked up her drink. "She didn't know you. And we all want to know what your intentions are toward St. Nacho's."

"I don't have any. I hadn't even heard of St. Nacho's before my brother wound up here."

Cam smiled. "Yasha loved it here from the beginning."

"You mean he loved JT."

"He loved both."

Izzie leaned forward. "Minerva floats some theory that St. Nacho's is a seat of awesome cosmic power and she talks a lot about Native American folklore, but I think once you stop here, moving on doesn't feel like such a great idea. St. Nacho's wraps itself around you, and it doesn't let go."

"Maybe," I said. "It doesn't seem to have the same effect on me, though."

"You did a lot of poking around when you first came here," Izzie pointed out. She cocked her head to the side and watched me in a funny, dissecting way that made me feel both transparent and on fire at the same time. "You were doing market studies, reviewing traffic patterns and sales."

"That's because my brother was looking to start a business here."

"But how are we to know it isn't about buying up everything and putting in a big-box store?"

"You have a big-box store just down the highway next to the community college. And for the record, I'm not in the big-box store business."

"I know that. Minerva can be a little protective. She's taken it upon herself to be St. Nacho's spiritual guardian."

"She has nothing to fear from me."

"That's good to know. We're awfully glad to have Yasha around, even though it's not doing my ass any favors. That boy's raspberry tarts call me out of a sound sleep. Add Miss Independence Pies to that, and I need my gym more than anyone else in town does."

"Mary Catherine is expanding into new markets, so Miss Independence taking on the second enterprise hasn't been too much for St. Nacho's even in this economy. That's what I hoped when I was getting a feel for the place. Contrary to popular belief, I wasn't planning a hostile takeover of your little town."

By this time, the way Izzie studied me had started to get damned uncomfortable.

"Most people who show up here take one look around and want to stay," Cam said tightly.

Minerva nodded. "I guess at first we assumed you'd feel the same way. Given your history, we figured you'd have big plans.

Minerva didn't believe you'd be satisfied with the status quo in a sleepy little town like ours."

The waiter put our pitcher of beer on the table between us and offered four glasses. Andy and Izzie declined the beer but didn't leave.

Izzie continued to look at me like I was a bomb she needed to defuse. "Plus, I can't read you at all, which never, ever happens to me."

"I wouldn't worry about that. I'm sure it happens to everyone sometimes."

"Not to me."

I was about to make some crack about psychic Viagra when Cam handed me a beer and asked her, "What do you see when you look at me?"

"Oh, darling, you are a sight for sore eyes. You're sunny yellow even when it's pouring rain, and your heart chakra is like an explosion of green palm fronds with pink tips."

Cam blushed. "Is that good?"

"When have you ever not been good, you big fire muffin. Gimme some sugar." Izzie rose and kissed him on the forehead. She was a little rough, but Cam was obviously pleased. "I'll let you two get on with your dinner."

"Thanks." Cam grinned up at her. "See you tomorrow at the gym."

"Sure, baby." She turned back to me. "You missed your appointment with Jordan today, so he'll be expecting you to call and reschedule. Maybe you should think about annual membership now that it looks like you'll be staying around."

"Who said I'll be staying around?"

Beside me, I heard Cam's intake of breath.

Izzie's tone cooled. She glanced from me to Cam and back again. "Why wouldn't you?"

It wasn't enough that my mind went blank. My mouth hung

open as I waited for something brilliant to occur to me. Three pairs of eyes watched me while I tried to come up with something both truthful and tactful.

"I haven't exactly planned that far ahead."

"I see." Izzie's lips thinned, but before she could say anything, Andy took her arm and tugged.

"I can see we've interrupted your evening out. We'll let you get back to it." He led her away. I watched them go, wondering if I dared to look at Cam.

When I finally turned to him, he was sipping his beer. "Cam…" I began, but he forestalled me.

"I know St. Nacho's isn't exactly your kind of place." His expression was closed again. He might as well have been a stranger.

"It's not that. I don't know what kind of a place is 'my place'. I just don't—"

"It's all right." Cam sighed and reached over to put his hand on mine. I realized my right hand had been jerking, reflexively trying to squeeze my fork/knife/napkin setup. "Relax."

I let out the breath I was holding. "Thank you."

"Most people who come here want to stay. If that's not the case with you, if you don't see yourself here, it's best for everyone if you move on."

"Are you telling me to go now? Before we start something?"

Cam shrugged. "I'm just saying you shouldn't feel you have to stay—not just because you like the people or because your brother wants to live here. St. Nacho's isn't a place you settle for. It's a place you choose."

I nodded. I understood, theoretically, how a man could come here and want to stay. I could see that Jake was growing roots here. That he was forming a new family—something he'd believed he'd never have. I knew how much it meant to him to finally have a place he could call home.

But despite the undeniable beauty of St. Nacho's, despite the peace and comfort it offered, it was something I couldn't relate to. As soon as that sense of place stole over me, I grew restless, almost achy, and I felt the need to get back on the highway.

"I don't know what I want," I said carefully.

Cam's lips curved in a faint, rueful smile. "Then it makes sense to find out, doesn't it?"

I nodded.

When the waiter brought us our food, we settled into a companionable silence. I managed to cut my carne asada—the marinated steak typically served with flour tortillas and the usual sides, beans, rice, pico de gallo, and guacamole. One thing about Nacho's Bar: the spicy food was plentiful. Plus, they made the tortillas by hand and served them piping hot in baskets that kept them that way.

A word from Cam and the waiter brought a fiery, hotter salsa with a smoky bite that was perfect for rolling up with the meat into delicious and filling soft tacos. Our second pitcher of beer was going straight to my fingers and toes, relaxing each molecule along the way. I was content, but I could swear Cam glowed only half as brightly. Izzie would say his sunny yellow had lost its shimmer and that his pink-tipped palm fronds had grayed a little at the edges. Once again, my heart hurt to see a dimly lit Cam Rooney.

"Next weekend, I'm planning to meet my business partner, Al, and his family in Pismo. His girls are horse crazy, and I found a place where they can ride on the beach."

"Yeah?" Cam glanced up from his plate. "I ride horses."

"Do you have a day off? If you have Friday night and Saturday, we can make a big deal of it. I'll find us a nice place to stay. If not, we can just head down for the day."

"I have Friday and Saturday off. I'd love to go."

"All right. We can head out Friday, and I'll see if they can join us Saturday morning. Can you be ready to leave around noon?"

Cam nodded. His eyes had taken on a faraway look from the

moment I mentioned horses. It was possible the key to Cam's heart was through the animal kingdom. I decided I had to investigate that, and I'd start with *the clue of the deluded firehouse cat.*

"Is there anything else you like to do? Golf? ATVs?"

"*Golf.*" He laughed as though I'd made a joke. "Do I look like a golfer to you?"

"I can't golf anymore anyway," I said, forgetting that I'd wanted to see him smile.

"You will." He was resolute. "I'm sure if you want to golf again, you'll find a way."

I felt better than I had since dinner arrived. "Thanks, Cam."

"For what?"

"For being a nice guy. For being the kind of guy who always makes people around you feel better." He smiled and took a sip of his beer, and I went for broke. "So…should I get two hotel rooms for Friday?"

He shook his head. It was the minutest, most tentative *no.*

"Are you sure?"

Again, he signaled with a brief, embarrassed nod. "One hotel room is fine. One bed." He glanced away. It was odd that it embarrassed him, considering we'd known each other for a while—we might even be considered friends—and I'd watched him get a blowjob from a stranger.

He ate the last few bites of his taco in silence. Its filling oozed out onto his fingertips—salsa and sour cream—which he licked off without taking his gaze from mine. His blue eyes glowed like the heart of a flame as the tip of his pink tongue snaked out to swipe over his full lower lip. *Fuck*, he was hot.

"I want to see if I can tie your dick in a knot with my tongue like a cherry stem."

"*Shit.*" Cam dropped his taco, which had somehow imploded, onto his plate. "I have to head to the station right after dinner because I'm working a double shift starting tonight. I promised one of the guys I'd come as soon as I ate."

I nodded. "Rain check?"

"Hell yes." Cam happily scooped the rest of his food up on chips. His demeanor had changed again. He'd gone from happy, to subdued, to happy again in the space of a meal, and ah, damn. I just needed that. I *needed* to see him smile.

At least when I was irritating the shit out of Cam, he didn't seem sad. I'd growled at him, taken potshots, treated him like a rube or whatever, and he'd given as good as he'd gotten from me. But ever since the fire he'd been vulnerable to even that, diminished somehow or damaged—- as fragile as my hand. I couldn't stop myself from doing everything in my power to protect him.

My gut argued caution. I told myself to watch out. I didn't want to find myself tied back down to someone and inevitably worrying about what he was thinking or how he was feeling. I didn't want to have to change my behavior at every turn based on what some guy thought of me.

I had to tell myself that Cam wasn't my dad, who was unstable and impossible to make happy, or my mom, whose happiness depended on my living a lie. He wasn't Bree, who constantly required me to adjust to an ever-changing array of rules, rituals, and magical thinking.

It occurred to me then what a chameleon I had turned out to be.

Well. *That* bore looking into. No wonder I'd become an adept obfuscator.

I frowned.

Cam had apparently been watching me. "What is it?"

"Nothing." St. Nacho's felt itchy again. It was closing in on me. I was sinking in it. It covered me like so much beach sand and swallowed me up. "Maybe I'll head up to the office for the next few days. There are a million little things I know Al wishes I would see to, but he's been trying to cut me some slack. It's not fair to expect him to do everything without me."

That was deliberately vague. If I'd been talking to Bree, I'd have said I needed to go shopping. Shopping was something she never questioned.

He wiped his hands on his napkin. "Okay."

"I think I need some time."

Cam nodded. What could he do? He'd demanded honesty, and I'd given it.

After that I stopped wondering whether he was happy and started worrying about why I cared as much as I did.

Cam continued to eat, and I continued to worry, and after we'd paid, we walked together to the parking lot.

I turned to him. "I guess I'll see you next Friday?"

"Sure," he regarded me thoughtfully.

I opened the door to my car, but Cam closed the distance that separated us, stopping me by grabbing the center of my shirt, buttons and all in his fist, and pulling me back around.

"I think you forgot something."

I gasped, both surprised and frankly turned on to be manhandled that way. In the darkness, he was little more than an immense silhouette, man and muscle, a huge presence. He was capable of astonishing tenderness, but I couldn't forget he could bench-press my weight and throw me around like a toy. He took my face in his hands and pressed his lips to mine, tentatively at first, and then tilting his head to deepen the kiss, slipping the hands that clutched me around my back to pull me into a tight embrace.

He reeled me in—like St. Nacho's itself—trying to drag me down with peace and sentiment and pleasurable sensory over-load until I stopped struggling.

I broke the kiss and pushed him gently away without—I hoped—sending the message that his kiss wasn't welcome. I was breathless and my skin tingled everywhere.

Cam's gaze traveled from my eyes to my dick and back again

like a god giving his creation the once over *and he saw that it was good.*

Cam's smile lit up the otherwise darkened corner of the lot.

"Fr-Friday." That came out weaker than I intended. He nodded, and I got into my car and headed home.

CHAPTER TEN

I made it back in time on Friday the following week to pick up Cam from his apartment just before noon. He answered the door wearing his cat around his neck like a workout towel. The animal hung there motionless except for a loud purr—completely content—while Cam made his last-minute preparations. He gathered his keys and wallet, lifted his duffel, and said, "Okay". Spot came to life and leaped down off his shoulders to rub up against his legs.

"Back soon," Cam told her. I watched him reach down and scratch one last time under her chin. "Jennifer will stop by while I'm gone to check on you."

When he was done reassuring his cat, Cam turned a happy face to me and took my breath away. He looked damp and freshly scrubbed but utterly casual. He hadn't shaved, so his cheeks were covered with a golden stubble that winked in the sunlight when we exited his apartment and walked to my car.

"Mind driving? I just drove in from Santa Cruz, and I could use a break."

"Sure."

I gave him my keys, and he took the wheel after throwing his bag in the trunk.

He wore a subdued Hawaiian shirt and a pair of cargo shorts. I'd gone with lightweight denim jeans and a long-sleeved T-shirt, and I'd thrown a sweatshirt in the back of the car.

"Are you sure you'll be warm enough?"

"I'm sure." He grinned at me as he edged the car out onto the street. "I don't get cold."

"Never?"

"Not that I can remember. It doesn't get cold enough on the coast here. I guess in the winter I might put on a jacket, or if it snowed or something…"

I watched the way he gripped the steering wheel with one hand while he let the other rest on the door. His forearms made my stomach do a funny flip. "You have all those muscles to generate heat."

He grinned, then flexed them. "Maybe."

"So where do you want to go?" I asked. I'd done some checking on the web, and made reservations in a nice Pismo Beach hotel, but other than that, I was completely open to suggestions.

"There are some tidal pools about an hour south, and we could stop for lunch near there."

"Sure." The car had hardly started, and I was already feeling the pull of a nice nap. I'm afraid I yawned.

He glanced at me and grinned. "Don't let me keep you awake."

"I didn't get much sleep last night." I grabbed my sweatshirt from the backseat and bunched it up. "I'll be ready to go as soon as the car stops rolling. The combination of being tired and the motion of the car knocks me out."

"All right." He turned on the radio and fished around for a clubby hip-hop station. He was going to hate my presets. "You rest. I hear old guys need that, and I'll wake you when we get there."

I flipped him off, but my heart wasn't in it. He was right. I pushed my sweatshirt up against the window and fell asleep.

I dreamed what seemed like a dozen different dreams: of New York, of Bree, of getting another—this time unwanted—tattoo. When at last I woke fully it was because the realization came to me that the car was no longer moving and hadn't been for some time.

I opened my eyes to discover Cam had parked in a lot at the top of a cliff with a startling view of the vast foamy gray-green sea. I could see him walking all by himself a hundred feet below, balanced on the rocky shore, bent over to peer at something in the tidal pools.

Cam's short hair, usually stiff with whatever styling product he used to make it stand up, was overpowered by the wind and ruffled gently across his forehead. Muscles bunched under his light clothing as he squatted farther down and leaned over. That youthful, boyish face of his was a study in earnest concentration on whatever he was watching as he put a gentle finger out to poke at it.

I'd seen some amazing things in my life because I was blessed: palaces, museums, great art, theater, dance, pricey cars, expensive men and women, but the sight of Cam carefully lifting up a rock to study what he found underneath was by far the most beautiful. My heart clenched around the knowledge that he was *wholesome*. He was honest and capable of kindness and a depth of compassion I would never have expected from someone as huge and pretty. He was simply good in all the ways that things can be good—good to look at, good to touch and taste and smell. And he was arguably good for others like me, who maybe had a little problem sorting out the whole good/bad thing at times.

I admired his beauty, I loved his heart, and I knew I would

have to live up to his expectations, which made the walk down a hundred feet of rickety wooden stairs to join him on the shore seem like the green mile—a treacherous path into the unknown without even a handhold for comfort.

When he saw me coming, his face lit with a happy smile. "Hey."

"Hey." I couldn't help smiling back. "Whatcha looking at?"

"Anemone." He pointed to a spiny creature in the shallow pools created by low tide. "They have little cells like spear guns that anesthetize their prey. You never touch them though, because they're holding their breath, and touching them would be like punching them in the stomach."

"I guess it's not a good idea then, huh?"

"You're not supposed to touch anything around here, really. It's okay to feel a starfish with a damp finger or something, but it's better to observe without handling the wildlife."

"I see."

He put his hands behind his back. "You can cut the ends off a coffee can and wrap one side with heavy duty plastic wrap—you know. You can secure it with rubber bands. Then you submerge the can and look through the plastic to see what's under the water. It's worth looking at. There's some pretty cool stuff down there. It's hard to get the wrap as tight as you'd like though."

"Is that something you learned when you were a kid?"

"Nah, I grew up in Northern New Mexico. I went to the Monterrey Aquarium when I first got here, and they talked about tide pool etiquette. California is amazing. I've been whale watching and hiked in the Channel Islands. We're damned lucky to have all this here, and it's essential to figure out the best way to take care of it."

I glanced around. Gulls wheeled overhead, and there were other seabirds. I might have recognized a cormorant or a sand-piper, but there were also species I'd never seen before. Glancing down at Cam, my inattention to details like that seemed to me—for the first time—like a senseless waste. As if I'd spent my time in idleness or on frivolous pursuits when I could have been observing everything he was effortlessly sharing with me.

"We are lucky." My voice seemed hoarse to my ears.

He turned to look at me and frowned. "Is something wrong?"

"No. I just don't think I've ever looked that closely at all this."

"Why not? It's amazing." He hopped happily onto another rock, and I stepped after him. "When I was a kid, I found a shell fossil on my dad's land. It made me wonder what it must be like to be able to explore the ocean. It's so much more than I imagined it would be."

"Didn't you ever go to the beach when you were a kid? The Gulf Coast?"

"No," he shook his head. "I grew up on a working ranch, and there was way too much to do."

"You what? A working ranch? Like…a cowboy?"

Cam rolled his eyes. "I guess."

"You're a cowboy *and* a fireman?"

"Yes, Daniel," Cam said dryly. "It's almost as if I'm half of the Village People all rolled into one."

"Why'd you leave?"

"Because my father told me to."

I couldn't believe what I was hearing. "You can't be serious."

"When they found out I was gay, my parents thought it would be best for the family if I left home. They believed I would be a bad influence or a danger to my brothers, so they asked me to leave."

Cam stepped away from me to explore a different little dimple in the rocks. "Wait, did they catch you in flagrante or something?"

Cam looked oddly embarrassed. "No. Of course they didn't."

I didn't think my question was absurd or anything. After all, I'd been sitting in a tree, perfectly innocently, and Cam had come along to get a blowjob underneath it. "So what happened?"

"I came out to them, and they asked me to leave."

I still believed there was more to it than that. "Really. They just said leave."

"That's about it."

"Without any kind of discussion?"

"Yes."

"Without asking you to change or take it back or...anything?"

"That's right."

"Oh, hell no. That is *not* right."

"You have to understand my situation. There were six kids in our family, and we lived in a kind of...Christian-family bubble. We were homeschooled but active in church. We went to Bible camp every summer. We rode buses down to Mexico to do mission work there twice a year. My dad enjoyed being righteous, but being right didn't worry him too much."

"That's awful."

Cam shrugged. "I miss my family sometimes."

"What about your brothers and sisters?"

"They have families of their own now." Cam refused to look at me.

"But surely—"

"They're not interested. I don't exist for them anymore. Leave it alone, okay?" He put his hands in the foamy water and swished them to rinse off sand. "I'm finished here if you want to move on. I just like to stop by every now and again and take a look."

When I glanced around, trying to think of something to say, two things occurred to me. "Their loss is St. Nacho's—and most especially, *my*—gain. And you need to show me around before we go."

Cam's smile was absolutely radiant. "Yeah? Okay." He took my hand in his and led me to a small natural shallow depression in the rocks. "First thing, it's best not to move anything. Most of the creatures you find here shouldn't be touched, but there are some you can feel if you're gentle. If you do, make sure you wet your fingers first because these organisms can be hurt by dry hands and killed outright by carelessness."

"I'll just look."

"This is an echinoderm, mostly called starfish or sea stars. There's a lot of different types. Some have long arms, like these, and some are like little pincushions."

Cam glanced up to make sure I was following and took off again. "There's a ton of interesting things about these guys. They have a hydraulic vascular system that helps them move around in the water, and they…" He kept on talking, and I just followed along, happy to be there.

I let him tell me all about the sea stars, and eventually he widened his lecture to encompass the entire tide pool. I followed him from rock to rock, watching as his strong bare feet found purchase while mine, still firmly in my athletic shoes, slipped a little so I had to windmill my arms for balance. No way were my feet made for hopping around on…whatever the surface was, lava rock or coral, or even the pebbly sand we encountered after he'd shown me all the things he'd come to see. He taught me to look beneath the surface of the water at things I'd never given any thought to, and he told me why they were important to the environment I took for granted.

At one point, he climbed up onto a boulder and stood above me, looking down—a smiling Titan, blond and healthy—his hands shoved in his pockets. I watched him a long time before I realized he was watching me too.

He said, "You look at me differently from the way everyone

else does. I like to think you see things no one else can. I hope that anyway."

Gazing up at him, I felt my skin flush with arousal. He was so...perfect. "You're kind of larger than life, Cam." He had to know that. *Didn't he know that?* "You take my breath away."

"But why?" He crouched down and leaned over, peering at me, and I felt exactly like one of his damned sea cucumbers or starfish, as if he was going to put out a tentative finger and give the side of my face a stroke to see how I'd react.

I could hardly find my voice. "Because just being around you makes me so fucking happy, you airhead. I like you. I want you. I see my unborn children in your eyes—okay scratch that one. I swear to fuck I'm not being flip here." I sighed. "What my heart does whenever you're near isn't just about chemistry, Cam. It's like...stargazing. I feel insignificant and dazzled. Hopeful yet completely unprepared."

His smile was slow. It started on one side of his face, a lazy lift of the muscles at the corner of his lips. Then it trembled across his mouth. From there it moved up his cheeks to his eyes and eventually the whole of his face. He leaped lightly down to stand before me and cupped my face between his hands. For what seemed like a damned eternity, he just stared at me, and then he pulled me in for a kiss so sweet I will never, *ever* forget it. It seared me, scarred me, made every kiss that ever came before it insignificant, and set the bar too high for every kiss that would come after.

"I make you happy." He grinned against my lips. "You know what? *That* was exactly the right answer."

"So I overreached?" I sighed into a second kiss and then another.

"Maybe just a little." He grinned and took my hand to lead me to the stairs, and if going down those weathered bits of wood was unnerving, going up, even being pulled along like a roped rodeo calf by Cam, was unbelievable. Steep step after step passed with the sea churning behind us and nothing but sky above us until we reached the top and the lot where my car sat waiting.

I was vaguely insulted when Cam suggested I do more cardio.

"I do cardio," I said between heaving breaths I was trying to hide.

He laughed and unlocked the car.

"Don't worry." He took a fiendish delight in my discomfort. "We'll get you in shape in no time."

CHAPTER ELEVEN

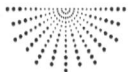

"Is it a problem for you if I eat shellfish?"

"Only if you want to kiss me." It was a pretty smug Cam Rooney who sat across the table from me. I'd laid my cards on the table, emotionally speaking, and I could tell, as far as he was concerned, he'd won whatever battle of wills we'd been waging.

"Is that true? You can't kiss me if I eat shrimp?" We'd planned a late lunch of wine and tapas on the patio of a local resort, but I wasn't about to order a food that would make him sick. We shouldn't even be there if his allergies were serious. I knew any cross contamination could be life-threatening for people with peanut allergies.

"Nah. My allergy is nowhere near that serious. In the past, whenever I've eaten certain types of shellfish—actually so far it's only been prawns and shrimp—I've broken out in hives. I don't take a chance it could turn into something worse, but so far I've never gotten hives from kissing someone who eats it." Cam's cheeks colored. "I admit I don't spend a lot of time *actually* kissing people, and I carry an EpiPen just in case."

"You kissed me."

Cam looked back at the menu. "You complaining?"

"That means you like me, huh?" I put the menu aside. "More than any of your tree fucks. I knew it."

If anything, Cam flushed a deeper red.

When the waiter got there, I ordered several small plates, manchego cheese and grapes, a cured Spanish prosciutto-like ham wrapped around melon, Spanish chorizo with marinated olives, and fiery garlic-seared shrimp with pepper flakes. We got a richly aromatic Rioja wine to go with it and settled in for the relaxing Spanish ritual of wine and nibbles.

"You eat like this a lot?" Cam surveyed the odd assortment of highly seasoned food. "It's pretty salty."

"It's meant to be. It's supposed to make you want to drink more."

"Seriously?" Cam flagged the waiter down and asked for water for both of us.

"Little bites of things that have extreme qualities, bitter, sweet, spicy, salty, are fun, don't you think?" He raised an eyebrow at me. "Jake could explain this better."

"I guess." Cam reacted to one of the olives by blanching and taking a big sip of his wine, which seemed to help not at all. "The salami is good."

"Chorizo."

He frowned. "Really?"

"It's Spanish chorizo, which is kind of like salami." Maybe this wasn't the greatest idea. "Try the melon."

He picked up the ham-wrapped melon and smiled. "I like this."

It was pretty clear he was humoring me about the wine too. "Look, you want a beer?"

He sighed with relief. "Please. And maybe some hot wings?"

I flagged the waiter down again and ordered a beer and a couple of different kinds of hot wings for Cam. Cam took his Corona with a smile, and as he jammed the lime into its neck, he picked up another melon slice.

"Red wine is supposed to be good for you," I said tentatively.

"I know it is. I don't like the flavor."

"Hot wings are deep fried, did you know that?"

"Mmmhmm." He spoke around a mouthful of melon. "I'm not going to stop you from eating your fancy munchies."

"Okay." I pinched the tail off a shrimp and dipped it into the spicy oil. "That's good. I'm only just getting used to being able to eat what I like."

Cam leaned forward to palm a couple of wings. "How come?"

I wondered how much I should say about Bree. Nobody wants to be with a guy talking about his ex on what could arguably be called a first date. "My ex didn't like food very much."

Cam paused, his wing halfway to his mouth. "What do you mean she didn't like food? Any food?"

I picked up my napkin to wipe my fingers. "I told you about Bree. She had some issues. One of her things was she was determined to stay slim. Plus she had this aversion to restaurants. And certain foods. It took an act of God to get her to eat out in a restaurant with me."

"Poor baby."

Cam's frown was formed from pure compassion, and I was quick to deflect it. "No, really. It was a lot harder on her than me. She just didn't seem to ever fit into her skin. Everything irritated her. Everything worried her. I could still go out for business meals but she—"

"I meant her. I meant, *poor woman.*" Cam put his wing down.

"*Exactly.* Wow. How cool that you see it like that. Sometimes Jake was a little hard on her." I breathed out a breath of relief and surprise. It was true she was a bitch sometimes, but I still felt a connection to her, and I hated to make her sound like she was crazy. "She had problems. I'm perfectly willing to admit that one of them was me."

"There are some people at the gym like that. They're way too thin, and they see themselves as overweight. They work like demons, and they're never satisfied. It makes me sad."

"Bree could be self-destructive," I admitted. "Occasionally I had some luck getting her to see a therapist."

"It's good that you tried."

"Not really. There were plenty of times when her problems were convenient for me. When she focused on herself like that, I never had to worry she was looking too closely at what I was doing." I pushed the food away and picked up my wine. In that moment I was ready to swear Minerva put some kind of spell on me. It was becoming impossible for me to keep very private, even painful, things from pouring out of my mouth, especially with Cam.

"I see." He sipped his beer, watching me carefully.

I shook off the mood I'd placed us in. "And just like that, I've become the guy who talks about his ex."

"It's all right." He shrugged.

It wasn't *all right*. "I know that I come with a warehouse full of baggage. For a lot of different reasons I blow hot and cold. I run, then I chase, and I act like I don't know what I want because I don't. But I know what I like. I know what makes me happy, and whenever I see you, it's like getting a face full of sunshine. Maybe that's all I need to know. I keep wanting to turn to you again and again because you make me feel so good."

"That's the nicest thing anyone has ever said about me." Cam put his hand down on mine. He stroked the backs of my fingers, and just that small connection between us lowered my blood pressure and sent soothing messages to my brain. *It's all right. It's going to be fine. You have time to figure this out.*

I lifted my glass to my lips to cover my embarrassment.

Cam asked, "You know what happens when I look at you?"

"Do I want to know?"

"Probably not." He huffed a laugh.

"All right though. Shoot."

Cam toyed with his beer bottle. "When I look at you, I just think...that one is mine." *Aw, man.* How do you resume an afternoon of casual dining after something like that?

"All right."

I'm not sure what I meant by *all right* at the time. Only that I'd heard him. That I understood, or maybe even that I was willing to capitulate, to fall in with his plans for me—to come when he called—like his cat. I might have.

Probably I would.

Cam smiled then and put his effort into his wings. While he did that, I was able to enjoy looking at him. He hadn't forgotten me, but he didn't seem like the kind of guy to spend a lot of time talking while he ate something he liked, so I paid attention to detail like never before. Every crunch of Cam's even white teeth fascinated me, every swipe of his tongue turned me on. He had a way of eating wings that would have made Bree faint. It was unapologetically carnivorous. Intrinsically dirty. He dipped the juicy, sauce-coated morsels into bleu cheese dressing and broke them into bits, licking and sucking both the bones and his fingers until I was hard as stone beneath the napkin in my lap. He wasn't nutritionally irredeemable like me. He seemed to enjoy the celery and carrots that accompanied his wings just as much, if not more, than the chicken itself.

At one point, he rubbed the tip of his nose with his thumb and smeared a bit of dressing there. It took all the sangfroid I had to keep my face blank—to keep from leaping over the table and licking it off.

One moment, our meal was laid out before us, then after what seemed like very little time passed, we had nothing but plates and garnish left between us. My bottle of wine was empty, but Cam was still on his first beer.

I paid the check, and we left, Cam leading me to the street, holding my hand in public as if it was just another day in St. Nacho's.

I pulled my hand away discreetly.

"Are you worried about what people will think?" he asked.

"This isn't St. Nacho's."

Public affection between same-sex couples was far more commonplace around St. Nacho's. It wasn't like living in a fantasy world, but it was easy to get into the habit of taking a lover's hand or kissing a date on the street there. In Pismo the populace was older, more conservative, and less likely to approve of open displays of affection from anyone, let alone two men.

"Fuck 'em." Cam opened my car door and waited while I got in. "I do what I do."

I grinned up at him. "That's one way to approach prejudice."

He knelt down next to the car, next to me, and brushed the hair back off my face. "I don't hide who I am. If I want to hold my date's hand, I do. I don't care where we are. Physically, very few people are willing to push a guy my size around. You're probably pretty safe with me in a place like this."

"I guess." I'd never take him on, and bullies are almost all born cowards.

"But people still talk crap all the time. That going to bother you?"

I couldn't lie to him. I wasn't supposed to lie anymore anyway. "I don't know."

"That might be a good thing to figure out." He closed the door and walked around to the driver's side. I caught him feeling his pockets for the key again and waited for him to remember he didn't need one.

"Where to now?" He got in and started up the car and glanced over, relaxed and ready for whatever came next.

Even though I told myself I'd planned to make this a real date, to take it slow and amble along the beach, to show Cam a good time instead of jumping him the second we reached our destination, I said, "We could check in at the hotel."

He shot a knowing glance my way and backed out of the space. "Sure. Put our stuff away. Take a look around and figure out what there is to do." He caught his lower lip between his even white teeth, trying to hide his smile.

"Sure. Read the informative hotel brochure." I really couldn't look at him when I said that.

It took only a few minutes to get to the resort where I'd booked our room. Cam insisted on carrying both our bags and my briefcase to the front desk. The clerk was friendly and didn't bat an eye when she handed us our keys.

"Have a pleasant stay, Mr. Livingston."

"We will, thank you very much."

Once inside the elevator we were alone. He pushed me against the wall, pinning me there, pulling my hands over my head and proving that he'd had the same reaction to our lunch that I had. I hooked a leg around his in a grossly indecent, needy maneuver that brought our groins together. A bright flash of heat surged directly to my cock when it came into contact with his, hard and ready, throbbing beneath the thin fabric of his shorts. He used it like a battering ram—rubbing and grinding it against me—until I saw stars.

For the first time in my life, I went weak at the knees, and Cam, who already had my duffel on a strap across his shoulder and was carrying two other bags, leaned over and lifted me in an effortless fireman's carry—probably just to prove he could.

I laughed like a kid as he carried me down the hotel hall that way.

CHAPTER TWELVE

Cam whumped me down onto the bed and divested himself of his other burdens. In no time at all, he was on me, wrestling me out of my clothes while I did the same to him. Finally clad in only socks, I wrapped my legs around him and let him pin me down.

I let go of my deeply rooted need for control and clung to Cam. I was smaller, weaker, and arguably drunker. He kissed me long and hard, opening my lips with a forceful tongue and probing my mouth. I opened for him, but I gave him a fight, and I guessed we both found that satisfactory, because Cam gave me little time to recover between forays. I barely had time to breathe, but he did no more than kiss me and grind for what seemed like forever.

What a sensualist. He ran gentle fingers over every inch of me he could reach, from my shoulders to my thighs to the bottoms of the feet I had locked behind his back. He gripped and squeezed my ass and nuzzled our cheeks and our noses together. At one point, I think he even brushed his eyelashes over my closed eyelids while he rubbed his lips over mine, his touch featherlight and then gone as quickly as it came.

Then with a great, rolling heave of his upper body our positions reversed, and I found myself on top, able to explore him in equal detail. He had soft, curly golden hair on his chest and in his pits. It grew darker the farther it traveled down his magnificent abs to pool in a thatch of red hair now hidden by his erection.

I thumbed the dark disks of his nipples, watching as they pebbled and flushed beneath my fingers. Laying the flat of my tongue on one, I sucked and swirled until he arched for me, offering both his nipple and his cock, trying to get more sensation, more contact between our heated bodies.

"Dan." His breath came in short puffs. "C'mon. You're killing me here."

I slipped my good hand around his back and insinuated a finger between his ass cheeks as I sucked his other nipple into my mouth. He was salty and delicious, tasting of sweat and man and sea, and I couldn't get enough. I reached for his jaw with my tender hand and touched his mouth. He licked my thumb and sucked it, shuddering as I teased the tight ring of muscles guarding his channel.

"Ride me." He panted. "Dan...I need you to ride me."

I nodded and left him long enough to scramble to my bag for supplies where I came up with a bottle of slick and a couple of condoms. When I got back to him, he lay there, one arm behind his head, one hand on his cock.

I couldn't believe he was mine.

A smile bloomed over his lips as he welcomed me back, grunting and accommodating my weight. Something in his eyes made my heart lurch, a giddy, thrilling little spike of adrenaline, a rush of happiness that surged through my veins on contact with his skin.

He took the lube from me and gave my hip a light slap. "Come up here."

One of Cam's large hands gripped my ass, and he drew me

up and up until I was poised over his chest—my legs spread impossibly wide—so he could nuzzle my balls. I shivered all over when the wet heat of his mouth surrounded my flesh, engulfing me in a moist cave. It was almost-pleasure and almost-pain while his hand kneaded and gripped my cock and his mouth teased and fondled my balls. I had to grab for the headboard because I thought I'd fall right over and crush his head. He flipped the lube lid open, and the hand that held me disappeared only to return, slick and insistent, on my perineum, gliding toward my hole.

I shook all over, weak with need, while he readied me for him. His fingers pumped inside me, and when I started to push against his hand, begging for more, he slipped it free, pushing me back until I hovered over his cock. I was almost senseless by this time, and he had to explain what he wanted.

"Get me ready." He pressed a condom into my hand. I must have looked at it like I'd never seen one before because he took it from me and opened it, handing the latex circle back unwrapped.

Feeling foolish, I rolled it down on him, giving him a pump or two, then held myself still.

"What are you waiting for?" His eyebrows rose.

"I want to kiss you while you push inside me."

He smiled faintly, gazing up at me, and then his entire body rippled beneath mine. It was like riding some magnificent, mythical animal as he rolled up onto his elbows. His abs strained, and when his lips met mine, I sank onto his cock, trying to relax. He seemed impossibly large, and I felt tight. I worried whether I'd be able to take him even though I wasn't exactly untested in that area. He pressed his lips to mine, and for that bright moment, we were connected by a circle of hunger and need that raced from my lips to his, down through his body and back to me through his cock.

I resisted him only as long as he resisted me. When my

tongue swept in to take his mouth, his cock surged past the tight ring of muscle, past my brief, unconscious resistance until my body capitulated for him. I rocked back, and he pushed up, and little by little our bodies joined. With a groan he dropped back, and I sat up fully, one palm flat on his chest, split open and spread wide, impaled on him. I felt him as deep as my heart, and I let out a noise I didn't recognize as coming from me at all.

"Dan," he whispered, shifting, drawing out and then pushing his hips up and around in tight circles to push deeper still. "*Daniel.*"

I didn't know where my hands should go, so I wrapped them around myself—across my body to grip my own shoulders— and rode him like that, letting him hold my hips so we could find a rhythm together. And fuck, it felt good and bad at the same time—confusing to let him in that deep. I opened myself so completely and yet I was still, for all intents and purposes, clinging to myself, alone.

I wanted more. I needed him to pull me down and engulf me completely.

I needed him to hold me. I needed skin. I needed to taste and touch more than I needed to be fucked, and I stretched and reached out for him, taking his face in my hands and bringing our mouths together for a searing kiss that I wanted to last forever.

One minute I was on top, and the next, he'd pulled out and rolled me over facedown so he was lying on me, crawling up, nudging my legs apart, spreading me once more while he licked and kissed all along my spine. He entered me again, this time kissing my shoulders and my neck. He breathed softly against my temple and said my name and *gimme* and *yeah, yes, mine* until he seemed to lose even the power of one-syllable words.

He fucked me slowly. Deeply. He drew grunts and satisfied little huffs of air from me until I couldn't breathe except to pant.

It was perfect. *Cam* was perfect, and at last, when he

wrapped his arm around me like a python to pump my dick with his hand while he fucked me into oblivion, I blew all over, howling my delight into a pillow.

He chuckled hot breath into my hair and rubbed his bristly face along my shoulders. "*Daniel.*"

I was boneless and sated and oh, so very content to gather his hand in mine. I kissed and rubbed my cheek along the knuckles like his damned cat.

His other hand, still splayed across my lower abdomen warmed me even though what spunk he hadn't wiped away with the sheet had started to cool and dry.

I felt his cock soften, and he slipped it out of me, dropping the condom over the side of the bed.

"Jeez." He sighed.

"Feel like a nap?" I turned and tucked my head between his neck and shoulder, shamelessly wanting his arms still wrapped around me.

"Mmmhmm." He sighed as our bodies came into contact again. I wrapped my leg over his to keep him close.

I had planned other things for the afternoon. Exploring the beach, the pier, the shops. Dining. Dancing, if he wanted to go to a club. I was just too comfortable to move. "Just for a bit."

"Mmmhmm."

I LAY BESIDE CAM LATER, FADING IN AND OUT OF SOME forgettable dream. I had the peculiar sensation that I was being watched, and when I opened my eyes, I found Cam's blue gaze fixed on me, curious, as if he were observing a slow growth of mold on my face.

I shot up, startled. "What?"

"Nothing." He ran the tip of his finger down my nose. "Did you know you talk in your sleep?"

Ah, *no*. I scrubbed at my face and glanced at the clock. Eight p.m. Perfect for a late supper and a walk on the beach. "Bree used to tell me that, but I can't say I've ever heard proof. What did I say?"

He grinned. "Mostly nonsense I think. You did say a name. Jack."

"Ah." *Jack*. I chuckled. He waited, but I ignored his curiosity.

"Who's Jack?"

Gotcha. "Jack was my zeyde's dog—predictably enough, a Jack Russell terrier. I haven't thought about him in years."

"Really."

I nodded, shifting so I could lay my head on his outstretched arm. Not a pillowy soft bicep, that. It was like sleeping on small boulders. I faced him. "I used to love that dog. My dad wouldn't let us have one, but we could play with Jack. I was eight when Jake was born, and Zeyde made me this grand presentation of a key to his place and asked me if I thought I could handle the responsibility of walking Jack on my way home from school. I think he just wanted to keep me out of the house so my mom and Jake could nap."

"Your grandfather sounds like a great guy. Yasha told me a lot about him."

"He's the one who always called Jake *Yasha*. He was a good man. He tried to make things better when...when they weren't."

"He was good to you. He took Jake to Israel?"

"Yeah. Jake had a hard time in school. When he was younger, I was always there to protect him, but when I went to university, things got bad. Mom lost it when he came out. She called me first thing, hysterical. She talked all that out to me so she wouldn't let him see how much it bothered her."

"That's why you never came out to her?"

"I'd never seen her like that. No way she could have handled two of us. She was devastated. But you've got to hand it to her. Regardless of how much that upset her, she stood by him."

"I see."

"They're gone now, though. I guess it's finally my turn."

CHAPTER THIRTEEN

C am and I had dinner by candlelight in front of an amazing panoramic ocean view. I hardly paid attention to the well-prepared California fusion cuisine which took the disparate aspects of French and Asian cooking and merged them with typical fresh California ingredients. Cam frowned at his plate like the waiter had presented him with soylent green, but dinner was lovely. Maybe it was the first time in my life that good food took a backseat to watching my date.

When the waiter presented Cam's dessert in a flaming shot glass, it was nothing less than priceless.

"Are you kidding me?" Cam asked, polite enough to wait until after the waiter left. He flipped the saucer from his coffee over the glass to smother the flame. "Pudding should never be on fire."

"What can I say? The reviews said this place was good."

The food had been delicious. I'd had black sesame seared ahi with greens and some sweet hot dressing with wasabi grits—or something. Was it white polenta? Cam had beef tenderloin with summer squash and wasabi mashed potatoes. It was first-rate, but maybe not Cam's style, because he pulled apart the self-indulgent little towers of food suspiciously, separating the dish's elements onto the plate like a child, after which he peered at each thing before he ate it like he expected it to move. He'd frowned in concentration to the point I thought sweat would pop out on his brow.

Note to self: save pretentious restaurants for business lunches.

"It is good," he admitted when he finally dipped his spoon into his dessert. "The fire kind of caramelized the sugar in the fruit on top."

I wasn't too hungry so I let my dessert sit for a while, preferring to slouch on the table in a way my mother would have hated, leaning my head on my hand and watching Cam like some lovesick teen.

"I've been watching every move you make, and next time I'll get the restaurant exactly right."

The gaze that had been focused on his spoon rose to my face. His cheeks darkened. Maybe he wasn't used to being the center of someone's rapt attention like that. I couldn't imagine why. I loved looking at him.

"You don't have to do that."

"I want to. I want to study you and figure out everything you like, everything that makes you happy, and then pour it all over you like…rain."

Cam's brows drew together. "That's—"

"I know it sounds creepy. Like someone should be piping in the soundtrack to *Psycho*, huh?"

"A little."

I shrugged. "I don't really always know what to do with people."

"I'm starting to get that."

"But there are some people I want to make happy."

He sagged a little and put his spoon down. "And you figure

that you'll watch them and see what they like and give them that?"

"Well…yeah."

"But there's more, right? There's more than just giving people things they like, or even experiences, like riding your bike or a horse on the beach." Cam took my hand. "What I like is *you.*"

Jeez. A bubble must feel something when it pops. It's only air, floating along separated from a vast ocean of other air by the thinnest membrane of soap and water, a microns-thick skin containing it, keeping it from melting back into infinite space.

Cam's words popped some rigid bubble that kept me isolated even when I was with the people closest to me. The pressure around me equalized as I came to terms with my new reality. I was dizzy with anxiety, and my heart raced like I'd run a marathon.

He pushed his dessert away. "Can you learn to give yourself away the same way you give away things?"

Ah, fuck. Could I? I didn't know. I was pretty sure I never had. Even looking all the way back, past Bree, past school, way back into childhood, I'd always functioned the same way with people. Like a cross between pet owner and classy Santa Claus, managing the environment for those I loved and gifting them with their favorite things.

I'd never even approached a dog without a treat in my hand.

"I don't know what I have to give."

Infinitely optimistic, Cam said, "There's bound to be something though, right?"

"Right." I dropped several bills into the leather folder left for us by the waiter. Cam let me. He probably knew there was no stopping me. The conversation we were having didn't warrant an intervention at that point. I worried that he considered the price of dinner a small skirmish when there were much larger wars in our near future.

Cam got up from the table. "Don't look at me like that."

I rose and picked up my jacket, shaking it out and pushing my arms through the sleeves. "Like what? How am I looking at you?"

His face softened. "I'm not trying to blow down your house of cards, Daniel."

I nodded, but whether he was trying or not, he had, and we both knew it.

———

THAT NIGHT WE WALKED HAND IN HAND ALONG THE BEACH. MORE than one person reacted to that. Some were positive, some not. I had to admit I wasn't anxious to wear my sexuality on my sleeve, but it felt all wrong to treat Cam like less, to hide what I felt for him away in the hotel room when I could have showered a woman with affection in public.

I sensed disapproval from strangers like waves of energy, whether I was looking at them or not. At one point, a couple of teenage boys spit on the ground in front of Cam's shoe and called us faggots.

I must have seemed pretty stricken, because Cam dropped my hand without rancor and kept walking, still close, brushing shoulders, but not overtly indicating that we were a couple. I knew it wasn't like him to hide who he was. In my surprise, I'd slowed. When he turned back to wait for me, his eyes held nothing but affection. I took his hand firmly in mine again, and we kept going.

"You sure about this?" he asked carefully.

My heart was so full of all the new things I was thinking and feeling that I almost couldn't answer. Mostly I'd never been sure, *really sure*, about anything. Well. Except one thing.

"Cameron Rooney, I feel lucky to be here with you. I don't care who knows it."

I heard him let out the breath he was holding. "All right."

We went back to our hotel, and I'm ashamed to say I fell asleep in his arms, listening to the susurration of waves through the open slider—even though he might have had other ideas.

I BLINKED WHEN THE SUN SLATTED THROUGH THE GAPS IN THE blinds. Cam had obviously just woken up himself. He looked around, disoriented, as if he was trying to put together a memory of the night before. I noticed when his gaze landed on me, he didn't seem disappointed.

"You should look away before you turn to stone. I need to shower, and my breath probably smells like ass."

Cam ignored my advice. Instead, he laughed and rolled toward me, giving me a good long, not unpleasant kiss. "Come on then."

I grimaced when I rose to my feet. I was definitely not twenty-five anymore and here it was. *The shower scene.* The full monty: vertical, naked, in the bright light of morning, without the heat of passion to gild us and blunt any imperfections. Cam was safe. He didn't have any imperfections.

I didn't think the harsh light of day was going to hurt me much, but I thought I looked better between the sheets in the moonlight. Most people do.

I let him lead me, clad only in our boxers, to the bathroom. I must have let on that I was feeling shy, because he joked around about it.

"You've been watching me wash the rig for months. Let's see how you like me soapy and wet without clothes on."

I rubbed my face and grinned, unwilling to break my truth-only vow so soon over trivialities that could be easily verified. "Watching you guys work is like free porn."

"It's a public service." Cam rippled the muscles in his

immense shoulders. He was a big enough ham to give me a little show. "That's why we have the cleanest rig in the state."

"Because we have the *dirtiest* firefighters."

"This"—he indicated his ripped torso with a sweep of his hand—"isn't something you hide."

"Oh, no." I could not agree more. I could scarcely catch my breath. "That would be a crime."

He flicked the elastic waistband of his boxers down, all the while pumping his slim hips so his crotch shot up at me like a 3D cartoon. His moves were practiced, easygoing, and flirtatious. He smiled that sweet-as-candy smile, but it was impossible not to lose a little of my confidence. I don't think he noticed because he hooked thick fingers in his shorts and pulled them down and off, kicking them to the side.

"Holy fuck," I whispered.

Cam stood before me naked except for his socks. The cut of muscles on his torso looked positively succulent. He had to know how fine he looked, and he definitely enjoyed showing it off. His cock lurched lazily—half-erect. All proud. He smiled at me, but there was something more in his eyes, a flash of uncertainty, the tiniest hint that it mattered to him what *I* thought.

"You're gorgeous. You *know* you're gorgeous."

"Yeah?" He flexed and preened a little. "You like?"

"Of course I do. How can you ask that after yesterday?"

"What do you like best?" He posed—the classic Mr. Universe —and, while he wasn't so serious about bodybuilding that he appeared veiny and bulbous, it was obvious he worked hard to maintain his physique. I knew for a fact he didn't juice. It took backbreaking work to look that good. Jordan had given me the heads-up on how much time Cam spent in the gym, and the result was just spec-fucking-tacular.

He stood before me: a magnificent, impossible specimen of manhood.

"What I like best"—I went to him and slipped my good arm around his neck—"is the way you say my name."

Long seconds passed where I thought I had totally fucked up.

"Like...Daniel?"

I nodded. "Just like that."

"How come?"

"When you say my name like that, I'm special," I said. "Or unique maybe. Jeez. Now I sound as batshit crazy as everyone else in St. Nacho's."

Cam shook his head and pulled me in for a tender kiss, and I could feel that caring, that instinct to protect that came from somewhere so deep inside him he didn't know it was there. When he slipped his tongue into my mouth, I welcomed him enthusiastically.

We stayed like that, locked together, warming up—breaths mingling and hearts pounding. His fingers traced lightly over my skin, glancing off my angles, stopping at interesting landmarks. He brushed his thumb over my nipple, and I arched.

"Come with me." He took my healthy hand to lead me toward the bathroom. Pulled nearly off my feet, I went.

He turned on the shower and moist air filled the bathroom. I watched the silken shower curtain flutter while I brushed my teeth. It was too bad the shower surround wasn't clear glass or something. I would have loved to see Cam's body under the showerhead, dripping wet, soapy, and nude.

His head poked between the fabric and the tiles. "Coming in anytime soon?"

I nodded. Was I stalling? The new, honest Dan Livingston had to admit it.

Yes.

I dropped my boxers on the floor. Maybe I tried to give them a devil-may-care kick with my toe. Cam watched me hungrily, and as far as I could tell, he didn't do one of those noisy cartoon double takes or in any other way indicate he found me wanting. In fact, he grinned at me like he liked what he saw and dragged me in with him.

"C'mere you." He dunked me under the spray and laughed when I realized he'd turned the heat way down, so it could barely be considered tepid.

"Aw come on. Heat it up, please."

He got right behind me and rubbed my ass. "I'll heat it up. Hot as you can stand it." He turned the dials, and the water grew warm again, but by then we were both wet and breathless, and he pressed my back up against the cold tiles. I grabbed the tiny squeeze bottle of body wash, and when he offered his hand, I squirted some out.

Our lips met as he slicked up my chest and shoulders, his hands soaping me in a haphazard way as I returned the favor, until we were sliding against one another and rivers of foam ran between our bodies. He tongued my lips and clutched me to him. Our bobbing cocks met sloppily, and we glanced off one another in a tangle of limbs and self-conscious laughter. Cam nipped my shoulder hard.

"You taste good," Cam whispered. He rubbed his nose against mine and seemed to like that, because it made him smile sweetly again, his lips curving up against mine. Our cheeks scrubbed together, and he trailed kisses down my jaw to find the pulse at the base of my neck.

"Are you marking me?" I asked and got a nip and a heartier squeeze. I nudged him with my pelvis, and he nudged me back, turning with me until I was under the spray. I blinked water from my eyes because suddenly there was cold empty space where his body had been, but he came back again, and I realized he'd only been reaching for the shampoo.

While he noogied it into my hair, I got a glimpse of unguarded Cam, blue eyes dominating that chiseled American face.

"You're so hot." I breathed the words, and even though he must hear that twenty times a week, his cheeks colored faintly from the praise. I lifted my good hand to his jaw, unable to stop myself from thumbing his full lower lip again. "So kissable."

I traced it with my tongue and then sucked it in. He tilted his head and pressed his lips firmly to mine. When his tongue slashed out this time, it was with a definite purpose, intended to let me know what he wanted from me. I surrendered to him, opening my mouth and wrapping my arms around him as he pushed me back under the spray again.

This time it was like drowning in soap and sex and Cam, and I didn't bother to hide my willingness to go wherever he took me. He could hold me under that water forever, and as long as I could see the intense, hungry way he looked at me, as long as those keen eyes kept their promise to take whatever he wanted from me—I would let him suffocate me under the spray and die happily.

He held me there and rocked me until my hair was free of soap, and then he lifted me and pressed my back against the wall again. This time I had no choice but to wrap my legs around him and cling.

"You like this?" he asked.

"Rhetorical que—"

He stopped my lips with a passionate kiss.

"I'm strong," he whispered, and I had to agree. If I'd had any breath left, I surely would have said something out loud to concur. As it was, I wanted to feel every inch of him pressed against me. I wanted to squeeze our dicks between us and rub them on the coarse hair of our bellies, and I wasn't thinking much beyond that.

He stopped moving. "You want me to fuck you again?"

I glanced at his face, and what I saw there wasn't the bluff, stripteasing Cam I'd met earlier. "Huh?"

117

"I…" He frowned. "I can fuck you just like this if you want. I'm strong enough to hold you here and do it just like this."

Oh…what a thought. It was a good one. I wanted Cam to do exactly that—to fuck me up against the tile of the shower, or over the back of a couch, or on a bed of nails if it came to that.

Still, as my mind raced off in that direction, I couldn't help the tiny tingle of something like caution, which I was unlikely to exercise at the best of times. I usually didn't even understand the concept when my dick was up and sliding soapily on a hot guy's slab o' abs.

Something in my brain shook loose and said…*Wait.*

"Cam?"

Lashes lowered over his eyes. "Mmmhmm?"

"I want to do what you like best," I said, feeling my way around something I sensed was a landmine. "I want to be the guy who gives you exactly what you want. Do you want to fuck me?"

"Yes."

Those eyes still weren't…I actually had to tilt my head to look Cam in the eye, and I have to believe that was the weirdest moment of my life, dangling there from Cam's arms, legs crossed against his ass, asking what he wanted most from me. "What do you want?"

"I like a guy's mouth. On me," he admitted with a fierce blush, "and in me."

A *whoosh* of breath left my chest when I visualized that.

"Most guys see how big I am and they only want me to top. Or they want to get all subby and blow me on their knees. Assume some weird-ass position. It's all good."

"I guess…"

"But sometimes…"

"Sometimes you want to let go and get *done.*"

He nodded, almost as if he was ashamed to admit it.

I shook my head *no*, and I felt him start to pull away. I clung to him and pressed my cheek tightly against his, brushing it with my lips like I'd kiss a particularly beloved child. I meant, not no but *no, wait. Why wouldn't anyone with half a brain spoil the fuck out of you?*

"*Cam.* Holy shit. Pick me...*Pick. Me.* I will tongue fuck you until you scream my name so loud they throw us out of this dump."

He laughed and shivered against me. "Yeah?"

"Are you kidding me? I'm your ass pirate. Heave to and prepare to be boarded."

CHAPTER FOURTEEN

I sent Cam into the bedroom without me while I toweled myself off. After that I made coffee in the minuscule pot on the sink and dug through my toiletries for supplies.

Whoa, had this day ever taken a turn I hadn't expected. Yet if I really thought about it, the whole thing made perfect sense. I'd always known Cam Rooney was far more than what, as they say, "…it said on the tin."

In some ways Cam was the ultimate bad boy. He'd grab a likely fuck off the dance floor and do whatever, wherever. He gave off an uncomplicated vibe but was far more intelligent than he let on. How many men took one look at those muscles of his and assumed he'd want to top. How many simply saw a guy who could pound them into the mattress and never bothered to ask *him* what he liked?

Stupid fuckers. *Their loss.*

I entered the bedroom carrying a cup of coffee for each of us and my toiletry kit. I wore only a towel wrapped around my waist. I found him sprawled on the bed, arms and legs akimbo, taking up most of the figurative real estate in the room and breathing all the air.

I shook my head.

"No," I told him. "This isn't how it's going to be."

Seriously, I would not let Cameron Rooney—or any man in the same circumstances—run my show.

I gave his thigh a light tap to let him know he needed to leave a little room for me on the bed. He looked up at me with what I thought was a kind of cocky disbelief. "You just turn over and draw your knees up under your chest. Put your head down and wait for me while I get ready."

He digested this with a sweet frown on his face. Maybe the reason he simply sat there and waited was surprise. "Are you serious?"

"How serious are you about liking a tongue in your ass?"

After that he moved faster than I thought possible, curling up into a ball around a pillow, knees drawn up to his chest. His naked ass stuck up in the air like two pale, perfect boulders—his glutes so tight I could probably crack pecans between his butt cheeks.

I swear to fuck there was a blush staining his entire body. He asked, "This okay?"

"Oh, yeah." I left the room wearing only a towel, to get ice.

At that point I have to say I was probably laughing inside. There's no telling what Cam was thinking. I didn't take forever. I came back to the room as quickly as I could, carrying a bucket of ice. Coffee, check. Ice, check. Supplies, check, check.

A lot of people like to just fall into bed with a lover; they want to be swept away by passion, carried off in the moment and out of control. I like that. We'd certainly had that the previous day when we'd arrived at the hotel with only one thing on our minds. But this wasn't about me, and when it's about my lovers, I employ the opposite strategy. I give them exactly what they need without getting too carried away myself, and it generally works out pretty well.

And *fuck*, I enjoyed the rosy glow that anticipation left on

Cam's skin. I loved the way his breath hitched when I climbed onto the bed, and I caught my own breath when he peeked back at me from under his arm. He was apprehensive, and I liked that too. I wanted him hyperalert, off-balance, even a little afraid.

"Are you into kinky shit?" he asked when I ran my hands over his ass. It felt just like I remembered, like velvet but crisp with hair, wrapped over rock. He couldn't get any hotter without burning us both alive.

"Define kinky for me."

"Are you going to hit me? Am I going to have to call you Sir, or—"

"I don't know. Do you want that? You tell me what you want and what you don't want. That's how this works. I like control." I'd never lied about that. "I like control a lot. But I'm not going to do anything you don't like."

He bit his lip.

"This shouldn't come as a surprise. Are you going to give me what I want? Are you going to relax and let me pleasure you?"

"Yes." He whispered the word.

"Excellent." I continued to massage his glutes. I missed the muscles in my right hand so much. I only had enough strength to smooth with my right while I could grip and squeeze with my left. I could penetrate him with my right thumb, maybe, but my other fingers still felt too tender. That was reality. It must have been a very uneven massage for him. "Do you like this?"

"Yes," came a muffled reply. A sigh escaped him. I pulled some massage oil from my kit and warmed it between my palms.

"You should have people to do this for you every day," I said, smoothing and polishing his skin. The oil made him glisten. "You need minions to anoint you like some South Sea island king or a Greek hero."

"Now you're just making fun…"

"I am *not*." I went higher on his back, up his rib cage to his shoulders, down his arms. While I was doing that, my towel fell off. I let him feel my arousal. As I worked the oil into his skin, my cock bobbed against his ass crack, leaving a damp trail—like kisses. I left a trail of kisses with my lips too, some gentle, some firm. Sometimes I nipped and left light marks from my teeth.

"You are the object of my desire, Cam. I plan to worship every part of you with everything I have. Do you believe me?"

Cam tensed again but nodded. I dropped my hand between his ass cheeks and smoothed oil there. When I indicated he should lift up, he did, pressing his face down into the pillow.

"This is mine." I rubbed his taint and circled the dark bud of his anus with an oiled finger. "Your ass is all mine."

He let out a sound like an embarrassed chuckle.

"Say it." I tapped his pucker to get his attention

Cam's self-consciousness was clear in his voice. "My ass is yours."

"When I want it, you'll bare it for me and let me have it. No questions asked." I rubbed my thumb over his perineum and fondled his balls with my other hand. When I gave them a squeeze, I felt him shiver.

"All right."

"It's a beautiful ass, Cam."

I swear he giggled.

"Do you like to be slapped?" Some people liked that. I liked a nice pink ass as much as the next guy, but I wasn't married to it. As far as I was concerned, whatever I did was about Cam, and I liked what he liked. He was out of luck if he needed me to really hurt him, but a little slap was fine with me. I could still do that with my left hand. His shoulders tensed.

"This honesty thing is really getting out of control with you, isn't it?" he mumbled.

"That's the deal," I told him. I rummaged around in my kit, throwing things on the bed: dams, gloves, lube, and scented oils. Maybe I seemed clinical to him and killed his mood. I could understand where he was coming from. He just didn't know where we were going. *Yet.*

"I'm going to rub your ass. I'm going to get it slick, lick it, penetrate it, and spank it if you want me to. I'm going to do all this while I'm mouthing your balls and jacking your dick. By the time I'm done, you'll feel like I electrocuted you. You'll give it up to me each and every time because I'm going to make it so good for you, baby. So good…you'll beg me for it."

He swallowed hard.

I leaned over and whispered in his ear. "And I'm going to get off without even touching my dick because just the thought of owning your ass makes me so hot I could come right now."

"You going to talk dirty to me?" he asked.

"You like that?"

"Yeah."

"Good then, baby. You're going to be my new fuck toy." I grabbed a glove and pulled it onto my right hand. It was a tight fit, a surgical glove liberated from my doctor. A lot of what I had in my kit was lifted from doctors and dentists. I popped an ice cube into my mouth. It was one of those small round ones with a hole in the middle. I pushed it with my tongue so it was clenched between my front teeth and rubbed it along Cam's spine. It wasn't easy to talk around ice, but I managed a little. "You're going to be my ash shlut."

"Ah." He squirmed, but I held him fast. "Ah, shit, cold."

"Mmmhmm. Cohd. Gonna get ya hot. Coo' you dow'. I' gonna 'ake ya shweat and 'eg and co'.'"

I kept going, down his ass crack, and circled around his hole, his taint, and behind his balls. He shivered and let loose a moan that I knew had more to do with the finger I was circling against his hole than the ice I was melting along his skin. I let the ice drip until it melted, and he stopped squirming.

I pushed on the skin around his asshole like a threat. My

well-lubed finger barely breached him, and he sucked in a deep, shuddering breath.

"You going to let me in?"

He nodded and tucked his head down without speaking.

"Open for me, Cam. Push back and show me how much you want me inside you." He shoved back hard as I rocked my finger in. He was so tight, so hot. I could barely get a finger inside him. He was all muscle, all power, yet he presented his most delicate, his most intimate skin for my touch. His feet lay visible between his ass and the bed, one crossed over the other, soles up. I brushed one with the tip of my finger, and it wiggled.

Ah, man. I was a goner for Cam, and he probably knew it.

But he was so tight, his ass fought me, and I took that as a sign that I needed to go slower, to be gentler. To try harder.

"Maybe you need a little convincing." I took a swig of coffee before laying a latex dam against the puckered skin of his ass. When I breached him with my tongue it had to be warm, nearly hot, by contrast.

"Ah." His hips jerked. "Ah, fuck. *Fuck.*"

I arrowed my tongue as firmly as I could and fucked him with it, licking around the hole and fluttering along the rim, then diving in, pushing as far as I could, digging until he cried out, until he tensed and twisted, begging. With my ungloved hand I got more ice, and put it in the side of my cheek, starting again, this time with a cold tongue, a cool mouth, while I used my cool hand to fondle his balls and start stripping his dick.

Hot, cold, tongue and *fingers.* I used everything I had, even the vibrations of my voice at different pitches as I purred and hummed against his skin. I brushed his sweet spot from the outside while I thumbed it from the inside. He began to moan, his body trembling, so I mouthed his balls and nuzzled his perineum. Finally, I had to have him roll over so I could suck him and fuck him with my fingers at the same time. I nudged him, and he turned and stretched out, unfurling for me like some big naked-man bounce house while I slipped a condom over his leaking cock and tongued his tight balls.

I gloved my left hand and lubed it, slipping in three fingers while I mouthed his dick. When he cried out, I gave his cock all my attention, letting him rock between my mouth and my hand until my fingers rubbed his prostate again and again and he jerked each time, out of control, hungry, and reaching for climax, incoherent with need.

His thighs trembled, and his jaw hung open. He gripped my head and fucked up into my mouth. Thank fuck I have no gag reflex to speak of because he used me like I've never been used, and I fucking *loved* it. I'd been humping against his knee and knew I would probably come when he did. I welcomed it. I let go, and he jerked a few more times and so did I, my hips snapping up and back, until my blood sang through my veins and climax was an unstoppable train for both of us.

He screamed my name once as he lost control—just said *"Daniel,"* as though he'd been Tasered, as though he'd fallen off a cliff or flown into the sun, and the last thing he thought about before oblivion was me.

The sound alone filled me with satisfaction, but the rest of it…I rocked against his muscled leg until that first electric tingling surge of my release hit my spine, and I let go and spattered cum into the sweat that pooled between us.

Fuck yeah, you are mine now, Cameron Rooney. Take that, you big bastard. This is as good as it gets.

His cock throbbed and warmed against my tongue, and he froze inside my mouth. I held my breath while he gasped for his.

Finally he fell back against the pillows, arms to his sides, still shivering. I crawled up to lie beside him, dropping all the latex and that used condom off the side of the bed. I admit I was proud of myself.

Cam rose up on his side and leaned over to kiss me. He certainly enjoyed intimacy after sex. I know I did, and I could have kissed Cam for hours—just lipped and sucked and nuzzled him—because he was sweet and I'd pleased him. He smiled against my mouth and rubbed my nose again with his. When I was a kid, we'd called those Eskimo kisses. I wondered what the politically correct term was now. Whatever Cam did, he did it with his usual bad-boy charm, and I had to grin back and nip his lips in return.

"You melted my brain."

I resisted the urge to ask him whether he believed that was a great loss.

He seemed content to look down at me with a stupid smile on his face. I was pretty content too, but I felt like I was still on the control clock, and I was trying not to let on.

He curled up then, lying with his cheek on my chest. It felt good to hold him like that. I wrapped my arms around his upper torso, one arm under his and one around his neck. It was like cuddling up with a tree trunk, but he was oddly childlike about it and it warmed my heart. He brushed his lips over one of my nipples and rubbed his face on my chest hair before falling almost immediately to sleep.

For a while I just held him there: a satisfied Cameron Rooney, who stretched out in my arms and whuffled little soft snore noises against my breastbone.

Score.

He lifted a knee and nearly emasculated me with it, trying to get closer. I kissed the soft blond hair at his temple and rested next to him, squeezing him a little harder than strictly necessary, because he was fast asleep, no one could see me, and I was too relaxed and happy to worry about wanting to hold him so much.

CHAPTER FIFTEEN

When I woke later, Cam was making use of my lube and pushing my legs over my head, and just like that, I realized he liked to be in control very much; it was simply that he liked it *all*, and a lot of men didn't bother tapping into the vast smorgasbord of *fuck yeah, let's try it*, served up all day, every day at Cameron Rooney's sexual buffet.

Any license to control I'd received earlier in the day had been revoked, and there was the distinct aroma of one-upmanship in the air.

Even then, even when he was stretching me and lining himself up, even when he was pinching my nipples and gauging my reaction, he was careful. Even as the popping of his hips plunged his cock into me inch by inch—eventually I swear I felt it at the back of my throat, driven by those thick glute muscles up my ass and beyond—he was so careful with me, it almost choked me up.

He'd put a pillow between my body and my damaged arm and settled my hand on a thick pad of folded blankets. While he wrapped my good arm around his neck and encouraged me to hold on, he gently stroked my injured hand every so often with his. It was curiously, dangerously tender—like inviting some-one's grandmother to dance at a wedding—even though he had his dick up my ass and his eyes challenged me to complain if he popped his hips so hard my head slammed into the headboard.

"You're just accident-prone, you know that?" Cam took pity on me and pulled a pillow up between my skull and the wood.

He reared up and shifted to get more traction, gripping my shoulder and my hip, and pounded me into that mattress like a fucking porn star. My head rang and my legs trembled, and I made this noise, *ah, whimper*, with every thrust. He angled his dick a whole new way so that it ground over my prostate as he gave my cock a few quick pumps. My eyes rolled back into my head, and the last thing I saw before I nearly blacked out was his face, grinning down at me.

"Good, huh?"

I responded by splattering cum all over. It ribboned through the air like the searchlights outside a movie premiere, all over both of us.

My ass clamped convulsively around his cock, and he jerked a few times, muttering, "Yeah, baby. Oh, fuck, that's it. Give me everything you got. Yeah...yeah...*yeah.*"

After a while he pulled out and dropped the condom over the side of the bed where I'd dropped everything else. "Fuck yeah."

He collapsed on my left side, leaving my arm uncrushed but the rest of me ringing like I'd been hit by a meteor, and for exactly the first time in my life, I wanted to be reassured that I wasn't just somebody's latest fuck.

Irony will kill you if you let it.

"This is...? You know." I asked when he wrapped an arm around my head and clutched me to him again. "It's not just *this*, right?"

"Hell no. I'm keeping you. I thought you knew that."

"Thanks." I tucked my head next to his chin.

He peered at me. "You?"

"Just try to get away. All I have to do to make you come running is start a fire."

He huffed a laugh and said, "Yeah, if you want to go to jail."

I kissed his bicep. "You'd be worth it."

I believed that. Cameron Rooney would be worth anything. Even being honest, which is what he seemed to want from me, damn it.

I'd try.

Heaven knew I'd try. But oh, man. Precedent for that shit was not in our favor at all.

———

I woke up and realized Cam had been watching me sleep again.

That may sound romantic at first—when you open your eyes and someone else's eyes are gazing down at you—but seriously, it makes you jump. It makes your heart race and your skin crawl. Even if the eyes looking at you are some of your favorite eyes in the world, if they're watching you while you're asleep, it makes for a rather unsettling few minutes as you're gathering your first thoughts on waking.

"*Jeez*. What are you looking at?" I asked.

"Don't think I didn't notice you fucking laminated me."

"What?" I shook my head to clear it.

"What's with the rubber gloves and the latex dams. I get why you might not want to let me come in your mouth. I know why we glove up for anal. But it was like you didn't even want to touch me."

"You didn't seem to mind at the time."

"You didn't exactly give me a chance to think about it then."

I sat up, resting my back against the headboard. "No, I didn't.

I didn't want to spoil anything for you. And judging from your response, you were flying."

Cam opened his mouth to say something then closed it again. "Daniel, if there's something you need to tell me. If you're HIV positive, now would—"

"No," I reassured him. "Hell no. If I were positive, I'd have told you long before this. Before I even touched you."

"Me too." He frowned. "You have to know I wouldn't let you touch me like that if it wasn't safe." I guess I was quiet too long, because he shifted away from me. "You don't trust me."

"Of course I don't." Oh, crap, honesty was going to kill me.

"Thanks." He got up and stalked to his duffel, reaching for a pair of jeans. "I'll just be—"

"Wait. Don't I get to have my say?" I smacked the bed, and he sat. "By any standards, what I did to you was risky sexual behavior. By public health standards, I might as well drink raw sewage. I'm not going in without a strategy. You can take it or leave it. It doesn't spoil my fun, and you certainly seemed to enjoy it, so I don't know what you're complaining about."

"I felt like"—he seemed to search for the words—"unclean. I felt unclean."

"Cam." I tried to coax him into my arms. "I never wanted you to feel like that."

"I know. I should applaud your efforts to keep yourself safe. That's better for me as your partner. But I kept thinking about it while you were sleeping. I'm not some fucking leper. I'd know if I were sick. I get tested regularly and—"

"Since Tree-Blow Guy?"

He shook his head.

"That's not good enough. Not for me and not for you."

Cam was silent for a moment. He looked away. "I know."

"Look. I'm not asking for a commitment. I'm not even saying I won't do whatever you need, whenever you need it. What I am saying is I always use protection when there's bodily fluids. Mine or yours. That's the way it is."

"All right. But you used gloves. Like you couldn't even stand to touch me."

I sighed. "I'll let you in on a little secret if you'll come back to bed, all right?" I patted the space next to me.

Uncertain, he got under the covers and pulled pillows around so he could lie on his side, facing me. I relaxed back down next to him and looked up at the ceiling. It wasn't going to be easy confiding in Cam. If I had any deepest, darkest secrets, they would all be about this.

"BreeAnna has…issues. That's why I started doing this—beside the fact that I trick. BreeAnna couldn't stand to have saliva touch her skin. She didn't want semen inside her. Even my bare fingers made her feel sick. She wanted none of that. She hated it. You spend the night trying to coax a woman out of the closet, where she's rocking and pulling her hair out, and you'll do whatever it takes."

Cam shuddered delicately. "I can't imagine fucking a woman."

"Maybe I'm bi or something. I don't know. It was okay. It was my trade-off to make. When we first got together, I thought I loved her."

"Yeah?"

"Of course. I'm not a monster. I wanted to please her. I knew I couldn't be everything she wanted, but I wanted to at least make her happy in bed. At first it just seemed like she thought certain things were gross. I made a game out of it, and she responded. That wasn't easy, but we were young, and I thought we were in love. I thought someday we'd have kids and we would concentrate on them. Drift apart. Cheat. The entire American dream."

"I wouldn't want to live like that."

"It's not like I believed I had a choice. Jake was gay. I was really close to my mother, and I knew what it would do to her if she thought neither of her kids would get married or have kids of their own. I had to be straight because Jake wasn't."

"So you made the best of a bad situation?"

"I made a *mess*. I took a bad situation and made it worse by marrying Bree. Her problems got so much worse over the years. Kids weren't ever a possibility. She said she could feel my sperm swimming inside her. That my spit burned, and semen made her feel bloated. It all made her feel crazy."

"So you McGyvered the sex so she could feel comfortable."

"Who am I to say everything wasn't as painful as she said it was? There was no point in arguing. It bothered her, so I tried to help. She deserved my compassion because she was my wife, and if I had to treat her like she was the heroine of 'The Princess and the Pea,' well...why not? We were together for twelve years. There was more between us than what happened in the bedroom."

"That must have been awkward."

"I kind of grew to enjoy control rather than sex itself. I get off on giving my partner the mindless oblivion you only get when all your senses are overwhelmed. I knew I could take Bree out of herself, and she needed that. Of course, then she fell in love with someone else, and now she's like...some kind of porn queen. I found videotaped evidence that it was just me she couldn't stand."

"Aw, shit, Dan." Cam's brows drew together. "I'm sorry."

"It's over. Who cares?" Maybe I thought if I said that enough, I'd believe it. It still hurt though, damn it, if only because I didn't see myself as some kind of freak show. "That was all Bree. No one likes to be treated like they're repugnant, but I'd always figured she'd be like that with everyone. It was kind of a shock when I realized she didn't have the same aversion to another man."

"That sucks. Overwhelming the senses is very nice, though." Cam shivered a little. "You've got that going like nobody ever."

I raised myself up on one arm so I could face him. "You like?"

"Yeah. Does that mean I'm your new princess?"

"Maybe. It means I want to treat you right. I want to give you everything I have to give and make you fly. Does that bother you?"

"Won't you get tired of having another princess? You're divorcing her."

I hooked my leg over his and pulled him toward me with it until our hips touched, until we were cock to cock, and I could feel his dick filling lazily. "We're not divorcing because she's a princess. We're divorcing because she's a cheating bitch."

Cam snorted.

"And despite even that, I'd have stayed except she fell in love and wanted to move on. I'm loyal. When I make a commitment, I keep it."

"The spirit if not the letter of it anyway," he reminded me.

For honesty's sake, I answered, "Yes."

I was probably going to have to do something about that. As things stood, Bree believed she was the only person to violate our prenup. I had done that early and often as well. If I wanted to live a life free of lies, that was another thing I had to come clean about and *that* would cost me money.

Well, *shit.*

Cam's cock nudged mine, and I forgot my troubles almost immediately. Moments later we were kissing. He rolled me over onto my back and—this time without any hint of competition—he ground against me. We rocked and kissed and came. No fireworks. Just comfort and quality friction.

I never thought I'd be able to have that, and it struck me how simple it could be to misinterpret it—to choke it off by squeezing it too tight or to lose it by not holding on tightly enough.

For the first time, I had to walk the line in a relationship with a man I could really care about, and it scared me.

We showered off quickly again and shaved in silence, then got ready to check out. I hung back a little. I didn't want to leave the quiet intimacy of that room.

"Hungry?" I asked after he picked up both our bags again. I got my briefcase and we exited our room. He caught my hand in his and led me down the hall.

"I could go for steak and eggs. I'm starved."

I handed him my keys again. "You can drive. I'm still half-asleep."

Cam laughed as we got on the elevator. "What you are my friend, is fucked out. That is a condition of total satisfaction, which follows getting laid by me. It's characterized by lack of focus and loss of muscle tone. Poor reaction time."

"It's also characterized by irritability and the constant sound of *bragging* in one's ears." I argued. "I've heard of this, yes."

"Shut up or no more free rides."

"Oh, yeah, the much-vaunted *Camshaft.*"

"Are you complaining?" Cam nuzzled me with his nose again. I was pretty sure he knew I was kidding.

"Nope. It was far better than advertised. Here," I pushed the button for the lobby.

We emerged with lips swollen from elevator kisses, and if anyone thought anything about that, I didn't care.

CHAPTER SIXTEEN

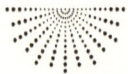

Al's wife Ellie's laughter was infectious. Cam was anxious to greet the horses, so they headed off to the stables with Al's girls, Katie and Jana, first thing. All three ladies sported jeans and cowboy boots, decorated denim jackets, and cream cowboy hats. Next to those girls, Cam looked like a city slicker in his jeans, T-shirt, and baseball cap. They had dark hair and laughing brown eyes and each one of them had eyelashes like long sooty brooms, they were so thick. I'd held both the girls when they were born, and at the time they'd looked like squashed grapefruits. I should have known based on Ellie's beauty they would turn out just fine. In reality, they'd turned out better than fine, and it always took a moment to adjust to them. They were far more gorgeous than you'd imagine if you'd only seen Al, and every time I saw them it almost took my breath away. They could certainly have been little pageant girls if their mother didn't have their feet firmly planted on the ground.

Cam was an instant hit with Katie and Jana—no surprise there. They took one look at him and burst into fits of hysterical, pink giggling. They fairly sizzled with excitement, but as soon as they saw the horses a reverent hush fell over them. Horses made those two weak in the knees, and as the unofficial uncle who spoiled them, I was marginally laudable too, for bringing them there.

I originally planned to sit out the guided trail ride on the beach with Al, who refused to ride, but Cam and the girls were so disappointed, I let our guide, Taylor, provide an unflappable, broad-backed mare named Buttercup for me.

I mounted Buttercup with some trepidation, but it felt more like heading up the gangway to a cruise ship than actually riding a horse. It's not that I couldn't ride. Bree was an accomplished horsewoman, and I'd learned because—in that odd, hit-and-miss way she had with her phobias—she lit up around horses like nothing else. I wasn't *incapable* of riding even a spirited horse like Cam's; I was simply still too afraid of falling off and being injured worse, of having to go through the surgeries and the early, terrifying physical therapy all over again. I think Taylor might have misunderstood, and I didn't set her straight. No way was I going to fall off a big hairball like that horse, so I kept my mouth shut. Buttercup's tail switched away flies occasionally while we waited for Cam and the ladies to mount up, or I might have thought she'd been stuffed.

Al informed us all loftily that he'd be getting coffee in one of the restaurants that dot the beach, and we could call him when we were done. He waved at us from his car and took off.

Cam's gelding danced beneath him, and they seemed delighted to have found one another. The damned horse was big; it had to be to carry Cam. And it looked like it was smiling. I'd never seen a horse do that.

"He's exuberant," I remarked.

Taylor lightly mounted her own horse, a gray mare named Shadow—*what else?*—and acknowledged that the horse was indeed a happy camper. "Blue Boy there loves a rider that knows what he's doing."

I snorted. Who wouldn't? *"Blue Boy?"*

Taylor blushed. "The boss's daughter named him. We mostly call him Blue."

Cam patted Blue Boy's neck. "I love blue roans. He's a handsome boy, and he feels like he likes to run."

"He does. He'll get away from you if you let him. I don't put anyone on him who's not an experienced rider."

"I've got experience."

Taylor's look was appraising and flirtatious. "I knew that the moment I laid eyes on you."

I looked away but not before I saw Cam soak up her admiration and return her interest with a little harmless flirtation of his own.

I asked, "Buttercup here isn't asleep, is she?"

"No, but you can hardly tell, can you? She'll follow along wherever we go at her own pace, so just sit back and enjoy the ride."

"Great."

Taylor took off, and I watched as first Ellie, then Katie and Jana nudged their horses into a walk after her. Blue followed and even though I gave Buttercup a squeeze with my knees, it took her a minute to realize what she was expected to do, and after that, it took a while longer for her to sally forth. I barely felt her placid, even footsteps. It was more that she sashayed ahead, swaying from side to side like she was on ice skates. She was the perfect nag for a three-year-old. I tried to cover my shame with interest in my surroundings.

"Not too much for you, is she?" Cam's blue eyes sparked with mischief.

"I believe I've let her know who's boss." The easy way he sat his horse caused my jeans to tighten.

Katie turned back to me and stuck her tongue out. "Uncle Dan, my horse is way better than yours."

I mock-frowned at her. "It's not nice to point out old people's shortcomings, Katydid."

"The girls are sure cute. How old are they?" asked Cam.

"Jana's in second grade. Katie's two years younger."

"Nice family."

I nodded. They were a nice family, and they'd let me be an unofficial part of it since it began. "I've been working with Al since we got our MBAs. He's got a level head on his shoulders and Ellie...she's the only kind of woman he could be with. She's as driven as he is, only in a different way. She's lively and smart and runs a business out of her house."

"What does she do?"

"It's one of those multilevel marketing things. She gets awards every year, and they end up taking free trips together. Cookware, I think. She has an army of underlings, and she's damned good at it."

"I see." Cam's horse danced beneath him.

"It's okay if you want to take off and enjoy your ride. You don't have to poke along with me."

"I'm fine where I am."

"Uncle Dan." Katie waved her little cowboy hat. "Look at me!"

"I see you, princess. You look like a cowgirl. Cam here is a real cowboy. He was raised on an honest-to-Pete ranch."

Cam flushed, and I realized he might not have wanted me to share that.

"I'm sorry if you meant to tell me that in confidence."

"It's not a secret or anything." Cam pulled his cap down to shade his eyes better.

I peered at him because he'd stopped smiling. "But it makes you sad?"

"I guess. I don't think about it too much." We ambled along in silence for a bit, but Blue was dancing sideways trying to tamp down his frustration.

"Look, I know it's none of my business, but sometimes a man can go along with a preconceived notion that's wrong."

Cam looked blank.

"If you have any doubts about how your brothers and sisters feel about you, you need to ask. Don't make the mistake of thinking that they don't want you in their lives without checking with them first. Do you know what I mean?"

Cam's expression didn't change but he said, "I guess."

"I know it takes balls to do that. To give someone you care about the chance to reject you. It can be easier and safer to make assumptions. I've done both. If I really care, it's worth the risk."

"That's what I admire about you."

His words surprised me. "What?"

"You know how to put your heart on the line. For all you twist the truth, you have the guts to step up when it counts. I've seen you stand by your brother, even when he makes mistakes. You push him to take chances that will help him grow."

"You make me sound—"

"A little heroic. Yeah. That's kind of how I see you, Daniel. Deal with it." He flashed me a grin and turned away, kneeing his horse forward. He and Blue caught up with everyone else who had left us behind by about two city blocks. If I'd wanted to catch them, I'd have had to jump off Buttercup and jog. I hated even thinking about making Buttercup try.

Did horses cry?

Did Cam just call me *heroic?*

I'd like to say I had some kind of personal epiphany while Buttercup and I moseyed along over the sand, seemingly by ourselves because everyone else was light-years ahead. That would make the story so much more fun to tell, and at the time I really could have used a moment or two of clarity. As it was, mostly we just provided a much-needed bit of comic relief to the many Frisbee throwers, volleyball players, and those hardy individuals who still scoffed at skin cancer.

I watched Cam from a distance and discovered that the mere sight of him made my heart do funny little twists in my chest. It was pretty easy to see how men in power, men with money, men of intelligence at a pinnacle in their professional lives could still lose their shit and fuck up everything over love.

My mother used to sing a nonsense song about the lovebug. "Oh, the lovebug'll bite you if you don't watch out..."

No shit.

Ouch.

I tried to cut myself some slack. Cam—my bona fide fire-fighter *and* cowboy for fuck's sake—was *riding a horse on the beach.* If my heart sort of soared at the near-perfect picture he made there, with the sun limning his skin and happiness bubbling from every pore, I shouldn't be blamed for it. I never stood a chance of keeping my heart in the first place, and if I had to lose my head, there were worse things to lose it over. I didn't catch up to them until they met me going back the way we came.

By that time, I was feeling so silly I was singing Sancho Panza's song from the musical, *Man of La Mancha*, out loud. I called Buttercup *Rucio, my dappled darling* from that point on, and even though the girls had no clue what I meant by that, it made them laugh.

When we got back to the stable, I was all kinds of out of sorts. I'd been bobbing along in a lazy stream of attraction, and before I realized what was happening, I'd gotten caught up in the rapids of full-on emotional involvement and gone over love *fucking* falls.

Cam dismounted first and in a show of misguided solicitude, he stood by my round little horsey and held up his arms to help me down. What the hell? Did he imagine I couldn't get off a damned barge like Buttercup without his help? It took all my concentration not to slap his hands away. I must have hurt him when I rejected his help, because I glimpsed his eyebrows draw together before I turned away.

I needed time with my thoughts, though. I needed to reevaluate what was happening to me.

In the first place, I'd been surprised and not a little angry that my attraction to him cut my much-anticipated wild and indiscriminate bachelor days short, and now...now I'd begun to imagine a future with him in it. Now I couldn't imagine a future *without* him, unless it was written by Aldous Huxley.

And how could a future between us even happen? Unless I was willing to settle in St. Nacho's—a town that made me itchy and tense—for good.

Cam and I were silent on the ride to a local diner to meet Al. We had Ellie and the girls wedged into the backseat anyway, and that didn't allow for any kind of private conversation between us. When we got there, we got caught up in Katie and Jana's delight that breakfast could be served all day, and chaos reigned until they had their little mouths full of chocolate chip pancakes and milk.

I ordered a Denver egg-white omelet with a side of turkey sausage and oven-roasted O'Brien potatoes, billed as a healthier alternative to hash browns. It came with a pancake the size of a pickup truck hubcap, which I handed over to Al's bottomless pits. Cam had a ranch style breakfast—he seemed to be taking the whole cowboy thing to heart—consisting of a mass of eggs and meat and potatoes with a side of whole wheat toast on which he slathered an awful lot of those single-serving-sized packages of strawberry jam. He seemed subdued but content.

As always, Al had a yellow legal tablet with a checklist of things he wanted to tell me, and a number of papers for me to sign. I didn't even think anything of it when he opened his briefcase and handed me a thick, spiral-bound and laminated presentation booklet of the project he was calling St. Nacho's Resort and Card Club until Cam's gaze met mine.

Too late, I realized what it must look like to Cam. He would take one look at that prospectus and assume we were a lot further along in the process than we were. Al was very good at his job. He'd designed a mockup of what he imagined the facility would look like and created a splashy sign and logo for it. He had no doubt filled the booklet with numbers and charts and graphs and persuasive arguments in favor of building that particular type of project on that particular site.

We produced project pitches like that all the time, but not every project got a green light, and fewer actually made it through the rest of the process of acquisition and building.

But Cam couldn't know that. All he could see was a splashy little gimmick intended to persuade investors that his home-town should become a gambling mecca. I knew as soon as I saw how he looked at me—as soon as he took into consideration the many lies I'd admitted to telling, my self-serving relationships, and my inability to perceive St. Nacho's the way everyone else did—I knew he'd put two and two together to come up with the wrong answer.

After that, he shut me out so completely I might as well have been on Mars.

We said goodbye to Al and his family, and then we were finally alone. On the way back to St. Nacho's, he drove my car.

I tried to tell him the way things work. "So…you see, anyone is free to propose a project. They prepare their ideas and make a presentation. Al and I do the math and the research, and we present all the possible projects that have crossed our desks to our other investors. Then a larger pool of people consider each idea and more time is required while they do their own research. It takes a long time before we green-light something like that, but it's not unheard of to work for months, sometimes even over a year, deciding whether an idea will actually fly."

In response, Cam only gripped the steering wheel tighter.

"Seriously, Cam, just because he had the prospectus doesn't mean he has my support."

"Then let me ask, so there's no misunderstanding, does he have your support?"

I hesitated to give an answer one way or the other, mostly because I wasn't about to let either my business partner or my lover tell me what to do. I admit it wasn't the wisest choice. Of course I should have said, *No. He does not have my support.* Because he didn't. I'd already told Al I didn't like the idea.

Instead, I said, "I haven't had a chance to read it."

"But...you think putting some sort of casino in St. Nacho's would be—"

"For your information, you know even less about this project than I do. I don't know what I think yet, but I don't base my decisions on my emotions."

"Well maybe you should."

"Right. Because that's such a good business practice."

"I don't care about business practices. I care about my home."

"From what I understand what he's proposing isn't within St. Nacho's city limits."

"You mean if it's not in our house, we don't have to worry that it will impact us? How'd you like me to open a twenty-four-hour fast-food drive-through in your backyard?"

"You don't understand."

"I'm not an idiot. That plan will be great for whoever builds it, but it will suck for St. Nacho's."

"Times change, and land gets built up. It's bound to happen sooner or later. Even St. Nacho's started as—"

"So it's okay because it's inevitable? It's okay because someone is going to build on that land, so it might as well be you?"

"I didn't say that. Stop putting words in my mouth."

"What then? What do you mean? 'Cause it sounds like you're saying suck it up. If it's not me it will be someone else."

"Does that mean you don't mind if it's someone else?"

"Hell no, it does not mean I don't mind. I won't allow anyone to come in and put something like that in my backyard. But for your information, it hurts more that it's you. Maybe I believed you when you said you wanted your brother to be happy. Maybe I hoped we were building something solid together. Maybe I was thinking you'd stop spreading your money around like it was salvation."

"Wait, what does any of that have to do with—"

"Maybe I saw you as the kind of guy who would understand what it means to be at a really low place and just...fetch up in a town like St. Nacho's and *belong* there. I believed, wrongly it turns out, that you would understand why St. Nacho's means so much to those of us who live there."

I couldn't argue with that. I understood it. I just didn't share it. I said nothing.

"I have to say"—Cam spoke to me in a way that I believed would hurt forever—"you are not the man I thought you were."

Ouch. I turned and looked out the window. "Just get in fucking line behind everyone else who's ever said those words.

Lovebug bite victim dies ignoble death. Film at eleven.

CHAPTER SEVENTEEN

We arrived at St. Nacho's at around four in the afternoon. Cam pulled into the parking lot of the firehouse, but he left the car running when he got out and pulled his things from the trunk. I was left with little choice but to get out and go around the car to the driver's side. Cam maintained a frosty silence until he came around to say goodbye.

"Thank you," he said formally. "I had a nice time."

"Cam—"

"This is where I work, Dan. I'd appreciate it if you didn't make a scene."

Okay, that stung. I wasn't exactly the scene-making type. "Sure."

"Thanks for everything." Cam turned and walked away. Damned if he didn't catch a little piece of my heart, because it started to unravel with each step he took.

"No, thank *you*." I called as I backed out. At that point I knew he couldn't hear me. "*Really*. Thank *you* for reminding me why I don't do itty-bitty fucking inbred towns."

I wished I still had a manual car because getting up as good a rant without one has so much less *oompah*, and right about there

I might have gone a little faster or a little longer than necessary before shifting into second, and my old car would have growled, *grrrrr* and then shot off like a rocket.

"*Thank you* for reminding me why I don't do wide-eyed, corn-fed, delusional-cat-walking cowboys who think things can be all idyllic and shit."

Grrrrr...A little grinding and then third, and the power, well...I wanted to hear that *vroom vroom*...How childish is that?

"*Thank you* for putting a little perspective on what turned out to be a great weekend of hot sex. I want you to be the first to know: tomorrow, I start looking for hot men who don't *mind* me leading with my wallet, *at all*. It's a shallow pool, but somebody's gotta swim in it."

Note to self: buy chlorine.

I DON'T KNOW HOW BIG ST. NACHO'S ACTUALLY IS, BUT I HADN'T even shifted into fourth before I arrived at Nacho's Bar where I decided to get out and have a drink or three. After that, I took a little walk to clear my head. I must have gone up and down all the little beach access streets at least twice. The interesting thing about that slightly inebriated stroll around town was that for the first time ever, I didn't see anyone I knew. Everyone seemed like a total stranger, from the dog-walkers to the beach-goers, to the soccer moms herding their kids into Bêtise for ice cream.

I passed my gym without going in, which was a shame because I'd missed another appointment with Jordan. I blew off apologizing in favor of wandering, unhappy and alone, and chain-smoking, which was gradually making me feel sick and gray and dirty. The *third* time I passed Rune Nation, I finally stopped.

I wasn't thinking anything more profound—or less

desperate—than *why the fuck not?* Let's see what the oft-quoted Minerva from Rune Nation has to say to me.

Bring it. The fuck. On.

There was a light chiming sound when I pushed open the door, and I was immediately overpowered by the smell of incense. It wasn't unpleasant, I guess. It had light overtones of sandalwood and maybe jasmine. The scent wasn't refreshing in the way walking along the boardwalk had been, but it offered something vaguely weighty to the moment, like putting words in bold type, that made my initial meeting with Minerva feel portentous.

I'd seen Minerva, but only out of the corner of my eye—brief flashes of the colorful fabric of her clothes when I'd glimpsed her dodging me. Now that I was to meet her in person, I was nervous and self-conscious—aware I smelled of sweat and cigarettes and probably the alcohol I'd drunk only a little while before.

When she came through the beaded curtain, I knew we were equally surprised. I don't know what I imagined, but it was possible I'd prepared myself to face down Medusa.

In reality, Minerva was nothing more than a middle-aged, slightly dumpy lady with dark curly hair and brown eyes in a benign, moon-shaped face. She didn't walk, she sailed, yacht-like, from behind glass cases that held a myriad of crystals and jewelry, glass bottles and books, and when she took my hand in hers to shake it, she frowned at me as though I were the biggest disappointment she'd had in a long, long time.

"Daniel Livingston, I presume?"

I smiled tightly. Because that never gets old.

I looked into her eyes, which were expectant and maybe a little frightened, and said, "I'm not the Antichrist."

As an icebreaker, it didn't do much good. She drew her hand back and frowned at me like a teacher who had just discovered a dead frog in her desk.

"What brings you here, Mr. Livingston?"

"I don't know, really." I glanced back through the tinted windows of her shop, which were covered in great billows of gauzy fabric. "What exactly do you do here?"

She folded her arms across her ample bosom. "As you can see, we sell jewelry, incense, charms, books, crafts by local artisans, and I do psychic readings."

"I want *that*." There would never be a better day for me to take a swan dive into the occult. "I want one of those. A psychic reading."

"Are you a believer?"

No. "Yes."

"Is there something special that's troubling you?"

Yes, everything. "No. Not particularly."

"Do you have something in particular that you want to change?"

"No." *Yes.*

"I see." Minerva took my arm and led me to a table set up on the far side of the shop. It was dainty and small—covered with a couple of pretty tablecloths and topped with a round of glass. It looked like it had been designed with a little girl's ideal tea party in mind—or a teddy bears' picnic. There were stones and crystals scattered across the tabletop, mostly different types of quartz, from smoky to amethyst to some pretty milky rose quartz shards.

At that point, I didn't feel like I had a lot left to lose, so consulting Minerva made as much sense to me as anything else I'd done. It was like discovering the flaws in a business plan or educating myself about my opposition before going into a tough negotiation. At best it was an excellent practice and at worst it couldn't hurt.

"Do you use tarot cards?" I asked because it seemed to me that most people in her line of business used cards or some such thing. From what I'd read—and it wasn't much—modern day fortune-tellers read palms, cast runes, or laid out cards. They called themselves seers or psychics.

"I have used cards, yes." She eyed me as she placed an incense stick into a holder on a small tray of fresh flowers and fruit I thought might be an offering and lit it. "I don't need them."

"I see."

Her lips thinned into a tight smile. I guessed the joke was on me. "Using things like runes or cards or coins works best when you have a specific question in mind."

"Mother nature only answers when we know what the question is?" I asked. If that was the case, I was shit out of luck.

"I should say not. In those cases, casting or divining objects help the subject answer his or her own questions better than I ever could. With you, though…You don't even know the problem."

"How can you tell that?"

"You're a blank slate."

"I get that a lot, actually."

She folded her hands on the table and took a deep breath. I have to say that the sickly sweet fragrance was killing me up this close. Anyone who bitched to me about secondhand smoke was going to get an earful about incense the next time they did it.

"So what do I do?"

"Just relax, Mr. Livingston. This won't hurt a bit." She put her hands over mine as she closed her eyes. "Probably."

I don't know much about psychics, but she was doing a credible job of acting like one, I guess. She sort of hummed deep in her throat and swayed a little. She seemed to hear something from far away. She paused, poised like she was listening, and nodded as though being instructed by an unseen entity. I rolled my eyes.

She wasn't really selling it. I'd seen better psychics at a school carnival—neighborhood moms dressed up like gypsies with painted-on beauty marks and designer knockoff scarves...

When at last she spoke, I gathered my patience for the harangue I felt coming, and she didn't let me down.

"Dan Livingston, I have foreseen many things. You've come to St. Nacho's for a member of your family, but it is you, most of all, who needs what St. Nacho's has to offer. You are to be pitied. You are empty of all but dross."

Okay, *dross*? I didn't even know what dross was, but I resented the implication.

Her voice was positively stentorian when she spoke again. "Heed this warning for it comes not from me but from *the Mother herself*: you are on the precipice of change. You can be humble and teachable, or you can stay your course and destroy St. Nacho's forever. Stop what you're doing before you rend asunder the fabric of the very town that will *save your life*."

I pulled my hands out. "You are certifiably insane."

When I got up to leave, she stopped me.

"Here, all right. *Okay*. Wait." Maybe she was done—finally—doing her shtick. "I have something for you."

"What?" I was still wary.

"I keep seeing this." She took out a pad of paper with some cartoon kittens on it and a black felt marker. She worked on a drawing for a minute like a little kid, the tip of her pink tongue stuck out at an odd angle as she turned the paper this way and that to get it right. She sighed and dropped all pretense, and in that moment she looked a lot like a teacher I liked in high school, someone for whom I'd caused a lot of trouble. I'd been extremely competent with numbers and science—really I excelled in every subject—but my persuasive writing skills were poor, and it consistently dragged my grades down. Mrs. McCall worked with me privately, time and again, until I could write an essay that was good enough not only to pass her class but to win a local essay contest and be reprinted in the newspaper.

The words *humble* and *teachable* brought the memory back so clearly that tears stung my eyes for a second. I *was* humbled back then. I learned to admit there were things I had to struggle with, even though I was considered to be highly intelligent. I believed at the time that I'd never forget the lesson—that even the best and brightest have areas in life where the work is really hard and the outcome uncertain.

I watched her silently as she drew what looked to me like a plus sign on top of a bookcase over the symbol for pi. Under that she drew a curved vertical line with four horizontal slashes through it. There were odd little apostrophe marks and things, but it was basically just those two symbols, one stacked on top of the other.

"I need to know if it means anything to you. Does it?"

"Yeah," I said without reacting, even though I was stunned. "I've seen that before."

Tattooed on my back.

The only people who had ever seen it on me were the girl at the Santa Monica tattoo parlor where I'd had it done, the man I'd slept with the night I'd gotten it, and Cam. My doctor hadn't seen it, nor had Jordan, my PT. Not even my brother had seen my tattoo yet.

I studied her face to see if there was some subterfuge there—like maybe she was in on some kind of con with Cam, or she'd seen me through the window of my house. I'm good at reading faces, and I found no subterfuge. It was entirely possible that she didn't know anything about my tattoo.

"Okay, so what is it?" I asked.

"Hell if I know." She glanced up from her work. "But it's something important. Whatever this is, you have to carry it with you always. No excuses."

"Okay." That wouldn't be hard. It was a damned tattoo, after all.

"When you find out what this is"—she waved the little paper at me—"you'll have all the answers you'll need."

"Okay," I said again. *Doable.*

"The junior college has a Japanese language department. This looks like kanji, at least, so you can start there."

I thanked her and gave her a credit card to pay, then shoved the note she'd drawn for me into my pocket when she asked me to sign. Before I left, she stopped me briefly.

"Thank you, Mr. Livingston, for stopping by."

"My pleasure," I said and meant it. If nothing else, it reminded me I hadn't written to Mrs. McCall in years, and I wanted to. I remembered I could learn new things, even hard things, and become better for it. That was worth something, even if it came from a charlatan psychic in a dinky town like St. Nacho's.

Once I'd stepped back out into the twilight, I returned to the real world. Everything that happened in Minerva's incense-scented bubble seemed almost unreal. I'd met the famed Minerva, and she hadn't turned me into a toad. It became harder to believe she didn't have some sort of inside information about my tattoo.

She probably knew all about it beforehand, that was all.

I was okay. Everything was going to be fine.

My good mood fell like the Hindenburg when I passed the firehouse on the way to get back to my car. I was *afraid* to go inside—afraid to see Cam at all, in case he was still angry or in case I would do something stupid like grovel at his very attractive feet. I skittered past quietly and headed for my car and home.

I remembered someone I knew who could—theoretically—tell me what my tattoo meant.

At least one of my problems could be solved that night.

CHAPTER EIGHTEEN

T*ruth.*

    I hung up the phone after talking to Hana Ishikawa, a woman I worked with from time to time when I needed a Japanese-language translator or a cultural liaison at Livingston Properties.

I don't know why I didn't think of Hana when I got the damned tattoo in the first place. Maybe because I was embarrassed, or maybe because she was a good friend of Bree's.

I worried she might hold the whole girlfriends' pact sacred and would no longer speak to me, plus it would have been awfully hard to scan my skin. She was pleasant, though, when she picked up the phone and helpful, indicating that all was not lost from that quarter.

I used a wand scanner on Minerva's little drawing and then e-mailed the image to Hana, and it turned out the symbol I'd let some hot girl half my age inscribe permanently on my skin was *shinjitsu.* Truth.

Which was ironic, really.

I'd carried a lot of things around with me, but truth wasn't known to be one of them.

After I found that out, every time I thought about my tattoo, it burned like a brand, searing me with guilt and anxiety and plain old shame.

I walked to the liquor store, acutely aware that I had nothing to do that night—or for that matter, in St. Nacho's at all—but get hammered and live up to everyone's worst expectations of me. Which is how I came to be passed out on the couch in my underwear when the phone rang at some ungodly, brightly lit hour the next morning.

———

I LET THE MACHINE PICK UP, BUT SECONDS LATER MY CELL RANG. When I finally got up and found where my phone had dropped between the cushions, it had stopped ringing too. I looked at the caller ID and saw it was Jake, so I called him back.

Without preamble he said, "You need to come down here."

I shook my head to clear it. Not only was he brusque, he sounded pissed. "Where?"

"Bêtise."

I was about to say, "Give me a minute to take a shower," but he'd already hung up.

I made brief ablutions and ran out the door, worried. What the hell was that all about? Had something happened to the bakery? Was one of the workers hurt?

I checked to make sure my phone was charged enough that I could make some calls if I needed to. It was my lifeline to lawyers, insurance agents, and medical professionals. I feared the worst when I walked into Bêtise, and I didn't see Jake behind the counter or through the windows into the kitchen.

Muse wasn't working; in her place was my brother's partner, Mary Catherine. She didn't say hello but glanced over from where she was ringing up a customer. I must have looked hungover, because she frowned and pointed to the table by the

155

front windows. I looked and found my brother sitting in the corner of the restaurant with a woman. Her back was toward me, but I could see his face clearly. He seemed upset, and when I got closer, I could tell he'd been crying.

Crying?

"Jake?" I hurried over. "What's going on?"

He glanced up at me and then down at his hands, which were clasped tightly in his lap. The woman turned, and I knew who she was immediately. There was no mistaking her resemblance to our father or to Jake. But she was just a girl. Really, hardly more than a teenager. Suddenly I felt vile for ignoring her letters, for forcing her to come up all this way to deliver something, for making her track me down in person.

In a million years, I never imagined Joyce Livingston would come to St. Nacho's.

In my defense, I'd tried to find a way to tell Jake our father had been in touch with me. My time was obviously up. I couldn't tell if Jake was more upset by the news or by how he received it.

He seemed devastated, and he was looking at me like this was somehow all my fault. How was that fair? I wasn't the one who thought a note every so often could make up for an abusive childhood. I wasn't the one who'd left my family behind and started another. *I* wasn't the one who'd chosen to write to one of my children and ignore the other.

I swallowed down my anger. "I don't believe we've met."

"I'm Joyce." She stood and held out her hand. I gave it a perfunctory pump while I looked her over. She had our brown hair and eyes. Jake's were wider set than mine, and in hers I could see their echo. She was tough. I could see that. In that new Livingston family, this was the protector. But she was so very *young*.

"So I assume you told my brother who you are? Everything?"

"Yes." She bit her lip. "I didn't realize—"

"I guess that's just another thing I've fucked-up lately." I sat down and patted my pockets, looking for my pack of cigarettes and lighter to stall, the first of a number of nervous gestures I'm likely to exhibit when I feel fear.

"What?" she asked. Maybe she disapproved of my language.

"Nothing." I turned to Jake. "I'm sorry I didn't tell you."

"How long?'

"How long what?" I didn't want to tell my brother that his father had been writing to me and only me, for years. That I'd kept that fact from him, *for years.*

"Never mind." He turned to her—to Joyce, our *sister*—as if he already liked her and she would be able to make things right. Because obviously *I* never had. "If you give me the address, I'll make time to come down in the next couple of weeks."

She nodded.

"Of course," I said. "By all means, let's just drop everything and run because the man who beat our mother, terrorized us as children, and then left without a single word is asking for us."

"Dan," Jake's lip curled in a way I knew meant he was losing his patience. But I couldn't help it. This was simply *wrong.* Maybe it wasn't okay for me to withhold the information from Jake, but just because our father wanted us didn't mean we had to jump when he called. As far as I was concerned, he'd lost the right to ask me for anything except the not insignificant financial support I'd given him over the years.

He did *not* have the right to suck up to my brother. He didn't have the right to hurt Jakey again. I'd always protected Jake from him, and I always would.

Jake said, "I can't believe—"

"*No,*" I barked. "Have you forgotten everything? I know you were young, but—"

"What about when he contacted you the first time? I wasn't young then."

It was then I realized Joyce brought along a shoebox full of mail with her. That seemed damning, all those letters, but they were mostly just cards that Bree sent and a few terse notes from me. I'd only really written in the beginning, acknowledging I'd gotten his letters. Bree was brilliant at those kinds of things, though. She was organized and thoughtful. She sent cards several times a year, signing both our names, Love, Bree and Dan Livingston. She sent long, newsy letters at Christmas with a quick handwritten note at the bottom. Very efficient, but hardly personal. I don't believe she even knew my erstwhile siblings' names. But the end result made it look like I had cared a hell of a lot more than I actually did. It made my father look like yet another thing I'd lied to myself and everyone else about.

And Jakey—he was looking at me like I'd stolen the sun from him. Like I'd taken all its warmth and its light and hidden it so he'd had to live in darkness.

That wasn't the first time I discovered that lies come home in really unpleasant ways. Given the way I'd kept my mouth shut on my dad's whereabouts, that shoebox full of holiday greeting cards sat on the table between us like a smoking gun.

I could almost hear Cam ask me if I ever told the truth about anything.

"That's not what it looks like."

"What it looks like," my brother said, "is you've been hiding the fact that our father has been in touch with you for years. You've hidden the fact that we have half siblings, and you didn't bother to tell me that our father is dying and this might very well be the last chance I will ever have to confront him about—"

"Wait."

"For what?" Jake stood abruptly. "For you to bend the truth some more? For you to make up some excuse?"

"Jake—"

"I don't want to hear it," Jake told me. "Go home. I just wanted to see you to tell you…Go home."

My mouth dropped open. *I was home.* I mean…what passed

for home. Right now, for better or worse, St. Nacho's was home because Jake was home. There was nothing in the world I cared about more than Jake. And Jake was telling me to leave. The thought filled me with blind panic.

If I fucked St. Nacho's up—if I fucked things up with Jake—everything I cared about was gone.

I went back to our place and cleaned up properly. I had some calls to make—things I'd put off for too long. I knew it wasn't going to be easy to reach my attorney, but it turned out to be much harder than I'd planned. Apparently he was participating in a triathlon, and wouldn't be home until much later in the day.

He was nearly fifteen years my senior. He must be fit like a god to do that. *Shit.*

I could hardly lift my vodka shots. The afternoon crawled by. I had a fleeting thought of Jordan in Izzie's gym, helping me relearn to use my hand, and Cam offering to get me in shape. In fact, I took stock of everything I had and everything I'd lost, mentally putting little pluses in the win column and little minuses in the loss column. It was so much to think about I couldn't grasp any kind of unified concept of what I'd become. For once, the figurative spreadsheet in my brain failed me.

Eventually, my brother would forgive me, but it would be painful in the interim.

Physically, I wasn't that far gone, but the accident put paid to most of my usual workout routines—biking, rowing, lifting weights, even jogging jarred my painful arm. I flexed my hand a few times and got out the little bag of balls and webs and the tiny trumpet-button machine that Jordan had given me. *Maybe if I kept them in the console of my car and used them at red lights...*

Spiritually, I had turned some kind of corner and sure enough, there were awful growing pains to experience, and—just as I'd suspected all along—everything I'd done lately had gone all to hell. My life was going to hurt a lot before I could make it right.

If I could make it right.

Last but not least, romantically, I...Well. That hurt too. That hurt more. I probably couldn't fix that. Because in the end, Cam loved St. Nacho's, and I couldn't wait to leave.

IN THE LATE AFTERNOON I SPENT A WHILE WITH SOME COFFEE AT one of the tables on the patio at Nacho's Bar, watching the beach. It was a place I could smoke and think, and—my new conscience told me—it was a place where if I was lucky, I would get a glimpse of Cam. I'd seen him at the firehouse when I drove by. He'd been talking to one of the guys out front, but when he saw me, he headed back inside. That was a direct hit, but it didn't stop me from sitting at Nacho's for a while longer, toying with my coffee and smoking one cigarette after another, hoping to get another glimpse of him. The firefighters who were off shift stopped for beer at Nacho's in the evenings to hang out with one another. Cam drank there pretty regularly because he lived within walking distance.

Just when I'd gotten to the point where I considered giving up, he came into the patio area and headed right for me. I held my breath when he sat down. Maybe there was hope after all.

Without much in the way of warning, he said, "What were you thinking?"

"What do you mean?"

"I talked to Jake and JT today. They told me everything. Isn't it Jake's decision whether he should contact your father? What if you'd waited too long and your father died?"

"You don't know the situation."

"Of course I don't. But I know what you said just yesterday about making assumptions."

"Aren't you assuming some things? Pop could have contacted Jake if he'd wanted to get in touch with him. Jake could have googled Pop's name. He hasn't changed it. A private detective could have found either one of them in less than an afternoon. So please don't act like it's all on me."

Cam's face registered anger. "Why the hell wouldn't he get in touch with Jake? That's..."

"Our dad was a bastard, Cam. I'm not making that up."

"Okay, maybe your dad was a bastard, but you and Jake have siblings, and you don't know them. And you won't until you step up and take a risk. You said yourself that sometimes the risk is worth it, and you took that choice away from Jake by not telling him."

Cam was genuinely trying to help. His gentle face had tightened with worry, and his hands, which lay flat on the table, clenched and unclenched with emotion. This was obviously important to him. I guess maybe I understood why.

"I know you don't understand why I might keep this from him, but—"

"You're ignoring your own advice."

"Cam, it's not that simple."

"It *is* simple. He needs to know whether his family wants him, one way or the other. If it goes badly, well, that's when you can be there for him. But it might not. They might care about him. How could you cheat him out of that?"

Ah, *fuck*. I wasn't cheating Jake out of anything. Well, maybe I was. Joyce looked nice, and if she hadn't been poisoned by our father, it was possible having a sister would turn out to be a really good thing. I could see getting to know Joyce and her brother. I could see taking a chance that whatever had affected our father's behavior didn't also affect them. For all I knew, our dad was the father of the year with them. What if he had just needed a different family. A better family...That was like an abscessed tooth I didn't want to probe. *That* fucking hurt.

But no. This was *Pop* we were talking about. I knew Pop.

"I am not cheating Jake. I swear to *fuck* I am trying to protect him. You know I love him. He's the one person I"—*but maybe not anymore*—"I'd lay down my life for him. And you have to know —I've let you see more of me than I've ever let anyone see, so you of all people *have to know*—that I would never do anything to cheat him."

"Then what gives?" Cam leaned toward me urgently, his blue gaze tender but resolute. "Make me understand, because it just isn't right. Explain it to me, Daniel. Practice on me so you can tell him." His words embodied his faith in me and burst my heart into a million little pieces at the same time.

"My dad nearly killed him, Cam. He had Jakey in the bath- tub. He was holding him under the water. I swear to God Pop nearly killed him. Jake doesn't remember, but I-I snapped and nearly killed Pop that same night. The next day Pop was gone like he'd never existed. My pop acted crazy where Jake was concerned. Pop nearly killed him, and I will never, ever let him get that chance again."

CHAPTER NINETEEN

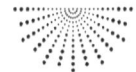

C am stared at me incredulously. "You can't be right about
that."

"What I can't do is make shit like that up."

"Jake really doesn't remember?"

I shook my head.

"What does he think happened?"

"He thinks Pop hit him hard enough that he blacked out for a
bit and fell into the tub. My mom grabbed him out of the water,
and I went after my dad like...I don't know. A maniac. Jake
thinks I grew a pair and finally stood up to our pop, which I did.
But he doesn't know why. I clocked Pop so hard I broke his nose
and kept on beating on him even after that, until a neighbor
pulled me off him. My dad left the next day. Jake thinks it was
his fault. He always has. But is that worse than knowing your
father actually tried to kill you?"

"Jeez." Cam's brow furrowed, and he put his hand on mine.
"I'm sorry. I didn't know."

"Of course you didn't. I've never told anyone that, and
everyone else who knew took it to their grave."

"And now Jake wants to see your father."

"Jake thinks he needs to make amends. Can you imagine? He thinks he needs closure." I ground my cigarette out and motioned the server over. "Far as I'm fucking concerned, somebody tries to kill your ass, that's closure enough."

Cam blanched. "I guess."

He looked so unhappy that I took his hand in mine. "C'mere, you. I know you're mad at me. I know you don't think you can trust me when I tell you that I'm trying to do the right thing, but I swear, Cam. I swear to you, I will not lie to you anymore."

"I don't know, Daniel."

"Aw. Just…c'mere, Cam."

He balked at first, but eventually after I scooted my chair closer to his, he relaxed. I wrapped my hand around the back of his neck. He was reluctant, but I could see he wanted contact. Like a wary animal he hesitated, inches away, waiting for me to press my cheek to his. When I did, he melted into me with such sweetness, I melted a little too.

"Daniel." He breathed the name in my ear. "Tell me we're not going to fuck this up."

"I—"

"Tell me money isn't more important to you than what's right."

"It's not, Cam. I swear it's not. You have to trust me. You have to believe that I know what I'm doing. That I wouldn't hurt you or Jake for anything."

His lips pressed to mine, and when I opened to him, his tongue swept out, and *fuck*, the taste of him was so fine, and I'd craved it so much it was like I was starving. I wanted to feel the shelter of his arms around me and the heat of his groin against mine. I had the fleeting, absurd thought that Cam was made for me, that if I'd sent someone out with a shopping list for everything I wanted in a man, they could only come back with Cam.

I must have smiled against his skin, because he pulled back and said, "What?"

"I missed you. After you left the car yesterday, I just—"

"I don't want hard feelings between us. But I don't believe in happily ever after, you know?" He took my hand in his.

"I know. Me neither, really." I drew a lazy finger up the inseam of his jeans and watched as a faint pink color washed his cheeks.

No one was staring or anything, but we sat in the last of the patio tables closest to the boardwalk—on display to anyone out for an evening stroll. I would have liked to drag him to my place, to bed. His infamous tree was closer, but just when I was going to suggest it, the waiter arrived. I glanced up and didn't recognize him. It might have been uncomfortable if it had been Marius, who still seemed to be crushing on me a little, even though I had it from Muse—who knew Marius from school— that he wasn't exactly pining away in solitude. But the waiter turned out to be one of Cam's conquests, and they sized each other up, all eyes and innuendo.

"Want something?" I asked Cam.

"Beer." Cam gave the waiter a tiny what-can-I-say shrug of his shoulders. The boy raised his eyebrows and pushed his lower lip into a sultry pout but said nothing. "And maybe some of those appetizer burrito things?"

He took our order and glanced back at Cam once more in open invitation when he left. Cam ignored him. Until that moment I didn't realize I'd been holding my breath. Maybe Cam wasn't that angry with me anymore.

"You'll have dinner with me?"

"I've gotta eat."

"That's good anyway. You had me worried, and I—"

"Look, answer one question for me. Are you staying in St. Nacho's?"

Damn. He would ask point blank like that. "I don't know what I'm doing yet."

"But what does your gut say?"

"I don't know. I really don't."

Cam sighed. "You don't really belong here, do you?"

Words failed me.

I could *always* count on words to get what I wanted—or to get me out of a tough situation—whether I was honest or used spin or prevarication or glib flattery. Yet now words failed me, when what I wanted *most* was sitting right in front of me and he needed to hear me say them.

Feeling cursed, I whispered, "No I don't belong here."

Cam reached for my hand and stroked the back of it as he had so many times. "I don't belong anywhere else, Daniel."

Well, that made things pretty clear. "I see."

Cam's voice was flat after that. "So how about we agree to disagree and give your brother and JT the best wedding they could ever want? How about we work together to make them as happy as two men in love could ever be?"

Oh, fuck. *The wedding.* How could I have forgotten about that? I'd have to see Cam every time I fucking turned around until the end of June. "I wish everything was different. You don't know how much. No one has ever gotten to me like you do." I swallowed hard. "I really think I love you."

Way to bury the lede.

Cam shot me a sad smile. "I almost believe you mean that."

Aw, shit. I *did* mean it. "Cam—"

"*Almost.* I'm asking you to think about your brother. He needs what St. Nacho's has to offer even if you don't. A lot of people do. And none of us will allow you to come here and take that away. Do you understand?"

"I'm really not the enemy." I took out my wallet and dropped some money on the table. When Cam tried to shove it back, I gave him my fiercest *not negotiable* glare, and he pulled his hand back. "I don't know how I came to represent all the evils of the outside world, and I don't blame you for protecting what you have. I couldn't prove myself to you even if I wanted to, but let me tell you in terms you'll understand. St. Nacho's doesn't want me, she can't wait to be rid of me, and *I don't want to be here.*"

Cam leaned forward to rise when I pushed my chair back to leave. I put my hand out to stop him. I didn't want to hear anything else he might have to say.

"Just stay there and enjoy your food and whatever else is on offer. I'll be seeing you around."

MY PHONE RANG AS I MADE MY WAY BACK HOME, AND I TOOK THE call, flinching reflexively when my lawyer, Ted, barked out my name.

"*Livingston.* You blew up my phone today. What's so urgent?"

"I've had an attack of conscience, and I need to change the terms of the divorce settlement. I need to admit I broke the prenup conditions first and take the consequences."

"What? No. That's insane. Did you get religion or something?"

"Not exactly."

"Is she blackmailing you?"

"It's nothing like that."

"Then what? Help me understand here." The implied *so I can talk you the fuck out of it* wasn't lost on me.

"I don't want to be that guy, Ted. I don't want to be the guy who does what's expedient and only tells people whatever they want to hear. I want my new life to be built on something more substantial than convenient lies."

"*Shit.*" He didn't bother to hide his annoyance. "If you do this, you'll have to split everything down the middle, fifty-fifty. Are you prepared for that?"

"Yes. I'm sorry."

"Don't tell me you're sorry. You're the one that's going broke. First of all, I'm going to bill you for the time it will take to go over the figures again, and when you get over that crippling blow, you'll be more than fiscally naked because you're giving Bree the clothes off your back."

"Too late."

"You need some time to think this through."

"I can't live with myself if I don't come clean. I have to do this. If it makes you feel any better, you can go after restitution for the things she destroyed."

"Hell no, it does not make me feel better. You should be distracting your *conscience* with what money can *buy*. There's a lot to be said for that, Dan. Did I teach you nothing?"

"*Conscience* is not a dirty word."

"It is if it makes you throw perfectly good money away."

"I've made up my mind."

He heaved a sigh that sounded like bagpipes. "You need to be locked up for your own good. You can do a month or two of rehab, and I'll forget we ever had this conversation."

"Ted. I'm serious about this. So serious, in fact, that if you refuse to go along, you could find yourself out of the loop when it happens."

"You'd fire me over this?" He was hurt. I knew he looked out for my best interests; he had since the day we met. He was protective, a surrogate father. A *business* father. I liked him a lot. But not enough to let him talk me out of this.

"Of course not, but I might leak the information and proof so Bree can control the outcome. Is that what you want? She'd be awfully smug if she thought she found something to use against me. If we go to her and come clean, we're occupying the moral high ground and she has to suck it up and behave."

"What you say makes a certain, pleasurably vindictive sense. We give her money and make it a bitter pill she has to take with the knowledge we're better than her."

"Now you're seeing the big picture."

"I still don't like it."

"But you will do it." I wasn't asking. I was telling, and he knew it.

"Yeah."

"All right then. *Make it so*, Number Two."

"Ah, I *hate* when you say that." Something thumped on his end. My guess is he threw one of his executive toys, maybe the little man whose eyes bug out when you squeeze him, or one of his many wooden puzzles. "*Number Two*. It's Number One, damn it."

"Keep your head. Just say to yourself, Bree will hate this, over and over while you're doing it. That ought to get you through."

"You really don't hate her, though, do you?" His voice held wonder. I got that. Bree might hate me, but I had cut her so much slack my lawyer had to be reeling from shock.

"No, I don't hate her."

"You should. The bitch totally fucked you over with Anderson."

"I know."

"Her *lawyer* for fuck's sake."

That bothered Ted more than the cheating. That she'd cheated with the man who later became her lawyer really pissed him off. He was funny that way. He'd always been morally conservative and determined to be ethical where his business and his dick were concerned. He wasn't a homophobe, but he wasn't having the easiest time since I'd come out either. He'd been supportive as hell, though, and I was grateful. Mostly I used humor to break the tension between us.

"By the way, the offer still stands. If you'll let me fuck you to get even with Bree, I'm there."

"Fuck off." He hung up the phone.

Okay, humor broke *some* of the tension. If Ted didn't find me funny, he hung up the phone. But he'd do what I asked. And that was one thing off my mind. But, jeez. *Cam*. My entire body vibrated with wanting him, and I couldn't do a thing about it. I went to sleep with his image stamped on my heart. His taste on my tongue. I went to sleep wishing he was there beside me, wishing that I could pull him so close—open my heart so wide —he could crawl inside me.

I said I loved him, and it was all too true.

And just like that, the boy who cried wolf got gobbled up and became an object lesson for liars everywhere.

CHAPTER TWENTY

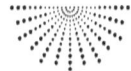

Jake got home at one a.m., stumbling drunk. His clumsy footsteps woke me up. When I went to make sure he was okay, his fist came out of nowhere and connected so solidly, so painfully with my jaw, it whipped my head around.

Jake didn't wait. He marched out the door, still talking to himself. "Motherfucking, control freak, douchebag rich, stick up your ass…"

"Wait, *wait*." I hauled my ass off the floor and took off after him. "I know I deserved that."

"Damn right you did."

I tested my jaw by opening and closing my mouth. *Still hinged.* "Is that what passes for anger management these days?"

"Shit," he hissed, and slumped sloppily against our fence. "Do you even have any idea what you've done? How huge a deal this is to me?"

"Obviously not, judging from your reaction. Why don't you come inside the house and we can talk about it."

He eyed me, and I knew he wanted to say no. But I eyed him right back, and fortunately I could still stare him down. He clumped after me and went ahead when I opened the door.

"Joyce wanted to say goodbye. She left around seven. We came by here, but you weren't home."

"Sorry. I was…"

"With Cam. I know."

Shit. "How the hell…?"

"It's a small fucking town, what can I say? I heard you two were canoodling at Nacho's."

Did I belong in St. Nacho's? Hell no. A guy couldn't get a drink without it making the news.

"You could have called."

"She said you should call her. I think she was overwhelmed."

"No doubt."

I had to hit the head, and when I got back, I found him pouring ice-cold vodka into chilled glasses for both of us. He started the ball rolling. "So now what? Have you figured out how you'll spin this? I have a brother and sister I've never met. I can't believe—"

"Just a damned minute." I took my drink from him and sat in one of the chairs at our little table. "I'm not the one who let you down here."

"The hell you're not."

"Not the only one. Pop could have written to you if he'd wanted."

"How could he find me? Half the time I wasn't even in the country."

"He could have found you through me. But he didn't." I wouldn't have let Pop find Jake either, but it was *true* he didn't try. I watched each word break Jake's spirit a little more. *Shit*. Was I so fucked-up that I couldn't keep that from him, at least? Better he should hate me than let our pop make him feel like less, yet again, after all these years.

His eyes broadcast his pain. "Then why? I suppose you'll fucking tell me."

"How should I know? I don't know the way his mind works.

And if you've read my letters to him, you've seen that more than once I brought it up."

Jake was silent for a long time. "What did he say?"

Had Pop ever explained himself? For anything? I put my glass down and clasped my hands between my knees. "Have you forgotten what he was like?"

"No."

"He ignored what didn't suit him. He evaded and blamed and twisted the truth until you didn't know what was real and what was made up. He broke Mom's heart over and over."

"I know that," Jake said miserably.

We sat in gloomy silence for a while, one of hundreds—thousands—of silences spent contemplating just exactly what we'd done or what we hadn't done to make our father act the way he had toward us.

"Do you ever...?"

When he trailed off, I lifted my gaze to his. "What?"

He put his drink down and placed his head in the palms of his hands. I had rarely seen him this defeated as an adult, and it scared me.

"Do you ever wish I'd never come along?"

"*What?*" I stood so fast my chair slid back against the tile floor and battered the kitchen cabinet.

"Do you ever wish it had just been you and Mom and Pop? Maybe if I'd never been born—"

"You wait just a damn minute." The intervening years melted away, and I got angry with our pop all over again, as if I'd caught him hovering over Jakey with his fucking belt out again, because that's what it felt like. That's what Jakey's face told me—that our pop could reach out through time and space and fuck him up all over again.

"You stop that this second. Pop was insane. It had nothing to do with you. He drank, and when he came home, he took his disappointment and his anger out on *us*. It was his *job* to protect us, and instead he terrorized us."

"He didn't want me, Dan. You know he didn't."

I shook my head. "I know nothing of the sort."

"Everyone said he snapped after I was born. Zeyde and Mom talked about it when they didn't think I could hear. Like…like I was the last straw, and Pop couldn't take it anymore."

"That's preposterous. How can anyone blame a baby for—"

"I don't know. I only know that he did. He blamed me for everything that was wrong, and if you think about it, you know it."

Thinking back, I realized what he said rang horribly true. Perhaps I'd never realized it, perhaps I'd never wanted to understand, but certain things, neighbors talking, veiled comments, insinuations disguised as idle speculation suddenly fell into place like tumblers in a lock.

Holy fuck. "Maybe…"

I remembered Jakey's birth vividly because he'd come weeks early. He'd been jaundiced—the color of pumpkins—and like me, had our mother's thick, curly hair. Pop, who'd been in the habit of drinking heavily already, left us alone a lot at night after that. Maybe I hadn't noticed because a steady stream of well-meaning neighbors and friends had come and gone with food and sundries, helping my mom by cleaning and shopping for her. More than one person I'd never seen before showed up, seemingly interested and kind but more curious to see the baby than the new mother. At the time I thought it was the novelty of a new baby that brought them over, but now…in this context, I wondered if they'd come to see…

Oh, *fuck*. "No way. You and Joyce both have Pop's eyes."

He turned to me then, and in those very eyes I saw what he'd believed all along.

Damn. "Did you honestly think Mom had another man's child?"

"No." He hid his face again. "*Yes.* I didn't know what to think."

"Why didn't you ask her? She'd have told you. She'd have set your mind at ease or given up her secret if she'd known it was eating away at you like this."

"And how was I supposed to ask our mother if she'd cheated on Pop?"

"You've been carrying this around for how long?"

Jake shrugged. "He hated me. He always hated me. I just never knew exactly why. While I was in Israel, I started thinking about whether—"

"Well, *shit.*"

He refilled my drink, and it took a while before I could talk again.

"Surely Zeyde said something about all this at some point? Did you ask him outright?"

Jake shook his head. "We had a huge fight about it once. I had to fill out some paperwork, and I said it was a shame I had to claim my father. He muttered something about my father never claiming me, so it would serve him right."

"He did?"

Jake smiled ruefully. "I pressed him about it, but it just upset him. He asked me if I loved our mother. Of course I loved her. I wouldn't judge her. He said it was none of my business unless she made it my business."

"Maybe even Zeyde wondered."

"Maybe we'll never find out the truth."

"I don't know. Looking at you with Joyce today, there's little doubt in my mind that you're Pop's kid."

"Maybe."

"I've seen pictures of Joyce and her brother Lonnie as children, Jake. There's a lot to be said for genetics."

"Did you ever wonder? Did he ever tell you I wasn't?"

"Oh, hell no. Do you think I would keep something like that

from you? Jeez, if I'd had the slightest suspicion I'd have had us DNA tested and rid you of him once and for all. The very thought of a *blood* connection to him, of sharing traits and maybe temperament, the idea that someday I could become like him freezes the blood in my veins and keeps me awake at night. Are you kidding?"

"*Dan.*"

"If I'd believed you weren't his natural child, I'd have taken you out to the best steakhouse in New York to celebrate."

Jakey's eyes swam, and for a second, he looked about five again. It was funny how that could just empty my sails. All my anger—all my righteous indignation—was gone, *whoosh*, in the face of some kind of crazy, protective love. His voice was hoarse so he whispered, "You will never be like him. Never."

I shook my head, unable to speak.

"It's time the Livingston brothers declared their Independence Day." He held up his glass, and I knocked it gently with mine. He looked right into my eyes as we drank and then heaved a last shuddering sigh. He put his glass down but didn't refill it.

Maybe things were going to be okay after all.

We still had a decision to make. "What I don't understand is why Joyce approached you."

Jake huffed a rueful laugh. "She didn't. Or she didn't mean to. Someone in your office told her you could be reached through Bêtise."

I told Jake about the note Joyce had left for me in Santa Cruz. "Bree forwarded it, but I wanted to sit on it while I decided how to respond. I guess I waited too long." *I'd been doing that a lot lately.*

"What are you going to do?"

That was a really good question. I wanted to lob Pop's letters into the trash and forget about them. I'd planned to ignore his pleas for a face-to-face indefinitely, and I guess I imagined that

176

one day the letters would simply stop coming. Sooner or later the old bastard had to die. But Jake looked like he needed some kind of closure.

"What do you want to do?"

He shook his head. "I have no idea how to respond. I never expected this. Joyce came for you, not me. I told her if she gave me the address, I'd go down to LA to see him but the more I think about it, the more I wonder, why should I bother?"

"I honestly don't know. I'm not sure I would."

"He wants you not me."

"Pop's a piece of *shit*, Jakey, and Joyce doesn't even know us." I clenched my hands into fists. Even my worthless right hand gave the impression it was in it to win it, the knuckles nearly white as pain shot up my arm. "You are the only family I have."

His brown eyes shimmered again. "Maybe you should meet them. It's got nothing to do with me. Maybe you should go just for you."

"There's nothing there I want, Jakey. You're all the family I will ever need."

CHAPTER TWENTY-ONE

For the second day in a row, I walked the short distance to Bêtise hungover. It was early enough that I didn't think it would be crowded and I was right. There was only a scattering of people seated at the many tables, some nursing coffee, some hidden behind newspapers.

Mary Catherine worked the counter and several Miss Independence Pies employees manned the kitchen and waited tables. My brother and his core staff typically took Mondays off, and Mary Catherine's pie ladies came in to handle things while he was out.

"Hey, Dan. What can I get for you?"

"Morning, MC." I flashed her a grin from behind dark glasses, trying to look less dissolute than I actually was. At least I'd opted for clothes. At one point I'd almost headed out in my sleep pants. "Can I have your biggest coffee and one of Jake's bran muffins please?"

"Sure, why don't you have a seat, and I'll bring it over."

"Will you join me?"

Mary Catherine motioned one of her newest workers—I

think her name was Andrea—over. She was a quiet, nervous woman in her midthirties with a nice smile.

MC brought over coffee and muffins and settled into the chair opposite me. "Slow today."

"Yeah? I guess." I acknowledged I hadn't seen the place much emptier. "But work is mostly going well?"

"Yeah." She smiled. "Better than I thought."

"I knew Bêtise would be great. You just had to have a little faith."

The little French café had been MC's dream long before Jake and I came along, but it had taken Jake's expertise as a pastry chef and all Ken Ashton's powers of persuasion to make her believe it could be a reality.

"What about you?" she asked. "What are you planning, now that you have a new life to look forward to?"

I took a swig of my too-hot coffee. "I don't know."

"You have time to figure something out. Plus we have a wedding to look forward to."

In my experience, all women of a certain age sparkled when they talked about weddings. MC was no exception. Her eyes took on a dreamy look. "It's going to be beautiful. I've never been to a Jewish wedding, but I saw one in a movie once. There's that canopy thing."

"The chuppah. Yeah." I nodded. "Great tradition. The ceremony is supposed to take place outdoors under the sky. The chuppah represents the new couple's home."

"They're going to have the ceremony on the beach, and we're going to decorate the chuppah with all kinds of flowers and branches."

"That will be lovely."

"Jake has designed a cake, but he won't tell us anything about it, other than it will be a gift for JT, and it has special meaning."

"Ah. Must be in the shape of a giant closet."

"Whoa there, Dan. Pot, kettle." Despite her words she smiled at me.

"But with me it's like that Monty Python skit. *I'm getting better.*"

"We all grow. Even you. I see the way you look at Cam." Mary Catherine's maternal laser-beam eyes missed nothing, apparently.

"The abominable fireman. Yes."

"Am I mistaken, or have you been wearing your heart out in the open lately?"

"I have." I took off my shades and winced. "But it's not going to work out."

"You don't know that."

"He loves this town, but my life and work are elsewhere. For me it was a pit stop, you know? For Cam, this is his home. Jake's getting married, and as soon as he and JT move into a place of their own, I'll be moving on."

From behind me, I heard a man say, "Don't be so sure of that, son."

JT's dad, Carl, walked past me and put his arm around Mary Catherine's shoulders. "Hello, my dear."

Mary Catherine blushed prettily and lifted her cheek for his kiss. "Hello, Carl."

"Well, well, *well.*" I wasn't above giving Mary Catherine a hard time for having a boyfriend of her own. "Looks like I'm not the only one to slip on the banana peel of romance here in St. Nacho's."

Carl cleared his throat. "Mary Catherine has kindly accompanied me to several plays at the community college. We're working our way up to dinner and dancing."

"That's nice." I wouldn't have minded seeing a play or two with him myself. Carl was a great guy, and he'd saved Jake's life when Jake first wound up in St. Nacho's. "The pretty girls get all the good ones."

Mary Catherine rolled her eyes and got up. "I'm just going to go back to work now."

"You don't have to go on my account," I picked up my coffee. "If you two want to sit in a tree *K-I-S-S-I-N-G*, don't let me stop you."

Mary Catherine gave my shoulder a swat and left.

"So you and Mary Catherine, huh? How long has this been going on?"

"JT and Yasha have been throwing us together for a while now. Those two aren't exactly subtle."

"I guess not." When I looked around, business had picked up some, and the noise level increased.

Carl nodded to MC when she came back with a coffee for him. "Thanks, hon."

She scooted back behind the counter to help other customers with an extra spring in her step.

"That there is a gorgeous woman," I admitted.

"She is that."

"It's about time she found her prince, from what I hear."

"JT told me a little about her past. She's filled in the rest. I don't know if I'm any kind of prince, but I'm certainly not a toad like her ex."

It was no secret that Mary Catherine's personal and business life revolved around helping women overcome abusive relationships as she had finally done when she came to St. Nacho's to start over with her son, Jordan.

"No, man. You are a mensch. I'm happy for you. Life is good sometimes."

"It looks like we're going to be related too."

"Yeah. We are. How about that? I can't think of two nicer guys to have as family either. Don't tell Jake, but I heartily approve."

"You've changed your mind? I thought you weren't all that enamored with the idea of them getting married."

I waved that off. "I tried to explain. I'm a bitter old guy in the middle of a divorce. I want Jake to be happy, and I've never seen him as happy as he's been with JT. They're lucky to have each other. Maybe my reaction was sour grapes."

"Why is that?" He peered at me curiously. His eyes, so much like JT's, held intelligence and mischief. "Seems like I've heard you found your own firefighter."

Did no one in this town have anything better to do than gossip? "That is *exactly* what I hate about small towns."

"Me too." Carl grimaced. "No matter how long I've been here, I cannot get used to having everyone all up in my business."

"I heartily agree. I can't wait to get back to my regularly scheduled life."

"I understand that." He draped his hand casually next to his coffee cup and leaned back as though he had all the time in the world. "So tell me, why are you still here?"

I broke my muffin apart and picked up a small bite. While I chewed, I thought about it. "I don't know. First I had nowhere to go, so I came to hang out with Jake. Then we had the accident. Jordan is a great PT, and now there's the wedding..."

Carl simply watched me. "Seems to me you've been here quite a while. Maybe you like it more than you think."

"I don't like it at all." I was adamant. "As soon as I'm done around here, I'm going to buy myself a loft in San Francisco and get back to work."

"Gets a little tight, doesn't it?" Carl gestured around his throat with his hands. "Right around here, huh? Like you can't breathe? Like if you don't get on the road, you'll never be able to get a breath of air again?"

"Oh, yeah," I complained. "You feel that too?"

"I have, yes."

"How can you stand it?" I asked. "I walk out to get my paper, and this town curls around me, squeezing at me until I want to crawl out of my skin. Everyone talks like St. Nacho's is this big comfortable shoe, and to me it's like I'm wearing some woman's size zero stilettos with the antitheft tag still inside."

Taciturn, understated Carl laughed so heartily he startled the women at the next table over. "Welcome to my world. I hate this place."

Get out of town. "Seriously?"

"Sure." He waved and winked at MC. "With certain notable exceptions, St. Nacho's doesn't do a thing for me."

"Haven't you been here forever? Why the hell did you stay?"

He shrugged. "St. Nacho's was my Meg's comfortable shoe. She loved it here, and here is where I had to stay if I wanted to be with her. After she passed, there were the children to raise. JT got his job with the fire department here, and I had the motel to run. There just never seemed to be a good time to escape. Everything conspired against me."

"Oh, man." I gripped my coffee so hard the lid popped off. "Muse says you can tell if St. Nacho's wants you."

"For a long time I might have said St. Nacho's most certainly did not want me. Now I have to think she fought pretty hard to keep me here, even though I didn't want to stay."

I started to speak, then closed my mouth. Is that what was going on? A battle of wills? And when had I become the type of person to anthropomorphize a whole town and let it run my damn life?

It sounded like a Martin Short comedy sketch. St. Nacho's is a fickle mistress.

Fickle mistress my ass.

"I've come to believe it's not my cup of tea, you know? Nothing wrong with it, but I don't belong here."

Carl's gentle eyes studied me for a minute and then he said, "I don't know if we always get to pick where we belong, Daniel. I don't think I did."

So what? St. Nacho's was quicksand, and I should just stop

struggling and let it pull me under? Because that's what it felt like—the inexorable pressure of being crushed under a ton of sand.

"I don't…" I tried to get up but felt light-headed. "I just—"

"Whoa. It's not as bad as all that." Carl frowned at me as I picked up my coffee and muffin. "It can be nice here. That's what I wanted to tell you. There are things here you'll never find anyplace else. It's compensation for the freedom you lose."

"Oh, my fucking—" I admit to having a panic attack right there in my brother's café. "This is *The Town That Ate My Life*."

Carl laughed again. "That's funny. Okay. Sorry I said anything. You can relax. You're free to go, you know. Any time. Just leave."

I felt in my pockets for my car keys. "Okay. You're on."

The highway was calling again. Carl watched me with an amused grin on his face, then shot me a minimal wave. "Buh-bye."

"I'll see you later, Carl. Okay?"

"All right. See you. Drive safely."

I'd begun to make my way to the door when JT and Cam rushed into the place, calling my name. JT was obviously upset about something. Cam had his hands shoved in his pockets. He looked as tired as I felt.

"What is it?"

"Where's Yasha?" JT asked.

I glanced from one of them to the other. "He's at our place. He was asleep when I left."

"We were just there, and he's not."

"What?" I guess I'd just assumed he was still there because it was his day off, but I hadn't really checked. "Seriously? Did you go in?"

"We did," Cam acknowledged. "We used the spare key you keep in that fake rock thing. Jake isn't there, and neither is your car."

"Well"—I had given him permission to use it anytime, but —"so call him. He must have needed to go somewhere. He's a grown man. Why are we even having this conversation? Were you supposed to meet somewhere and he didn't show up?"

Cam spoke first. "JT thinks—"

"He went to see your dad." JT folded his arms. "I'm sure of it. He was talking last night about confronting him about your childhood once and for all, and the fact that he's gone this morning...It's no coincidence."

"Ah, shit." I looked at Cam. "He probably did. We talked about that last night too. About why Pop might have written to me and not him."

JT slumped. "I told him I'd go with him, but I was working today. He told me he'd wait."

"He didn't, apparently." I asked, "He isn't answering his phone?"

"Nope."

"That little shit. I'm going to text him that if he doesn't pick up his phone, I will kick his ass."

Cam's lips twitched into a smile. "That will make him laugh."

"Not if I'm speeding down Highway 101 after him. Tell him I'm on my way, and he is not to even enter that house without me. Got that? Tell him I need to be there with him." I felt in my pockets for my key fob and realized. "He took my fucking car!"

Cam flipped me his keys. "I've got your bike. You go. Take my truck."

"Are you sure?" I couldn't help it. I drew him aside and stood way closer to him than I probably should have, given that we'd decided the thing between us was fairly hopeless. "I might be gone a couple days. A while..."

"I'm sure." Cam reached out to me, and I sought the comfort of his arms. I got sucked into his heat—his warmth and his goodness—like I was gravitationally predisposed to be there. It seemed whatever freedom of motion I ever had suddenly shrank in size until I was locked into orbit around this one man. *"Cam."*

"Drive safely, Daniel." He held me there for a moment with his cheek against mine, and I knew, *I just knew* the sands of St. Nacho's thought they had me sucked under for good. I loved him. I fucking *loved him*. I didn't have to look at Carl to know he had a mocking grin on his face.

"I'll be back soon, Cam."

A tiny smile played over Cam's lips. "I know."

In Santa Barbara, I got a text from Cam telling me they'd been in touch with Jake, and he would wait and walk in the park for a couple of hours. Despite driving like a maniac for most of the day, I didn't hit the LA traffic until three in the afternoon. By that time, I could kiss going over twenty miles an hour—for the most part—goodbye. Yet, mercifully, it was still light when I reached Long Beach. I got off the 605 Freeway on Spring Street, in unfamiliar territory, and headed north a short way until I got to Studebaker Road. On my left was a huge regional park, and on the right, a tree-lined neighborhood full of low-slung fifties ramblers, ranch-style homes with cutesy shuttered windows and curving driveways. I could no more picture my father here than I could picture him in the pricey ocean-view home I had lived in with Bree. I couldn't picture my father at all, anymore.

I texted Jake's phone when I got off the freeway. It had been a grueling drive, but I pulled up in front of my dad's poorly kept, modest house at about six p.m.

I could smell the sea and feel its moisture on my face when I opened the door of Cam's truck. Someone was grilling meat, and it reminded me I hadn't eaten since that muffin from Bêtise. The wide, blue sky had only just begun its burning lightshow in the west, ready to put on one of the Southland's spectacular sunsets—enhanced courtesy of LA's grimy air.

While I waited, my car came creeping around the corner with Jake at the wheel. He parked behind me. I could tell he was nervous. Maybe he was ashamed he'd sneaked off without me. I wasn't going to give him a hard time over it. I was too worried about how all this was affecting him to give a damn how we got there. The main thing, the important thing, was that he knew I would stand by him.

"I get why you came alone." I told him.

"I'm sorry." He looked small, just then, and I hated that.

"Aw, don't be sorry. You know what? You can do this alone if you need to. I can deal with that. What I can't handle is wondering if you need me and I'm not here."

"Yeah." He nodded. "I know."

"I've been doing this a long time, Jakey. I have this thing inside me that kills me if I don't—if you need me and I'm not around. Maybe it's more like I need to be here, just in case. Maybe it's more for me than you, after all."

"I know, *Danilo*. No worries."

I felt tears sting my eyes. "I wasn't there so much lately though, huh? Bree wasn't big on family stuff."

"Not your family anyway."

I rolled my eyes. "Yeah, if I had a dime for every time I had to go to one of her cousins' insufferable weddings…Hell. Her parent's fiftieth wedding anniversary was like *Tales from the Crypt*."

Jake laughed. "I never could have stayed with that bitch as long as you did, man."

"Aw. Bree was all right," I responded automatically. "She was my wife for a long time. I owe her some loyalty for that, anyway."

I was going to pay handsomely for the privilege too.

Contrary to what I thought I'd feel, it was kind of...okay, actually.

"So. What's it going to be? You want me to wait here while you go? Or do you want me to come with you. Either way, man. No pressure."

"You really drove all that way to stand by Cam's truck?"

"I drove all this way to stand by you, Jakey. You tell me."

Jake flung himself forward and wrapped his arms around me, and maybe that's what I'd come for. Maybe that's what we both needed, right there.

Nothing the old man could do or say, nothing our new siblings could ever have to offer me, would eclipse that moment when my brother pulled me into a hard hug and let me know that no matter what, no matter who had actually fathered us, who entered our lives, or what happened to us, we were solid. We were the Livingston brothers. And nothing could take that away.

He threw an arm around my shoulder and pulled me with him. "Let's go find out what Pop's been up to all these fucking years."

CHAPTER TWENTY-TWO

A middle-aged Asian woman answered Jake's knock. She wore one of those smock aprons with wide, stitched-on pockets over scrubs and introduced herself as Sally. She was a smiling, nodding type of woman, pleasant and probably very nice. We didn't know what to expect, so I told her who we were and why we were there and asked about Joyce. Sally said Joyce didn't live there but her brother—Lonnie—would arrive home from school soon.

There were a few signs that a young person inhabited the house. A console table where stacks of mail sat unopened also held a bowl of movie-ticket stubs and what looked like the detritus of someone's social life—receipts for fast-food restaurants, CDs, and change—as though someone emptied their pockets out there when they arrived home in the evening. A colorful gym bag and some well-used athletic shoes waited by the door.

I wasn't sure what to do, but Sally took us at our word that we were Elton Livingston's sons. She led us deeper into the house. Despite fans and open windows, it reeked of cat and illness. That was the first time it really hit me. Pop was a very,

very sick man. Sally turned the television she'd been watching off, and took us past the living room, down the hallway to the master bedroom. There was no door—only hinges. Maybe they'd had to take it off to get the bed inside.

The room—repurposed as a sickroom—was cramped and stuffy. Besides the standard hospital-style adjustable bed there was a recliner and an old dresser. A television mounted on the wall was tuned to *Animal Planet*. Poor quality paintings graced the walls, along with a few pictures of what I assumed was Pop's new family in happier times.

Sally turned the sound down. "He likes to watch the nature shows." She said this to us, then raised her voice to almost shouting and turned to Pop. "Don't you, Elton. You like the animals, huh?"

Her head bobbed enthusiastically, and Pop nodded back once, almost reflexively, as if he didn't really know what he was saying yes to.

For the life of me, I couldn't really make myself believe it was him. Internally, I knew that brittle human shell was our pop. Who else could it be? But at the same time, it wasn't. Jake stepped closer to me, and automatically, I put my hand on his back.

I'm not sure Pop recognized us either.

"Pop." I made a marginal effort. "It's me, Daniel. And here's Jake."

Pop's salt-and-pepper caterpillar eyebrows drew together. His cheeks had sunken into hollows beneath high cheekbones. A nasal canula fed him oxygen in rhythmic bursts. He hissed something through dry, open lips, but I didn't catch what it was. What teeth we could see protruded a little, unbrushed for the most part. A tray by the bedside held water. Sally offered this to him, and he drank greedily. It made me think the television in the living room had claimed her attention for long enough that he'd grown thirsty. Whatever I felt about him that made me unhappy, that he'd had to lie there thirsty while she watched *Jeopardy* or whatever.

"Dan." His lips twisted into a rictus grin, and he extended a corpselike hand. I wanted to pull away, but something made me take it. "Dani."

"Yeah, Pop. It's me. Dani."

Beside me, Jake's rigid form had gone completely still. He barely breathed.

"And 'ake." Tears clouded the old man's eyes. He licked his lips. "*Christ*. Jake."

Jake walked stiffly to the other side of the bed and took Pop's other hand. The old man crushed us in his grip. You wouldn't even have thought he could squeeze a blueberry and my knuckles were white where he held my hand. Thank heavens I'd given him my left.

Jake's gaze was fixed on Pop, filled with horror. I could see the whites around the soft brown of his irises. I could never bear to see my brother scared. I felt like I had to do something to make it better; the emotion driving me was as insistent as hunger, as relentless as thirst. A physical need. But what on earth...? This—this *living corpse* was the monster we'd feared since childhood, and right then all I could feel was pity. Pop was way, way too young to look like that, but he was dying and his body was ravaged by disease. Pathetic.

It was as confusing to me as it was painful.

Pop didn't *deserve* my pity. I wanted my righteous indignation back. I wanted my anger. I wanted to hate this man because the alternative, the horror I was bound to feel if I gave into it, was unthinkable.

"It's okay, Jakey. It's just Pop. See?"

Jake nodded.

"Your daddy talks about you sometimes," Sally said.

I frowned. "Yeah?"

"Yeah. About his very smart boy who owns many, many apartment buildings."

"Yeah." That made it easier. I turned away so she didn't see my disgust. "I'll bet he does."

"I'll be back." She left us alone with him. Jake's gaze met mine from across the bed.

Everyone always said it was best to make peace. To say what needed to be said. To get closure—but for the life of me, I had not one single clue how to even begin. I'd had Pop in my life for a lot more years than Jake—early years, I admit, that I didn't remember too well. And what stuck out from those father-son moments wasn't games of catch in the fading summer light. It was hiding with Jakey in the closet while my mother pleaded with my dad not to scream at us anymore.

I wanted to drop the scrawny hand that held mine onto that sheet and walk away. Then I heard Jake's voice.

"Pop?"

The old man's eyes turned to his.

"I'm not anyone's fucking punching bag."

Jake peeled the skeletal fingers from his hand and left me and Pop in the room alone. My throat burned like fire, so my voice was raspy when I spoke again.

"Joyce seems nice."

As openings go, it wasn't very wide. I didn't let much of my pop through, but in the ensuing five minutes or so, I think I said what I needed to say.

Because, really, all I needed to say was goodbye.

When I left Pop's room, I was ready to move on. Oddly enough, my heart felt hollow and empty, but not sad like I thought it might. It felt...naked. *I* felt naked. Stripped bare and completely, totally new.

I found Jakey in the kitchen, filling the sink with soapy water. Dirty dishes were stacked high on the counters, and flies buzzed around old cat food. If Lonnie was still in school, he shouldn't have to come home to this. What the hell was going on?

Already, I was thinking of Lonnie as my brother. I *did* have a big-brother complex. Cam would have laughed.

Ah, Cam.

Cam would have wept too. He was such a softy. I'd have to make this situation easier for Lonnie or Cam would never let me hear the end of it.

When Lonnie finally came home, he seemed shocked to find strange men cleaning his kitchen. Sally stayed in the living room and left us to introduce ourselves.

Lonnie and Jake looked so much alike it was uncanny. Our pop was a total idiot. Either that, or he was going to spend the rest of his limited life lying in that bed contemplating what might have been.

"Sorry. We just kind of took over," Jake said over his shoulder. "I think it's all my years in food service. I can't stand a dirty kitchen."

Lonnie blushed hotly. "I meant to clean things up before I left for school. My bad. It's nice to finally meet you." Lonnie held his hand out, but Jake's were covered in soapy water. He took mine instead and gave it a hearty pump. "Joyce told me all about you."

"Yeah?" I asked. "Good or bad."

"All good." He shrugged. "Well. She said she kind of messed things up. We didn't know there were two of you."

I rolled my eyes. "Yeah. We figured."

"What the hell was that about?" Lonnie's young face creased into a frown. "Dad never talked much about his time before he came to California, but he's talked about Dan a lot, lately."

"We can only guess, but we think he didn't believe Jake was his son for some reason."

Lonnie glanced at Jake, then me. He pointed to his face, which was...wow. Genetics. You just can't fight the facts. There were three Livingston brothers and a sister, and we all looked like clones.

Lonnie chuckled. "I'll bet he does now."

He was so young. I realized we must seem like foreign invaders to him.

Jake only had eyes for the dishes. I think that was his way of coping.

I was numb. I was Izzie's blank slate, so I said, "Where's Joyce? I think we need to talk, Lonnie. We'd like to get to know you."

Joyce, it turned out, worked at a movie theater and didn't get off until ten. "She lives with our mom in the apartments on the other side of the park."

"So you live here alone with your father, and the nurses come and go?"

Lonnie shrugged and looked away. "It's…I'm still in school, and it's just easier for me."

"Are you saying you've been helping to take care of your father all by yourself?" I asked incredulously.

"No. It's nothing like that. There's always someone here. Dad's on hospice. I just…look in and stuff. Joyce and I both do. She comes here after work."

Jake and I looked at each other.

"He doesn't respond much, really. Mostly, lately, he sleeps."

Jake let out a muttered expletive. "And your mother?"

"She pays his bills and things. Takes care of his insurance."

"Shouldn't you be living at home with her and Joyce?"

"I couldn't just abandon him like that. It's not going to last much longer."

"Was he good to you?" Jake asked. "Does he deserve your loyalty?"

"Jake," I warned.

"Sorry." Jake looked away.

"No, he wasn't really that good to us," Lonnie said, an icy edge to his young voice. "He wasn't particularly *nice*. My mother divorced him and took us away because it was pretty awful living with him. But he's still a human being. He's still our dad."

"The best revenge is living on the high road," I said. "I like you, Lonnie. I like you a lot."

Lonnie shrugged.

"Are you hungry?" Jake asked. "Or do you normally eat before you come home?"

The kid shook his head, and it made me smile. He was like Jake in temperament too. He wouldn't ask for anything. Didn't want to show any weakness. "You could order pizza. My treat."

Lonnie brightened a little. "Sure."

I took out my phone and held it between my palms. "You order, whatever's your favorite. I'm starved. I eat anything on a pizza unless it swims. Jake can pick it up if they don't deliver. Oh, and get salad and garlic bread. In the meantime, if you give me your mom's number, I'd like to talk to her too."

He spouted off the number, and I entered it into my phone.

"I'll call her in a bit." *But first...*I jerked my chin at Jake and mimicked smoking with one hand. He nodded to me as I stepped outside into the now-indigo night. The crescent moon and evening star were visible, but other than that, the sky was dark blue and limitless. I dialed Cam's cell number. He picked up on the first ring.

"Daniel?"

"Yes. It's me. Hello. I hope I didn't catch you at a bad time. Are you fighting fire?"

"Sure," he said dryly. "But I still have one hand free so I can talk. How's it going?"

"Fine. I just...I need to hear your voice. Got a minute?' I lit up and blew my smoke into the salty breeze.

"I can hear you smoking. We're going to have to talk about that habit of yours, but yeah. I have time for you."

My heart...*wow*. It caught fire. Cam had my back. My throat closed, and I had to swallow before I could talk. "Thank you."

"Tell me about your dad, Daniel. I'm listening."

CHAPTER TWENTY-THREE

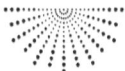

Jake and I stayed in Long Beach for several days, even though an unplanned leave of absence was the last thing we expected. Mary Catherine and some of the Miss Independence Pies staff filled the void at Bêtise while we were gone. Some of MC's pie employees had been working in the bakery—some even planned to go to culinary school eventually. They did double duty, and while Jake's highly sought-after fancy pastries were missing from the refrigerated case, they kept the patrons in pies, brownies, bar cookies, and muffins.

Al kept me posted but let me have the time for family. If something needed my immediate attention, he forwarded it to me via e-mail, and I did what I could.

Pop's hold on life was tenuous at best, and it seemed to lessen day by day. He slept most of the time, and when he didn't, he managed few words. Even so, our final goodbye before we left to head home wasn't as easy as I hoped.

Jake took it hard.

I spent an hour or so in El Dorado Park—a place I'd found made a great refuge when things became tense and I needed to walk off heightened emotions—talking to Cam on the phone.

"Yeah. It rained hard last night. It's still spattering us a little. Everything smells really fresh here. I'm at the duck pond, and some geese just charged a couple of little girls and scared the shit out of them. Geese are ferocious."

"I miss you." Cam's voice was as soft as the little droplets of misty rain. I could picture him in one of the recliners at the firehouse, one big hand wrapped around a coffee mug. More than once he'd shushed some of his coworkers. It sounded like they were playing cards. Maybe Cam was watching television with the sound turned way down, relaxing.

"I miss you too."

"Is it difficult? Seeing your pop like that?"

"Not like you mean. I don't really have anything invested in him. I know that sounds bad, but for me he died a long time ago. Jake is more conflicted, although if you asked him, he'd tell you I was full of shit."

"Did you ever tell him? About how your dad tried to—"

"No."

He let the silence draw out between us. "Are you going to?"

"How can I?"

"Maybe the truth—"

"I know what you're going to say, Cam, but I just can't. There's no reason he has to know that his father tried to kill him. I know you think every lie leaves a black void inside my heart, but that's one corner that's going to stay dark forever, and I swear to fuck if you tell him—"

"I won't tell him."

"Good." *That was one relief, anyway.* "I know how fucked-up you think I am, and if that's a deal breaker then...I know my brother, Cam, and I'm begging you, please, don't tell him."

"It's all right, Daniel. I was going to say maybe the truth is better left unsaid this time."

"Yeah?"

"Before you went off on me."

"Sorry."

"Is it going to burn a hole in your gut?"

"I've been carrying this around for a long time. It's like a sick gray fog, but it's mine."

"I know." The phone went silent for so long I thought maybe he'd hung up. Then I heard a door close and less background noise. "You're not carrying it alone anymore."

Ah, *Cam.* There was so much I could have said—wanted to say—right then. I could have filled the airwaves between us with all the shapes of words: of relief, of grief, of longing and hope and loneliness, and most of all, of love. What I felt for Cam was so big I couldn't dislodge it from my heart right then.

I held the phone with both hands and clenched my teeth against everything I wanted to say. Lies hurt. They fester. There's an unexpected weight to secrets I never realized existed until I started to let go of them. I had no idea what this secret—this last lie of omission—would cost me. I'd never tell Jake our father had tried to kill him. If he remembered...maybe I'd rethink that.

But I wasn't going to carry it alone.

I cleared my throat and said, "Thank you."

Cam chuckled. "Anyway it sounds like you have a pretty good family. The younger generation anyway."

I felt awkward talking about them all the time. "Have you thought any more about talking to yours?"

"No."

"Will you?"

"Trust me when I say it's futile."

"Tell me why."

"My brothers said if they ever saw me near their kids, they'd put me down like a rabid dog."

"*No.*"

Silence fell between us until I couldn't stand it anymore. "I'm a better man because of you, Cameron Rooney. You enrich—

you bless—every life you touch. I don't think even God can ask much more of you than that."

I heard a shuddering intake of breath, and I'd have given everything—all my worldly possessions and the balance of my time on earth—to put my arms around Cam right then.

"Just come home, Daniel."

"I'll be home soon." Ah, *great. Home.* Carl would have a good laugh over that.

SOMETIMES I THINK I WILL NEVER UNDERSTAND FAMILY. THEN, other times, I believe I understand it all too well. It's not rational, and you can't get around it. You get the family you get, and then if you're lucky, you get to choose the family you want.

Jake was on his way to happiness. We just had to see this through.

St. Nacho's and JT were waiting for him.

For a lot of different reasons, the biggest of which was having to stand at Pop's bedside and look into the abyss, I drove Cam's truck back to St. Nacho's wearing a nicotine patch and a pretty unhappy, I'm-quitting-smoking-so-fuck-off-and-die scowl on my face. Jake drove my car.

We arranged to meet at the Boathouse in Santa Barbara for lunch on the way back up the coast. Neither of us had been sorry to leave Long Beach, but I know returning to business as usual filled me with a kind of dread as if from this moment on everything was more important, or it had to be more perfect. Maybe we stopped more to slow our reentry.

I tried a smile on for the hostess who seated us and handed us menus while the bus boy served us water. Jake wrapped his hand around his glass, but didn't drink right away.

I asked him, "Do you ever feel like your life has gone into sudden-death overtime?"

Jake shook his head. "I'm not sure what you mean by that."

"I feel like everything I do now counts. Like I've had my very last do-over." I glanced through the menu quickly, but when I saw the faraway look in Jake's eyes, food became the last thing on my mind. "What?"

"What, what?" Jake finally opened his menu. "Nothing."

"Come on. Something."

Jake closed his eyes. "I was scared of Pop my whole life. And he turned out to be just an ordinary old man. Even if he'd been healthy, he's not—"

"Not a monster?"

"Not a monster." Jake rubbed a damp spot on the tablecloth.

"Jakey, he terrorized us, then made it seem like it was all our fault, remember? Or he'd be all nice one minute and then explode the next. Pop's the worst kind of monster—the kind that makes you afraid of everything. The kind that makes you afraid to trust yourself."

Jake acknowledged this with a nod

"I worry people will turn on me, and I've never given myself to anyone—not really. I don't have faith in my instincts. I thought if I had enough money, enough power. A pretty enough wife. A big enough house. But what's enough? You search and you search and there's always something more and you think, *ah*. If I have that, I will finally be safe."

Jake's expression went from unhappy to mild surprise while I talked. "You seriously feel like that?"

"To see him crumpled and old. Vulnerable. Utterly vanquished." I shook my head. "I don't know how that makes me feel."

"Me neither."

"I've got to put Pop behind me. Not just ignore him, but really get rid of him. I've got to believe that not only is he in the past, I'm perfectly capable of avoiding anyone like him in the future. That I will never be like him."

"You never will. I told you. You will never be like Pop. It's just not in you." Jake picked up his menu and studied it.

It was time to change the subject. "Cam is planning an engagement party for you. Did you know that? I promised him I'd help."

Jake smiled. "Yeah."

"They're having it at our place, and I was asked to man the grill. How does Cam know I can be trusted with fire?"

"I told him you're great with the grill."

I blew my cool and made my brother laugh by asking, "What did he say to that?"

"I don't know if he said anything. I just told him you were competent."

The waiter came by to take our order, preventing me from hotly replying that I was far more than competent with the backyard grill. I'd gone to Barbecue University in Colorado and taken Stephen Raichlen's class a couple of years before. "You making a cake for the event?"

"Yeah."

"What kind?"

"I'm only saying that it's going to be a red velvet cake with cream cheese frosting."

"Really?" I glanced up at that. Maybe I was hungrier than I thought but that cake sounded delicious. Maybe I was one of those ex-smokers who replaces cigarettes with sweets.

"Red velvet seems to be the firehouse favorite."

I'd been meaning to do something nice for Cam to let him know I was back in town. Flowers were a little girly. I was considering wrapping up some fancy cat food for Spot, but this might be better. "You do red velvet cupcakes?"

"Yeah. I do all kinds."

"Does anyone ever send them as gifts?"

"Sure. I make up baskets sometimes. It's a particular favorite gift for new moms."

"Would you wrap a couple dozen different kinds up nice and take them to Cam at the firehouse for me?"

Jake shot me a knowing grin and sang, "Somebody's got a boyfriend..."

I glanced out the enormous picture window at the ocean view. "Shut up."

"Somebody wants to send his boyfriend a basket of cupcakes."

I said, "Kiss my ass, Jakey." But *no*. He kept on singing.

"Somebody wants me to write 'I love you' all over a whole bunch of cupcakes and make all the *o*'s in the shape of little hearts."

"You do and I'll end you."

"Never fear, your not-very-secret secret is safe with me." He looked at his phone and thumbed another text message. "I'm letting JT know we'll be back this afternoon. While I'm at it, do you want me to ask him if Cam *likes you* likes you or if he only likes you like a friend? Do you want me to make it seem like I'm just curious, or—"

"Give it a rest, will you?"

The waiter brought our beers, and for the first time, I wasn't really certain I wanted to drink one. The image of our father's wasted life was too fresh, and alcoholism had played a major role in his irrational behavior and declining health. "Do you ever worry? That we'll be like him?"

Jake seemed to know exactly what I meant. Maybe he'd been thinking along the same lines. "Alcoholics, bro? I don't think so, but you should talk to someone about that if you're worried."

While I wasn't precisely worried, I wondered. Fear of turning into Pop wasn't going to go away easily if it ever did. Plus, there was avoiding his fate to be concerned about. I didn't want to die like that. Especially not like that.

I did drink too much, and I wasn't going to be comfortable taking my health for granted ever again.

Sudden-death overtime.

Jake grinned and in a respectable act of defiance, clinked his beer to mine. "I really think we dodged that bullet."

I raised my bottle to salute him. "Maybe we just took the bullet and lived."

Jake's smile was contagious. "Yeah. Maybe we did, at that."

CHAPTER TWENTY-FOUR

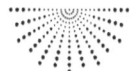

Two weeks later Jake and I hosted his engagement bash at our house. Already there were a mountain of coats on the bed in Jake's bedroom, and I added another leather jacket and two purses to that. One of those purses belonged to Izzie, and one—a tiny, studded leather bag with a long thin strap that went across her body—belonged to Muse.

Jake was both touched and delighted that almost everyone we knew showed up. Gifts piled up on every horizontal surface that wasn't covered with food. I'd hired a caterer to do the honors so Jake could enjoy the event, but he'd still spent three long days working to provide desserts.

The red velvet cake, a monstrosity that he'd topped with a massive car wreck, was...probably not something he'd seen in *Modern Bride*. Each of the figures: the cars, fire trucks, victims, and firefighters, showed off an amazing level of skill. He'd even fashioned my sporty little Lexus from fondant and cut it in half, immortalizing in pastry the twisted wreckage of the accident that nearly killed us, which was also the night JT came out to his family and friends.

It was both awkward and one of the most delicious cakes I'd

ever eaten, and I couldn't imagine, given that this was only his engagement party warm-up cake, what his actual wedding cake might look like.

"Did you get a piece of your car?" Cam asked from close behind me. I closed my eyes and enjoyed the sensation of his breath on the back of my neck, shivering a little even though the night was far from cold and I was wearing a jacket over jeans and a light sweater.

"I'll pass. I got a bit of the middle without too much frosting."

"I snagged a corner piece."

How like my guy. He liked things sweet. "There'll be plenty of leftovers. I'm sure you'll be able to take some back to the firehouse."

"We're still working off the cupcakes you sent. Everyone's been spending twice as much time in the gym since Bêtise opened." He turned me so he could reach my lips and drop a soft kiss there and one on my nose, making it itch a little. I wasn't sure I should enjoy that sort of thing as much as I did.

"That didn't take long." I heard the familiar voice and froze. *BreeAnna.* What the hell was she doing there?

I turned and saw Al next to Bree. Jim—who for a reason I utterly failed to understand—stood holding a gaily wrapped gift in his hand.

My mouth dropped open, but before I could say anything, Al stepped in and grabbed my arm in a firm grip. "I need to talk to you for a minute."

I let him lead me to the patio, past a couple of our guests who were sitting and having a smoke. "What on earth?"

"I hoped I'd get the chance to tell you she was coming before she got here, but no such luck, I see."

"*Why* is she here? She hates us. This is Jake's night. If she does anything to ruin it for him, I swear to fuck I will personally throw her out." I felt Cam behind me. There was no mistaking him, even here in the shadows, because of his size. He dropped a hand on my shoulder, and I leaned into him.

"I don't know why she's here." Al glanced back through the window. "I just know that since you told Ted to change the settlement agreement, she's now a partner in Livingston Properties. Or didn't you realize that would happen."

"I realized. I initiated it. But I didn't invite her to Jake's engagement party."

"I didn't realize I needed an invitation to a family event," Bree said stiffly. "Can I talk to you? This will only take a minute."

Cam's hand tightened, but I nodded. He and Al drifted a short way away and left me facing my ex-wife for the first time in months. Her hair was different. She'd had it cut in a sleek, square style with short bangs that made her hazel eyes look enormous. It suited her delicate features. As always, she was dressed impeccably—a Chanel jacket over menswear trousers and soft, high-heeled calfskin boots and leather gloves. She was as beautiful and brittle as ever. Fragile and poisonous at the same time.

"Hello, Bree. You look lovely."

Her smile was sad. "You don't have to do that anymore. It's not your job." I must have frowned, because she explained. "Lie to prop up my ego."

"What are you doing here?"

"I came to tell you…" She cleared her throat. "Thank you for what you did about the settlement. You didn't have to. I probably wouldn't have."

"It wasn't right to let things stand like that, with you thinking you were the only one who broke our agreement."

She nodded regally. "I guess I should be pretty horrified. I mean…that you were out there fucking every queer piece of trash you could find."

I closed my eyes and prayed for patience. "I never took a

chance with your safety, Bree. Not in the way I behaved with others, and especially since things were fairly…safe…when we were together, not with you."

"I got tested anyway. I'm negative."

I shrugged. "So am I."

Her eyes found Cam's bulky shape in the dark. "But for how long?"

That was irritating, but not unexpected. "I don't know, Bree, Jake and I were in a massive car accident, and I could have been killed. Life seems like a crapshoot any way you live it. At least I no longer have to live it with you."

Her face changed. I saw something flicker there—regret, resolution. I wondered what it was. It wasn't vicious, at least. She appeared to be reining herself in.

After she took a deep breath, she spoke. "I apologize for that. That's not why I came. Since we'll be working together, I felt I ought to put my best foot forward with you, Jake, and Al. With the other partners and investors. With your friends, some of whom"—she glanced back toward the party—"I haven't ever seen socially. I'm trying to put my anger away for both our sakes. I thought a family event might be a good place to start."

"I see."

"I admit I'm not doing a very good job of it, but I'd like you to believe I'm really trying here."

Wow. Sincerity? That was unexpected. Unless she'd finally learned to fake that too. "Thank you, Bree."

"So may I congratulate the new couple and visit for a brief time?"

"Can you do it without your usual bitchy homophobia?"

"I said I am trying to get beyond all that, Dan."

"All right. But I'll throw you out if you do one single thing to hurt Jake tonight. This is his special night."

"I understand that." She glanced around. "What I don't

understand is why you're going to all this trouble and expense if gay marriage is illegal in California?"

"Try the cake, Bree. It's delicious. And you can even eat my sugar Lexus if you want. Your half of it." Bree would no more eat a piece of cake than she would wear plastic shoes.

"Ha-ha." I think she actually shuddered.

Somebody had to be the grown-up. It might as well be me. "In the kitchen we've got some seafood on ice." That was more her style. Shrimp with a little lemon. Maybe a piece of sushi or two if she would eat. She'd have to take her gloves off, and I didn't think she would.

"Thanks."

I nodded. "It's—" It wasn't good to see her. That wasn't right. But if she behaved herself, since we were stuck together as partners of Livingston Properties, I could make the best of a bad situation. "It's going to be all right, isn't it?"

She tipped her head, again putting on that air of deposed royalty. "I think so. Yes."

"So that's the infamous BreeAnna?" Cam found me on the far edge of the yard, fully regretting that I'd quit smoking. No way was I going to bum a cigarette and light up with the patch on; that would have been begging for trouble. I was chewing gum, but it wasn't helping.

"Yes indeed."

"She's a tiny little thing."

"That she is."

"You all right?"

"What, because of her? Yeah. She gave me a start. I thought she was going to be like that witch in *Sleeping Beauty*, you know? Maleficent?"

"*Why was I not invited?*" Cam mimicked with a laugh.

"Yeah. But she actually…I don't know. She thanked me."

"For what?"

I hadn't told Cam I'd come clean, and for some reason, I didn't want to. "For trying to be fair."

Cam rested that big heavy head of his against mine. "I see."

"She wants to bury the hatchet because we're partners at Livingston Properties."

"I'd be afraid of where she wants to bury it. You'd better tell her I've got your back and an ax of my own."

"No." I let him enfold me in his arms. Cam was way better than gum. "It's going to be all right. She's nothing if not image conscious. She won't do anything to make herself look bad in front of our friends"

"That's good."

We stood together like that for a while and looked up at the sky. Clouds seemed to be moving fast, racing across a nearly full moon. "I miss the stars, Cam. I think we need to get away to the high desert or the mountains. Someplace dark where we can count the stars together."

"Maybe go camping?"

"In your dreams, baby. I wasn't much of a camper when I was a kid, but now? Not a chance. I was thinking of renting a cabin or something."

"I like camping. We could go out on horseback. I can show you how much fun it could be."

"Oh, jeez. Hell no."

"You wouldn't? Not even if it meant making love under the open sky?"

Okay that sounded enticing as hell. Until I thought about bugs and bears. "I'd probably go with you a couple of times because I am a total fool for you, but please don't count on me ever being much of a camper."

"You just don't know what you're missing yet."

"I know there are snakes and wild things out there."

"All right. Okay. Maybe I'll rent one of those luxury RV things and drag your ass off into the desert with some high-thread-count sheets and gourmet coffee. Then what would you say."

"I'd say, what are we waiting for?"

"I'll look into that." He chuckled, happy with himself. "But you know eventually I'll get your naked ass on a bedroll out under the stars, and you'll wonder why you waited so long."

I felt like I got off easy. I didn't have to tell him I'd walk bare-foot on broken glass and bed down over a red anthill just to be with him. No man I'd ever known had been as kind or as cocky. No one had his beauty or his ability to charm. And I knew no one who loved unselfishly—from a deep down, bottomless well of compassion—like Cam did. If I were twice the man I perceived myself to be, or more even, I'd never measure up.

But for him I wanted to try.

After a long while spent like that, simply holding one another and standing in the shadows counting what few stars we could see and talking about the future, we went back into the party.

If there was a change in the mood, I didn't feel it right away. The place was still noisy, glasses clinked, soft music played while people talked over it. At some point, though, I became aware of an undercurrent in the room, like a drop in the temperature. I discovered Jake and JT packed tightly into the kitchen with the St. Nacho's irregular militia, Izzie and Andy the cop, Ken and Jordan, Candace and Bianca from Miss Independence Pies. Muse and Minerva, Mary Catherine and Carl, and—absurdly—Bree, Al, and Jim.

They seemed to be having some sort of heated discussion, and I registered the odd fact that Bree was urging calm seconds before I realized they were all holding copies of Al's St. Nacho's prospectus, the one about the gaming resort Al wanted to build.

"I'm just saying"—Al spoke slowly and patiently—"that as

residents of St. Nacho's, it seemed like you'd want to be part of the investment group. In that way you would all have a say in the decision-making process. As Dan's friends and family, it seemed only right to share whatever good fortune may come out of this venture—"

"What is going on here?" I asked, but I knew. Everyone turned toward me.

"How long have you known about this?" Mary Catherine's voice was calm, unlike some of the others.

"I—"

"Let's all take a minute," Carl admonished.

Muse glared at me. "I thought you understood."

"Muse, it's not like that." I grabbed the prospectus out of her hands. "This is only a proposal, yeah? There's a lot that has to happen before something like this becomes a reality."

Bree frowned at all of us. "I should think you'd want to develop this place. It hasn't even got a decent hotel."

JT bristled. "What we have is *fine*."

"That's just it," Al argued. "There could be so much more. More jobs, more revenue, more tourists, more income."

Izzie stepped up next to Muse. "Sometimes more isn't better. It's simply…more."

Al glanced at me. "What the hell does that even mean. You should want this. You should all be on board with this."

"Al—"

"We don't want this in our backyard. You should just go away now." Muse folded her arms.

I said, "I have to go with the crowd on this, Al. I've never felt comfortable with gaming of any sort, and I'm sure there's something better we can do. You know me. I don't work on emotion alone, but this has me tied up in knots. I have to go with my instinct here that this is simply not the type of project Livingston Properties should undertake."

Al clutched his copy of the prospectus tightly in his hand. "Are you saying you won't even consider this further?"

"I'm saying that I've been uncomfortable with it from the very beginning. And my brother's engagement party is unequivocally not the place to discuss it. I'll see you in the office first thing Monday morning and we'll talk about it there, but I have to tell you, I don't want any part of a project like this."

"Well, well, well." We all heard BreeAnna's voice—loud and clear. "I think you've forgotten you signed away half your right to make that decision. I believe the project is sound, and I don't have emotional attachments and sentiment to cloud my thinking. It's going to be Al *and* me against you, and I think you'll find it's a little harder to throw your weight around now."

Stunned, I stepped back to gather my wits. *She was right.* I don't know how long it took me to think things through. People argued around me. The action hit my senses in waves—too bright then dim, too loud and then quiet. I thought that was how it must be to drown. My chest felt tight as if my heart physically stopped.

I didn't have to turn to know what I would see on Cam's face, but I did it anyway. It was a compulsion, like picking at a fresh scab. It was surely a cure for the optimism I'd been feeling, because what I saw in Cam's eyes made things very clear.

I'd inadvertently brought Pandora's box with me to St. Nacho's, and Al had prized it open. It didn't take that glimpse of Cam's face to know that I'd find no hope there.

"Come with me," I told Cam. I expected an argument, and I didn't let him start one. I put my hand up before he had a chance to get a word out and hissed so only he could hear me, "If you don't come with me right this second I will leave you and St. Nacho's to deal with all the forces of rapacious greed by yourselves and you will surely lose."

"All right." He followed me out into the darkness in silence. I made my way toward the boardwalk where we could be assured of privacy, and eventually we got to the pier.

———

"HOW COULD YOU DO THIS TO US?" CAM WOULDN'T LOOK AT ME.

"I didn't. I told you. This was Al's idea. Apparently my ex-wife has taken it to her scant bosom in a unprecedented way."

What did she mean, you signed away half your right to decide?

I sighed. "Just that I agreed to be fair with our assets."

He turned to me, surprise etched on his features. "You came clean about your infidelities."

I shook my head. "Not exactly."

"Yes, *exactly*. And now she owns half your company and half your power to put a stop to this thing."

"Half my interest. Yes. But the power? No."

Cam leaned over to put his elbows on the railing and dropped his head into his hands. He looked like he was going to be sick. "I can't lose St. Nacho's. I don't know if I'd survive losing everything again."

"You won't. I promise you won't."

"You think you can promise that? You're kidding yourself. Al is a nice guy, but he only sees a balance sheet. Bree wants to punish you. I know you mean well, but—"

"You are so wrong, Cameron Rooney. I don't mean well. Not really. I have never *meant well*. I've done what I pleased."

Cam gave up a broken sob. "Oh, thanks for clearing that up."

I laid the flat of my hand on his back to sooth him. "You don't understand."

"You're right, I don't." He tried to flinch away from my touch, but I didn't let him.

"I love two people in this entire world, and I'd lay down my life for both of you. If you think I'll let someone threaten your home—if you think I'll stand idly by and watch you hurt—"

"It's not your company anymore. They think it's a great investment, and maybe they're right—"

"Maybe they are. But that's not what's important to *me*." I used both hands to turn Cam around to face me. "You're important to me. And St. Nacho's is important to a whole lot of people. And worse, I suddenly find myself in the awkward position of possessing scruples."

Cam laughed weakly at that.

"This is what I do best, Cam. Better than Al, and Bree doesn't count. She and Al may have the right to vote, but that's all they've got. I still have the contacts, and the business is mine. Who's going to trust Bree? She's never done anything more with money than buy shoes. Who's going to capitalize a Livingston Properties project if I am emphatically not on board."

"It's good business. If they get that land…"

"They *won't*. I can see to it that they never will, and I will do exactly that, for you."

"What about Al?"

"He'll be disappointed."

"He'll fight you. You're friends."

"And I will always be his friend. His friendship is his to give or take away. But yours? I couldn't bear to hurt you. I'm asking you to trust me."

Cam shook his head. "It's my home…"

"Can you trust me with this? Can you say you believe in me this one time, even though you have no reason to?"

"A leap of faith." Cam gazed into my eyes for a long time, and I swear, *I swear* he could see every lie I'd ever told. "You haven't earned it."

I swallowed hard. "That's why they call it faith."

He stared at me for a long time—too long—and then nodded. I kissed him like it was the last time I'd ever get to do it, because if I failed…

Cam's soft lips melted under mine until his mouth opened for me and our tongues tangled together. Our harsh breaths misted the moist salty air, and he pulled me toward him with such fierce desperation it caught me like a flash grenade in my gut.

Cam's dizzying, powerful kiss sent all my blood rushing to my cock. He gripped my hips and pulled me toward him until I could feel his nudge to life. I pushed back before I could be swept away by the sensual tide.

We gazed at each other, breathless, hard, and hurting. He didn't let go and I felt the connection between us throb through his fingertips.

I could stop Al and Bree. I *would* stop them.

"You're my heart, Cameron Rooney."

Cam gave me a tiny shake. "You have a heart of your own."

"You make it beat." I caught his hand and pressed it where my heart was thudding beneath my skin. "You warm it. Because of you it's overflowing with some kind of peculiar audacity. I need to see myself reflected in your eyes. I *need* to see you smile."

"Daniel."

"Ah, *jeez*. When you say my name it's like a jolt of electricity up my spine. What the hell is that?"

"I don't know." Cam grinned. "But that's why I say it."

"I'll fix this," I promised. I had to go before I got sidetracked. I had to get out of town because I couldn't save the day by standing on the St. Nacho's pier—even though it meant leaving Cam's embrace. "Tell Jakey I said hold on. Okay?"

"All right."

"I love you, Cam. You big damn—"

"I love you too, Daniel."

CHAPTER TWENTY-FIVE

Four months later, I was dreaming of angels. They weren't the fluffy, Valentine's Day kind of angels, but the full-on, fire-and-sword-wielding Old Testament variety, which seemed odd to me. I'd never made the time to study my faith, and I could honestly say religion—what I'd seen of it—didn't impress me much.

There wasn't anything to the dream itself. I was in the company of some hypermasculine, stern-visaged angel in an empty place—the thickest, blackest void. He pointed out the different constellations of stars as he knew them, but I couldn't see anything because ugly black clouds roiled overhead.

There was a loud banging sound, insistent and irritating, and the angel frowned.

"What?" I asked.

He said, "Even when you cannot see the heavens, the stars burn bright."

The dream faded, all except the drumming noise, and I realized someone was pounding on my door. The bell rang twice.

I got out of bed and went to answer it, not caring particularly that I was only wearing boxers.

When I opened the door, Bree stood there, holding two coffee cups in her gloved hands. She was once again dressed in understated elegance, this time in a St. John knit suit and pumps. Jim stood behind her.

"Morning." I blocked the doorway, wondering if I was still dreaming or if I'd begun to hallucinate. Bree never brought me coffee when we were married. I couldn't fathom why she'd be standing there offering me coffee now.

"It's afternoon," she told me and stood her ground. "May I come in?"

I wasn't ready to let her by me, so I stayed where I was. She'd have had to brush against my nearly naked, hairy form to squeeze inside, and I knew she wouldn't do that.

"I need to talk to you, Dan. Please let me in."

I couldn't even remember the last time Bree had said please, so I stepped back, waiting. Before she moved forward, she turned to Jim. "You can wait in the car, Jim. I need to speak to Dan alone."

"All right." He nodded. Apparently he was far more sanguine about being dismissed than I would have been, under the circumstances.

I watched Bree enter my dingy, cramped rental and smiled at her obvious distaste.

"You live here? It's like"—she glanced around—"the floor sample room in a cheap furniture warehouse."

"It's a crash site for the newly jettisoned. Everywhere you look, divorced people are bringing in single sacks of groceries and taking out small bags of garbage. No one meets anyone else's eyes. It's purgatory for the matrimonially deceased."

Bree looked up at the painting over the sofa. It depicted a road leading off through a stand of birch trees in autumn shades that matched the brown leather couch. "It came furnished?"

"Can you imagine me buying a painting like that?"

She shook her head and turned. Wordlessly, she offered me one of the coffees, then clutched the other between her hands.

I took a sip. Vanilla latte. *Nice.* "Thank you for this. You didn't come all this way to bring me coffee or redecorate my place."

"This isn't your place. This is a furnished rental in San Jose, a city you hate."

"All too true. But it's convenient, and cheap, and I find that it suits my mood. I only sleep here."

"It's four in the afternoon."

"I sleep a lot."

She didn't seem to know where to look, and eventually her gaze fell to my hand. "Are you still getting physical therapy?"

In truth, I wasn't. I was still doing the exercises that Jordan gave me as homework, but I wasn't seeing a therapist. "I need to find someone here."

"Isn't there a window of opportunity as far as the potential for healing? You should get on that."

"I'll do that."

"Jake told me about your brother and sister. And your father...I'm sorry about your father."

"I'm not."

"You don't mean that, really."

"Most of the time you think the worst of me. Pick a side, BreeAnna."

"Jake's in touch with your other siblings. Your brother and JT postponed the wedding."

"*Damn.*" I didn't want that. I'd never wanted that.

"You left without a word, and you haven't answered a single message. I can understand why you might not want to answer mine, but there are people who need to hear from you. It's been months."

"*My phone broke.*" That was true. It broke when I threw it off St. Nacho's pier.

"You need to get a new phone and let your brother and Al know where you are. I practically had to hire a private detective to find you."

I scrubbed at my face. Even at four p.m. it was too early for that shit. "Yet find me you did. Would you mind telling me why? I just got up, and I need to piss."

Bree flinched at my crude language. "Get cleaned up, and for heaven's sake, dress. You and I are going to talk whether you like it or not." She glanced around, looking for a safe place to sit. Finding none, she steeled herself to balance on the edge of the leather sofa. It let out a loud, flatulent sigh as she did, and color flooded her cheeks.

"I'll be back." I left her there to fidget and took my time getting cleaned up. I took a shower and shaved. When I came back out wearing a fresh pair of jeans and a rock band T-shirt I'd gotten at some club, she rolled her eyes. I sat down on the coffee table across from her, close enough to touch her—to breathe in the familiar scent of Chanel and woman. She didn't move away. I took that as a sign of the coming apocalypse.

"You look like a forty-year-old frat boy. You need to act your age."

"That's not what the guys said last night." I don't know why I needed to be flippant with Bree. I didn't care what she thought of me anymore, not really, but I was proud enough that I didn't want her to see how far I'd fallen.

I didn't want her to see how much what had happened in the wake of Jake's engagement party had cost me, personally and professionally, even though I assumed she was astute enough to guess.

Then Bree did something I'd rarely seen her do in a strange place: she took off her gloves and laid them in her lap. When I glanced up, she clasped my hands in hers and held them tight. She gripped them tightly when I would have withdrawn them from sheer shock.

"I know it must have seemed as though everyone you thought was your friend lined up against you."

"It didn't just seem like that. Everyone did."

"Speaking for myself, I never understood how passionately you were prepared to fight—not until after the fact. I thought you were posturing for the sake of your image. You should have talked to me privately."

"And said what? That I truly didn't want to invest in a venture because it would hurt people I care about?"

"You could have let me know how you felt."

"Since when have you given a shit about me?" I asked bitterly. "Since when has making money taken a backseat to emotions for Al? For any of us? You wouldn't have believed me if I'd tried."

"Neither of us realized how far you'd go to stop the project from going ahead."

I couldn't help the way my lips twitched into a smile. I couldn't hide what I was feeling, which was triumph. No one was going to underestimate me again. Ever.

"I guess you didn't count on my desperation."

"No. We didn't."

"So maybe you can tell me why you came. Why you've disrobed"—I nodded toward her hands—"and what you could possibly want from me now that I have nothing left."

"You *won*, Dan. You beat us. You got what you wanted. Why are you hiding here in this dump as though you're indigent?"

"I can assure you, the indigent can't afford to live here, Bree. And since I currently own a rather large parcel of land I can do nothing with, I will have to get a job, and soon, if I want to continue to live in this kind of luxury."

"You always make jokes when things get serious."

"Nobody needs a joke when things are going along just fine."

"You used every last bit of your liquid cash to get that property, and from what I understand, you've leveraged yourself even more. Why? Why did you do that for people who turned their back on you the second they thought you'd betrayed them?"

"Because—" *Crap.* My eyes stung, and not for the world would I show Bree that she could still get to me. I got up and went to the sliding-glass door. The vertical blinds were dusty and tangled, but I pushed them aside to look out. It wasn't the worst place to live. There was a parklike atmosphere beyond my back patio, complete with streams and a small play yard where the Sunday fathers took their children to swing and slide.

At least I didn't have kids.

"Because?" Bree followed me. "Why, Dan? I need to hear you tell me."

"Because I loved them. Because making money doesn't justify hurting people or destroying the environment. In the past, I've looked the other way, and I just can't anymore."

Bree's hand landed on my shoulder and rested there. "I'm so sorry."

"Don't be sorry for me, Bree. Like you said, I won."

"I'm sorry because you think you've lost the very thing you were trying to protect."

"Yeah, well. There's a lot of historical precedent for shit like that. If nothing else, you have to love the irony."

She peered at my face. "You aren't capable of subterfuge anymore. It's fascinating."

"Now you're just making wild assumptions."

"Yeah. Maybe." She stood beside me and watched out the window for a while. "I'm sorry I didn't stand by you when you wanted to block the project."

I laughed at that. "It would have made things considerably easier if you had, but at least you bought me out. That was the last little bit of cash I needed. I should thank you for that, if I didn't already. Are you going to change your name when you marry Jim? It will be odd to see Livingston Properties without a Livingston at the helm."

"I won't keep your name in any case."

"I see."

"I never should have had it in the first place."

Old news. "I've regretted using you for a long time. I hope you'll agree I've been fair enough that we can both put it behind us now. LP can move on without that land and I can move on to...whatever's next."

"How did you manage to get that land anyway? Al was furious. He says to tell you hello from Ellie and the girls, by the way."

I nodded. That was *exactly* Al. He could be professionally furious with me during the day, and at night we could still have cocktails and catch up as though we were back in school. That friendship wasn't going anywhere, at least. Unless I let it die of neglect.

"I still have one or two tricks I never shared with the folks at Livingston Properties."

She bit her lip. "There's something else I need to talk to you about."

"Oh, jeez." What more can there possibly be?

"I want you to know I've been seeing a counselor. I think...I may have always known what you couldn't tell me. I may have been hateful to your brother and...others like you because I sensed..."

When she didn't continue, I guessed. "You thought I might be gay?"

"I didn't need ESP to know you weren't that into me. You substituted precise, almost clinical control for passion pretty early on. I was angry and waiting for the other shoe to drop. I resented the hell out of you for not wanting me. It made me feel unattractive and...Whatever. I must have known something wasn't..."

What it cost her to say that, I couldn't imagine. Bree did not like to apologize. So naturally, I made her clarify. "What exactly are you saying?"

"I'm saying I've said some pretty hateful things. Things that —looking back—I can't believe came out of my mouth."

"And?"

"*Must* I say it? I was vile to you and your brother. I was vile about your sexuality and insulted you every chance I got. But I knew I was losing you. I had lost you long since, and I—"

"Stop." Suddenly I didn't need her to say it. I could let her off the hook and tell her what she needed to hear because after all that time, it just didn't matter anymore. "I understand. It's okay. We both—"

"I'm sorry." She wouldn't meet my eyes. "I'm sorry that I treated you the way I did. I never meant for things to get like that between us."

"Neither did I. It wasn't only you."

She blinked and tried to wipe the tears that glittered on her lashes from her eyes before they ruined her makeup. "I swore I wouldn't do this."

"I have a box of tissues around here somewhere."

"No doubt," she said dryly. "But you can keep them."

"I beg your pardon? They're not used or anything."

"You know I can't use anyone else's tissues. I have some in my purse." She snorted and gave my shoulder the tiniest shove. I got the briefest glimpse of the girl I knew before everything went so wrong. "You made me say that out loud."

"Looks like we're both falling apart."

She leaned against me then. Or rather, she slumped, and I caught her. I felt her arms slide around my waist and then she was hanging on, almost hugging me, and I put my arm around her shoulder and held her there.

"I never meant to hurt you," I said. "I swear I tried to do the right thing."

She shook her head but said nothing.

"I wish I could have been the man you wanted—the man you needed—I wish…" I couldn't say it out loud. I wished, at that point, that I had never been born.

I held her, and we both looked out the window as if there was something fascinating there. People walked to and from the parking lot with shopping bags, or they led dogs along the winding pathways. We could hear children playing on the swings in the distance. Her voice, when she finally spoke, sounded tired.

"When I met you, I saw something in you. A core of intelligence and passion and promise. I thought I could build a future with *that* man, not the successful con artist you became. I would have been glad for a life with a man who would risk everything he had for the love of his friends."

"Oh, *Bree.*"

"You've become the kind of man I can believe in, Dan." She swallowed hard. "And you could never have done that with me by your side. That's…hard to take."

"I'm sorry."

"So am I." She tried in vain to wipe her tears, then left to retrieve her purse from where she left it by the sofa. "I'm a mess."

"Bree, you are always, *always* beautiful. You need to believe me when I say that if for no other reason than because I can't lie worth a damn anymore."

Her lips formed what was sure to have become a genuine smile if she'd allowed it. "I know."

"It's a *curse.* Minerva from Rune Nation wrote these symbols on my damned driveway in sidewalk chalk, and I haven't been able to lie since."

"So it's a magic spell?" She didn't look too impressed. "*Right.* But good for her."

"Them. There are three of them, and they followed me around like the witches in *Macbeth*."

Bree was digging around in her handbag, no doubt to retrieve her tissues, but she stopped and glanced up at me. "You don't really believe in witchcraft."

"Of course not. But that's as good an explanation as any for my inability to hide what I'm thinking or feeling at this point. I'm so...extremely uncomfortable." Vulnerable. *Naked*. As things stood, I was afraid to leave the safety of my apartment. Apparently I could still *omit* some things even if I couldn't outright lie, because I didn't tell Bree that.

"Maybe," Bree suggested, "you simply don't *need* to lie anymore. I should think you'd be relieved."

"No such luck."

"All right. Well. Maybe you should see someone. I've had some success with my therapist. Maybe you need to see about getting yourself a good therapist and a good PT for that hand."

"This is odd, hearing you concerned with my welfare."

"Tell me about it. But it seems I have a conscience too." She pulled an envelope from her purse and left it on the coffee table. "Who knew?"

"What's that?"

"Don't open it until I leave. And do as you're told, Dan Livingston. Take care of yourself."

She crossed the room to me and rose up on the balls of her feet. On autopilot, I leaned over and let her kiss my cheek. For once, she didn't rub at the smudge of lipstick she left behind.

"I'll be off, then." I watched her put on her gloves then hoist the little chain of her handbag over her shoulder. She turned with a swish, leaving a Chanel-scented breeze in her wake. "Don't be a stranger."

"All right."

A LONG TIME AFTER BREE LEFT, I SAT QUIETLY ON THE COUCH, nursing a beer and staring at that envelope. Darkness fell all around me. I didn't know what she might have written, and I wasn't sure I had the strength to find out. Had her counselor instructed her to put her thoughts into words? Was this her final indictment of me for marrying her in the first place? Her last opportunity to tell me how I ruined her life?

I opened it with shaking fingers, eventually, and took it into the kitchen to read. But...it wasn't a letter at all. It was a legal document reassigning the ownership of Livingston Properties to me, both the portion I'd given up to her as part of the divorce settlement *plus* the rest, which I'd sold back to her to get the St. Nacho's land parcel. I was once again half owner of the company I'd started from a couple thousand dollars, a decrepit beach cottage, and a lot of backbreaking physical labor.

There was a pink Post-it note stuck next to Bree's signature.
Make me proud.

CHAPTER TWENTY-SIX

The miniature horse I purchased in the beginning of October was officially the best, and the worst, idea I'd ever had.

The best, because taking care of a tiny horse as autumn's brightly colored leaves drifted down from the trees around my new home turned out to be the most joyful work—and the best therapy both emotionally and physically—that I could have undertaken at that point.

The best, because it cemented my status as the coolest, most perfect adult who ever lived, in the eyes of Al's girls. All of them, not just Katie and Jana, but Ellie too, loved that tiny hairball with every fiber of their being so my place became the favorite weekend destination for their entire family.

The worst, because every so often my diminutive pintaloosa looked at me as if he knew he'd been purchased as a shiny lure for a certain firefighter named Cam, and since he'd heard me admit it once or twice, in the deeply personal dialogue we carried on while I cared for him, perhaps he'd begun to believe it.

"So. Who's the best-looking guy around, huh?" I groomed

him conscientiously, giving him a good, thorough daily brushing as well as performing a thousand other horsey chores. Even so I swear he was still lower maintenance than Bree had been.

"I guess I could have gotten myself a spirited little mini stallion in the first place and saved myself a boatload of alimony."

He nudged my arm.

"That's right. You need to stop me when I start bad mouthing my ex, boy. If it weren't for Bree, we wouldn't be here."

My new best friend, a thirty-two-inch-tall bay with spots on his hindquarters and a fiery copper mane and tail—aptly named Fireball—gazed at me reproachfully with one blue and one brown eye as I tangled my fingers in his mane. He was uncommonly vain about his hair. He nipped at my hand without actually catching it in his teeth and gamboled off to play in the small paddock.

It was a fine day to lean against the white rail fence and watch him play. I caught up a colorful plastic beach ball and hurled it. He jumped like a dog, charging it and nudging it around with his nose.

That just never got old.

I went into the paddock with him and kicked the ball away. He fairly flew after it—tail like a flag—and nudged it back, trying to dodge around me.

When I saw dust rise in the distance, I tried not to get my hopes up. I really tried, because most of the time anyone coming up my driveway was lost. I continued playing with Fireball, but I was aware at the same time that a truck that looked a lot like Cam's was heading purposefully toward me.

Finally. Oh, my fucking...Cam is finally, finally here.

Since I'd moved back, all the television news broadcasts had been full of California's wildfires. A spate of arsons—and the wild Santa Ana winds that make them particularly deadly—had caused even our own local firefighters to be rotated out for backup in the Southland as more and more men were needed to battle the blazes. I'd hoped and prayed for Cam's safe return, and I pried every single piece of news I could from Jake and JT, but until I saw him rolling up the drive, some part of me had been afraid I'd never see Cam again.

That I'd never get a chance to tell him why I hadn't come back sooner.

Cam's truck pulled to a stop by the barn, and I forgot to breathe when he opened the door to get out.

He was thinner. That's what I saw. That's all I saw as he walked toward me. His jeans were loose around his hips, and the SIFD T-shirt and jacket he wore didn't bind on his pecs and his arms the way they had before. An SIFD cap shielded his eyes.

I kicked the ball to Fireball and headed toward the gate. Fireball ran off and retrieved it, pushing it after me, disappointed that I'd called a time-out on our game.

I watched Cam's face when he caught sight of *my little pony* and realized exactly what it was. His head whipped around again, and he looked back at me, eyes wide.

As though he were trying to make sense of things, he said, "That, sir, is a horse."

"Be quiet. He'll hear you."

Cam smiled faintly. "Jake told me you were back, but—"

"I've been here for a while."

"I've been all over hell and gone. I was in the Angeles National Forest for a week, then in South Orange County. Then the Cleveland National Forest near Julian."

"I know. I saw all the fires on the news. I thought you weren't a wildlander."

"My unit was defending structures. It was like living in hell. High winds and arson fires. Southern California's unique cocktail for disaster. We lost one hundred twenty-four homes all told. No lives, thank God."

"I'm…" I was at a loss. Should I have said I was sorry about the fires? Or I was glad he was safe? Instead, I simply went with, "It's good to see you."

Fireball decided he didn't like being ignored. He poked his nose through the slats of the fence and nudged me.

Cam squatted to look him in the eye. "Who's this?"

"Fireball." I hadn't been the one to name him, but I thought Fireball fit rather well.

"He thinks he's a dog."

"There's a lot of that going around." I hadn't forgotten Cam's oddball cat.

I studied every minute detail of Cam's face. He'd been sunburned, and his nose was peeling. Did he look careworn? Surely he was drawn. *Tired.* This wasn't the laughing, lively Cam who filled my fantasies and eluded me in my dreams. This Cam had dark circles beneath his eyes, and his cheeks looked almost gaunt.

He pulled off his cap, and I saw his hair was buzzed off short, a golden fuzz next to his skin. He looked military.

He ran a hand over the top of his head. "Do you think I could have a beer or something? It's been a really exhausting few weeks."

"Of course." I gave the beach ball a last shove and made sure the gate was latched. "Follow me."

We walked up the tree-lined path to the house, a tiny, tidy bungalow with shuttered windows and flower boxes. It was a little run down but had boatloads of charm. It had *potential.*

"This isn't the kind of place I'd have expected to find you."

My heart quickened. Had he wanted to find me? Had he looked for me? "What kind of place did you think I'd have?"

"I don't know. Some loft full of steel and glass and leather. Abstract art on the walls."

"You forgot the coffee tables made of glass-topped statues of nude men."

He grunted a laugh.

"This suits me perfectly." When we got to the wide front porch, I gestured for him to sit in one of the rockers I'd purchased with Cam's very own, very fine ass in mind. "Have a seat. I'll go get us some drinks. Are you hungry?"

"I could eat."

"All right then. I'll be back."

"Thanks." Cam put his cap in the pocket of his jacket before drawing it off and laying it over the rail. "This is nice here."

"It gets the shade in the afternoon and a nice cool breeze." How shameless. I'd said that like I was selling the place—which I was. And myself...if he'd have me. I was prepared to use every trick I knew to make it happen.

In the kitchen, I pulled a couple bottles of Corona from the fridge and cut up a lime. Food was more difficult, because I found my hands shaking with anticipation—part terror and part longing—and it made slopping mayonnaise and mustard on a long roll and then trying to open little plastic baggies of lunch meats with slick fingers nearly impossible. I topped his sandwich with lettuce, tomato, pickles, and olives, and finally, I crowned the whole ugly creation with cheese and sliced it up, placing it on a plate with chips.

It was haphazard, but it would be filling. I grabbed the food, the beer, a bottle opener, and some napkins and headed outside.

When I got back to the porch, Cam was asleep. I tried to be quiet, but he gave a start when I put the plate down.

"Sorry. I didn't mean to wake you."

"No. I'm sorry." He rubbed his face, which looked red and painful.

"How'd you get sunburned? On the job?'

"Not like you'd think. I fell asleep in a camp chair on a break the other day. This looks good."

"If that's the case, you must be starving." He took a big bite, nearly half the half, and I worried that I should have made two sandwiches. "I can make more if you're still hungry after that one."

"This will be fine, thank you." He popped a chip into his mouth. "It's rude to invite myself over like this and make you work."

"Nah. I'm glad to do it. I'm happy to see you."

He glanced around. "You're happy in general, huh?"

"Yeah."

"I'm glad." He nodded. "It's not St. Nacho's."

"No." Jake had accused me of channeling Moses: I'd saved the tribe but was unable to live in the Promised Land. But St. Nacho's didn't feel like my promised land. I'd made the right choice for me. The question was, could Cam live with it? I worried about that—a lot. "I found this place, and it just called to me."

"Look," Cam said suddenly. "I know what you did."

My heart tightened. "What?"

"I know it took everything you had to buy that land. I know what you did to save St. Nacho's."

No one was supposed to find that out. What if he accused me of using money to solve every little problem again? "It's not like—"

"You didn't think you could keep your part in saving the day a secret, did you?"

"That part? Yes, actually, I did. But considering I couldn't keep my part in nearly ruining everything a secret, I can't imagine why. Apparently Jakey's still got a big mouth."

"It wasn't Jake who told me. It was Ken Ashton."

Ah, yes, St. Nacho's very own real estate mogul. He could easily have gotten wind of what happened. "I see."

"And I made sure everyone else knows. You're a local hero. Or you will be if you ever show your face in town again. The way he tells it, you were really hard up against it for a while. No one could find you. Jake was frantic. He said you'd live under a bridge somewhere rather than ask for help."

"Fortunately, it didn't come to that."

"How'd you get back on your feet?"

"Believe it or not, it was Bree."

"No way."

"*Way*. Of course, she kept the money. She hasn't changed that much. But she returned ownership in Livingston Properties to me and she's helped in other ways. Bree is—remarkably —a good friend. She and Jim have a baby on the way."

"No kidding? I thought she didn't—"

"Apparently she's over some of her objections to intimacy. She's been taking really good care of herself. Forcing herself to eat well and gain weight. It hasn't been easy. She's working with a therapist."

"A baby." He sat back and rocked for a bit. "It could have been yours. How does that make you feel?"

"Delighted for her." I really meant that. "Delighted for both of them."

"And you?"

"I am living the dream. I work from home mostly, but I travel up to Santa Cruz a couple times a week. Things are looking up."

"Who takes care of Fireball when you go?"

"There's a high-school kid who lives about a mile up the road. She comes over to do chores if I need her to. She loves the little guy, and it gets her some cash for school later."

"That's good."

"But she'll be graduating next year, so I was thinking about looking for a part-time ranch hand." *Oh fuck, if I blew this now— if he turned me down flat—I would never recover.* "Now that I've got a spread and all."

"Just part-time?"

"To start, maybe." I took a sip of my beer. "Of course, I've been reading about ranching. I was thinking about getting another miniature or two. Maybe some chickens. Even a cow."

"You?" His brows drew together. "A cow?"

"But I'd need a qualified helper if I did that."

"You would indeed." Cam's eyes met mine. "*City boy.*"

"Not so city I can't muck out stalls or take care of my herd." Okay, Fireball wasn't much of a herd, but I'd taken care of him just fine.

"You wouldn't know the first thing to do with a cow."

"Maybe not. But I've got time. I can learn. Or I could start with something smaller, like a goat."

Cam made a face. "Goats can be filthy, evil-tempered animals."

Wow. Note to self: ask Cam about his bad goat experience. "Or a sheep or two. I know. I could get myself a llama."

"A llama?" Cam sputtered. "You don't have the faintest idea of what you're getting into. You can't just buy farm animals willy-nilly and hope you have the right kind of environment and resources and—"

"It's pretty clear someone with some ranching experience is going to have to straighten me out, huh?"

The spark missing from Cam's blue eyes when he'd first arrived appeared like magic. "Are we talking hobby or business, 'cause let me tell you right now, you are not going to make this a viable business."

"I intend for this to be my *home*. I want to share it with some animals. And...uh...a partner. I still have my original business to run."

Thank you, Bree. Thank you, thank you.

Cam went very still. "You're going to have to say the words, Daniel."

I was ready.

In fact, as soon as I started, everything I'd been thinking

came spilling out like so much word puke. "I *love* you, Cam. I've loved you for a long time. Please don't think of this place—what I hope will be our place—as yet another way I'm throwing money around to solve a problem. It's not in St. Nacho's, but you live at the firehouse half the time anyway, and you could even keep your place there if you want. I'd take whatever you can give me.

"You have to see this place like I do—as something we can build together. It's the perfect setting for everything I want us to become. Can you believe me when I say that? Can you see us together here? Can you forgive me and make a place for me in that great big heart of yours, so I can finally, finally slow down and maybe even get some rest? Because I really, *really* don't want to be without you one more single stinking—"

"*Daniel.*" Cam stopped my mouth in the very best way possible. He pressed his lips to mine in a searing kiss that was both tender and ruthless, claiming and yielding. I barely breathed as I opened my mouth to let his tongue slide inside, and with that he swept the rest of my second thoughts, my doubts, and my fears away. He broke the kiss after what seemed like hours but was probably only a few brief seconds and exhaled a shuddering sigh.

"I love you too." Cam stood and held out his hand.

I looked at it for a long time before I took it. When I did, I knew I'd never have to let it go again. I was going to put a damned ring on it and hold on to it forever.

He pulled me to him, and I guess I surprised him by jumping up and wrapping both my arms and legs around him. He let out a shocked *oof*. He was more than strong enough to hold my weight, but the surprise of it rocked him back on his heels a little.

"Come on." He lurched awkwardly toward the front door and opened the screen to let us in. "You'll have to tell me which way."

"Turn right," I told him, directing him toward the master bedroom "At the end, last door on the right."

"You've lost weight," he remarked.

I had my face pressed into the side of his neck where I could breathe in the scent of his skin—sweat and man and a faint trace of fire. *Essence of Cam.* "You too."

"I've been working for nearly four weeks solid. I'm tapped out." He opened the door to my bedroom, and I held my breath while he glanced around. "This is nice."

"Thank you." There wasn't much to it yet, just an old iron bed and a dresser. A wonderful, colorful quilt that Ellie made for me. The mattress was new and the sheets crisp, and when he dropped me on it and crawled in beside me, he heaved a huge, tired sigh.

"I should probably take a shower."

I toyed with the hem of his T-shirt. "You could just get rid of these clothes and sleep for a while. Take your shower later."

"Would you stay?" Those blue eyes studied me.

"Of course. If that's what you want. I could use a nap." I pulled his T-shirt up and when his head popped out, he shot me a weary smile.

"I'm not going to be good for much else," he warned.

"That's all right. Rest now."

We shucked our clothes, and before I could even get up to close the shutters to darken the room, he drifted off. When I got back into bed with him, he settled, inching toward my body heat in the implacable way of sleeping men.

I wrapped my arms around him and let his legs tangle with mine until he seemed comfortable.

"Got you," I whispered against the fuzz of his hair. "Rest now. I've got you."

I held him close and felt his heartbeat against mine. I touched his skin and counted his freckles, listened to each breath like it was music.

My abominable fireman.

For the first time in months, I had hope. I had plans. I had the man I loved beside me. He'd come to me when he was exhausted and fallen asleep in my arms and everything was going to be okay.

That was as good a start as any.

Better than most.

EPILOGUE

J ake's wedding didn't take place until November.

It dawned cold and gray, blanketed by the usual fog off the ocean. Cam was working the last hour of back-to-back twenty-fours so I woke up alone and took my coffee on the porch to wait for him.

Soon enough, I heard the sound of my Ducati purring up the drive.

Cam parked right out front and took off his helmet.

"Hi." I stood. "Let me get you some coffee."

He stopped me before I could head into the house, arms banding tight around me from behind. The chill of his leather jacket gave me goose bumps. "Hey. I don't need coffee as much as I need a hug."

"Bad call?"

"No." He grinned down at me and maneuvered me against the wall. I felt his cock, hard and insistent against my thigh. "I just missed you."

We kissed our way through the door and down the hall, discarding our clothes along the way. His skin was fresh from a shower, and he was wearing a citrusy, green-smelling cologne. "You cleaned up."

"Well, it's your brother's big day."

"Not for hours yet. I plan to get you good and dirty before then."

"I'm game." He pushed me onto my back on the sheets, rolling over me and pulling me with him until I wound up on top. "Whatcha got?"

I dragged my little bag of tricks out from under his pillow and dumped its contents: lube, latex gloves, condoms, and dams. "Whatcha want."

"Surprise me." He grinned up at me like a ravished angel, golden blond and fuckable in the extreme.

"Roll over," I told him, and he complied. His skin was beautiful and firm, white where his ass never saw the sun. I nipped at his shoulder and opened the drawer by the bed. Our most recent—and best—discovery had been how much Cam enjoyed being tied to that big iron bed. I kept a drawer full of colorful scarves now for playing and tying and blindfolding him.

I couldn't imagine why I didn't see it right away. I looped the silken fabric snugly around one wrist and secured it to the post, then went around the bed to bind the other, letting the light, smooth fabric slither and slide over that massive, muscled back. I understood the impulse to bind and the beauty of shibari or kinbaku-bi—Japanese rope bondage—and I knew it would have a deeply sensual appeal for Cam as well.

Learning rope bondage was number one on my to-do list, right before building a chicken coop and exploring alpacas. Just another forward step into a future I'd never imagined I could have.

"Too tight?" I didn't want to cut off his circulation; this was for fun, after all. My own right hand was more dexterous than ever since the accident, thanks to Jordan, but it would never be like it was. Still, it stood to reason some intricate knot tying might be an excellent auxiliary therapy. I knew not to tie anything so tight I couldn't get it undone. I'd learned that the hard way, and even though Cam had shivered and gotten hard when I used a knife to cut him free, I couldn't go that far in play.

"You can pull a little tighter on my legs," Cam said helpfully.

"I have other plans for your legs today." I tapped his ass. "Knees up under. Like the child's rest pose in yoga."

"Oh." He did as I asked, and I tied two scarves together, hooked them around his knee, and pulled until I could tie the ends next to his hands on the headboard. "Whoa. What?"

"That hurt?"

"No."

"Okay, let's see if I can do that on the other side. You'll tell me if it hurts though, right?"

"Yeah." His voice was hoarse, and already his cock was hard and leaking on the sheets. After I did the same with his other leg, I rubbed his balls from behind. Ah, fuck. He was all mine. Spread and helpless and ready to beg for my tongue in his ass. "See? I've seen you do this in yoga class."

"Not trussed, you haven't. I'm not sure I'll be able to breathe." He turned his head.

"What if I put a pillow under your chest, like this."

"*Oof.*" He grunted, then grinned when what I did stretched his arms. "Oh. This has possibilities."

"You think you could get loose?"

"Uh...no." He shifted experimentally and probably discovered that the tip of his cock rubbed on the sheets just so. "Uhn. But you could get your knife again just in case."

"No way." I shuddered. "You actually liked that?"

"Only because I trust you with my life," he said quietly into the pillow. "And because I need it sometimes. That little pinch of fear and pain with my pleasure. I never did anything like that before you."

"Ah, baby." I squeezed a dab of slick out onto my fingers and rubbed it along his perineum and into the tight rosebud of his ass. "If that's what you need, I'm your guy."

I laid the latex dam down on his skin and lapped at his hole while I rubbed the smooth skin behind his balls. He squirmed pleasurably beneath my hands, making sweet, excited noises in time with the restless, noisy spring supports on the underside of the bed. The tight muscles that guard his ass gave way under my intimate assault while I stroked his cock, twisting a gentle hand over the delicate skin, rubbing the head while he hissed and groaned and bucked.

"You." He choked out the word. "I want you inside me, Daniel. Now. *Please.*"

"Bossy." I picked up a condom from the bed and fought to open it. In the end, I had to tear the foil with my teeth. I rolled the condom down the length of my cock and got more lube. Then I lined up, pressing in that first half inch, testing to see if he was ready. Despite being tied, he stretched himself and gave a mighty push back hard against me, taking me in, swallowing me in all that dark heat, and I knew that this particular extreme —the burning he probably felt just then—was exactly what he was talking about—what he needed.

"Yes." He groaned in relief as he flexed and dipped, riding my cock even though it stretched his arms until his wrists were red and his hands pale. "*Yes.*"

I took over then, pulling out and plunging back so he didn't have to stretch to get that burn, angling and pushing deep, deep, deeper still until I could feel him flat against my groin and my balls slapped his with each thrust. Until his sweat-soaked back arched, and his legs trembled, and he lost all control.

"Yes," he twisted his hands and clung to the scarves that bound him, "Yes, *please…*Daniel…*Daniel. Yes.*"

My own hands shook so I gripped his shoulders tight and kept on driving into him, giving him everything I had to give. When I felt the first deep spasms of his release clench along the length of my cock, I let go and lost myself to the sizzling heat of a deep and satisfying release. He spattered the sheets with cum, and I gasped and sobbed as heat and sticky wetness filled the condom that sheathed me.

"Baby." I collapsed onto his back, wrapping my arms around him, still inside. Still connected. I bit his back and sucked up a mark there, making him wriggle and jump a little as I laid my head down and let his fine, strong heart thud against my cheek.

"Ah...Cam. Love you so much."

"Me too, Daniel...Shit." Cam panted. "Me too."

When I would have risen to begin the process of letting him loose, he stopped me.

"No. Stay. Just for a minute." I felt his whole body rumble with an almost-purr that made me chuckle. "Just for a little."

"All right. But your hands are changing color, and I can't help but feel that's a very bad sign."

"Don't care."

"I do."

He sighed. "All right then."

"Coming out." When I grasped the condom and pulled my cock free, I heard him grunt. "Okay?"

Cam's voice was relaxed and sexy. "Oh, hell yes."

"Let me just..." I tugged at the scarves that held his knees at the knot where I'd tied them together, and they came apart, allowing him to relax one leg, and then I did the same with the other. After that I let his hands loose, rubbing them gently between mine. "No rope burns or bruises."

"Of course not. They weren't that tight." He rolled over and sighed. "I gotta climb five flights of stairs carrying like...eighty pounds of equipment at work. A little silk scarf isn't going to hurt me."

"Yeah. I know. You Tarzan, me...Wait. If you're Tarzan, what the hell does that make me?"

"You're mine," Cam said. "Just like I always knew you'd be." He put his hands behind his head and sighed contentedly.

By the time I got a towel and cleaned him up, he was sound asleep, so I pulled the sheets up around him and kissed him lightly on the forehead.

He opened one sleepy eye. "What was that for?"

"That was for perfect dreams, baby."

His full lips curved into a sweet smile. "I'm living my perfect dream."

I couldn't help kissing him again for that, but I didn't stay. I had farm chores to do. Well. I had Fireball to see to, anyway, and he could get surly if I didn't come out right after breakfast.

When I opened the door, Spot the cat sped in and took up her favorite position, tenderizing Cam's firm pecs with her paws and settling right over his beating heart. She gave me the stink eye and an indignant *meow* for locking her out of the room while we fucked.

"Yeah, yeah. You may be on top now, Spot," I told her, "but that thing thumping away underneath your ass? That's all mine."

LATER, DRESSED IN OUR MATCHING TUXEDOS AND, COURTESY OF Muse, duly covered with rainbow crocheted *kippot*, Cam and I were fully prepared to discharge our duties as best men. We stood on the beach with Jake and JT while Cooper played the violin. The afternoon had turned out sunny but not terribly warm, so the guests gathered in coats, knit hats, and an occasional scarf, which made me laugh because every time Cam caught sight of one fluttering in the gusty ocean breeze, his face burned like fire. I was willing to bet his blood was also making its way south. Mine surely was.

Of all the Cams I knew: happy Cam, sad Cam, angry Cam, working Cam, playful Cam, and so forth, the hottest by far was formalwear Cam. He was a massive living doll I would be allowed to strip and pleasure at the end of the night, and I couldn't wait. I wanted to get on my knees right there, right on the beach in front of every one of his St. Nacho's pals and peel him out of his trousers and worship him, but then the ceremony began, and I lost my chance because it's ever so déclassé to blow the best man while the rabbi is talking.

Silly rabbi, dicks are for…

Cam nudged me and whispered, "Pay attention."

The chuppah whipped around in the wind, but it held, thanks to some ingenious spikes and sandbags and children who kept it in place. The poles had been, as Mary Catherine promised, covered in vines and—in deference to the delay— brilliantly colored autumn leaves. As the ceremony took place, the sky went from blue to a dazzling orange to violet to indigo. The crescent moon shone in one part of the sky and the sun in another, as if there was some magic holding them both in the heavens at once.

Jana and Katie marched before the grooms like walking confections, scattering rose petals, which got blown all over by the breeze. Jana broke formation to gather them back and put them where she'd been told, but her mother caught her and motioned her forward and the show went on as planned.

Jake and JT observed the rituals of blessing, the unity cup, spoke their vows to one another, and gave each other plain gold bands. The rabbi spoke the seven blessings of the Sheva Brachot over a second cup of wine in her firm, clear voice, and they shared that.

For some reason, maybe just because it was natural—or it was inevitable—I caught Bree's eye and remembered what I'd said to her on our very different, nondenominational wedding day. She gazed back at me and placed her hand over the baby growing inside her. She dismissed me with a warm smile and turned toward Jim, who didn't really feel comfortable with a same-sex marriage but showed up with his game face on anyway. He clutched her hand like a lifeline.

When it came time to break the glass, JT positively crushed it beneath his foot, and everyone, Jewish or not, shouted "mazel tov" in one loud, loving voice. I had plans for that little bag of handblown glass; I'd ordered it special from a company that would take the shards and create a unique, one-of-a-kind decorative glass piece from it, something the newlyweds could enjoy for a lifetime, God willing and earthquakes aside.

Maybe I just liked the idea that something shattered could be made into something wholly new and beautiful.

Since Jake and JT had spent a solemn day fasting and praying, they observed the custom yichud. After the ceremony, they took themselves off to the tiny room at the top of the stairs at Nacho's Bar, which had been decorated by the ladies from Miss Independence pies and set up with a little champagne and a gourmet private snack. Cam and I ushered the rest of the guests into the dining room and offered a toast to the health of the newlyweds while we waited for them to join us for dinner downstairs.

"That was really something." Cam kept his hands in his pockets.

"It was. I don't think I've ever seen a prettier wedding." I couldn't help adjusting his boutonniere—just to touch him—but it wasn't really crooked or anything. He raised a knowing eyebrow.

"You just can't help yourself, can you?"

"Nope."

He took my hand and led me to a quiet place on the patio. "I didn't understand about the wedding ceremony."

"What didn't you get?"

"I didn't realize how much tradition goes into the words and the symbols."

"Tradition is important to both of them."

Cam brushed the side of my face with his knuckles. "Are you very religious?"

"No," I admitted. "But I'm not above thanking God—every single day—that I have you in my life."

"That's very nice." He pressed his lips together, and I turned to kiss his fingers. "So. You wanna do it?"

I sucked in a breath. "What? Get married?"

"Mmmhmm." Cam nudged my nose with his.

Did I? "I could. I would if it will make you happy."

"What about you? Won't it make you happy?"

I took his hands in mine. "They're only words, Cam. Words on paper. Words in legal documents. We have all that in place. Everything that's mine is yours, you hold my life in your hands if I'm injured, you have the right to shut off life support if—"

Cam pressed his fingers to my mouth. "Shh. I hate talking about that shit."

I shook his hand off. "All right. But I believe in you. I believe in us. I just don't believe in words because I know how easy it is to say and how hard it is to live."

"So then what?" Cam's blue gaze bore into me. "You don't want to be my husband?"

"I'll do anything for you. Anything. I'm just saying for me, for the first time in my life, I'm speaking with actions, not words."

"I want the actions. But I want the words, the ring, and the cake. The whole thing. I just..." Cam glanced behind me at the chaos inside the crowded bar.

"What?"

"I'd like it to be private, just between us."

"That's fine." The longer I thought about that, the better I liked it. "Better than fine. We'll have a stealth wedding."

He brightened. "Yeah. And then we can just start wearing rings and that will be that."

"We'll tell Jake we want a small cake, just for us, for something else. For…"

"New Year's." Cam's blue eyes were so happy. So full of his own brand of personal mischief.

I nodded. "Okay. All right. It's a date."

A commotion from the dining room caught our attention, and we turned to see what was happening.

"Oh, the cake." Cam had the advantage of height, so he could see it over the heads of the crowd. I had to push my way through. Jake wheeled it, all three tiers of it, in on a stable cart, and presented it to JT with a flourish.

I suspected the presence of red velvet cake beneath the thick, beautifully piped cream-colored icing. In essence, the cake itself was very simple. There were swirls and rosettes and lattice work climbing up the tiers. The top of each layer was decorated with beautiful fresh flowers.

At the very top Jake had created a tower of cartoon-like sculpted figures depicting everyone we knew: me and Cam, Lonnie and Joyce, the St. Nacho's firefighters, EMTs, and police, the Miss Independence Pies ladies, Izzie and Jordan and Ken, Minerva and Muse, Cooper and his lover Shawn—all of them stacked, one on top of another, shouldering the little fondant figures of our tuxedo-clad grooms over their heads on chairs in the traditional Jewish wedding dance. The grooms were holding hands and leaning together for a kiss. Every detail was perfect, right down to their tiny wedding rings.

"Brilliant." Mary Catherine clapped her hands. "Absolutely gorgeous. He wouldn't let me see it, and I've been dying of curiosity. She leaned over and peered at it closely. "Jake, does my butt look that big in real life?"

"It's a cartoon, MC." Jake buffeted her with his shoulder.

As soon as he saw it, JT grabbed Jake's face between his hands and brought him in for a passionate kiss. The delighted crowd went wild, clapping and whistling and egging them on. Glasses clinked together and champagne corks popped.

Pretty soon the firefighters, Andy, Al, Lonnie, and I had them up and bouncing on chairs for real, and they got the full treatment. The girls, led by MC, Joyce, and Ellie formed a circle around us. As the band played "Hava Nagila" faster and faster and the dancing grew more chaotic, I'm sure Jake and JT feared for their lives.

While I was cooling down from that, Cam took off to do the hokey pokey with one of Ellie's girls. I turned and found Minerva standing right beside me.

"Look at them go." She waved a blue cocktail napkin stamped with Jake and JT's wedding date to cool herself down.

"Yeah."

"So. Did you find out what that symbol I drew for you means?"

"I did. It means truth."

"Imagine that."

"Oddly enough, I had that very symbol tattooed on my shoulder blade a few weeks before I came to you for that reading." I glanced at her to see if she gave herself away.

She turned to me and clutched my arm. "For real?"

"Yes. And someday I *will* ferret out how you knew I had that tattoo."

"But I didn't know."

"Sure." Even though her eyes were wide with surprise, I doubted her word.

Minerva smirked at me. "I really *didn't* know about your tattoo. I took several semesters of Japanese at university, though. I drew that symbol because I knew what it meant, not because I'm actually psychic."

"The hell you say."

"The hell I *do* say."

"Well…" I admit to feeling something icy crawl up my back.

Muse and Izzie joined us to spirit Minerva away. Before Minerva let them take her, she called back over her shoulder, "If you got the tattoo before I said anything, I think that makes you the psychic one."

At that, all three of them—Muse and Minerva and Izzie—laughed, joined hands, and dived onto the dance floor together.

WHAT TO READ NEXT?

If you enjoyed Cam and Dan's story, please leave a review. The more reviews a book has, the more likely it will pop up on other readers' sales pages, meaning they'll get the opportunity to enjoy it too!

Reviews are the #1 way for you to help me keep writing the stories you love. Review The Book of Daniel today!

After you've read the entire **St. Nacho's Series,** try the first book in the brand new spinoff series, **"Men of St. Nacho's—A Much Younger Man.**

One man is older and not quite wiser. The other is young and living rough. Can they ignore the critics and let their hearts decide?

Veterinarian Linden Davies gets on better with animals than men. After a lifetime of always putting work first, he's resigned himself to one-night stands and shallow blind dates. But years of heartache evaporate when he offers a handsome young busker a free health check for his companion Labrador.

Christopher "Beck" Beckett vowed to care for his late friend's loyal dog. After falling out with his parents and ending up on the streets playing music for tips, he longs for a warm embrace and a compassionate kiss. Linden is perfect, and he takes Beck under his wing, but his hangups over a relationship with someone half his age have Beck's head spinning.

As Linden lets the sweet wayward guitarist into his world and gives him renewed purpose, he battles disapproval from his friends and family. And when Beck realizes the kindhearted vet could well be his true soulmate, he fears that their love is probably doomed.

Will this perfect match transcend the judgment of others?

A Much Younger Man is the first book in the tender The Men of St. Nacho's gay romance series. If you like heartfelt chemistry, unequal partners, and emotional rollercoasters, then you'll adore Z.A. Maxfield's poignant tale.

Buy **A Much Younger Man** to throw societal expectations out the door today!

If you like stories about tough men and hard choices, I suggest you try **The Brothers Grime Series!**

Life is full of dirty jobs. That doesn't mean you can't fall in love while doing them.

After disability ends his career as a firefighter Jack Masterson still helps people in crisis. Jack's company cleans crime scenes and biohazardous waste so victims don't have to. The job is all Jack wants or needs, until he gets the call about old flame Nick Foasberg's suicide.

Ryan only understands part of what happened between his cousin Nick and Jack Masterson in high school, but after Nick's suicide, Ryan agrees both he and Jack need closure. They decide to clean the scene together and despite the tragic circumstances, passion flares between them.

Jack is keeping a painful secret and fighting his attraction to Nick's lookalike cousin, Ryan. Ryan calls himself a magnet for lost causes and worries Jack might be the next in a long line of losers.

Jack gives Ryan something to look forward to, and Ryan gives Jack a reason to stop looking back.

Will love be enough to keep Ryan and Jack together?

ACKNOWLEDGMENTS

I could never have begun to rerelease the St. Nacho's series—and create a series spinoff—without the help of Susie Selva, who dove into the first four books to create a story bible, and then reproofed the original manuscripts.

To say this was a Herculean task is an understatement. I wrote those books, and even I couldn't keep anything straight in my head.

I have long been aware that the little town of Santo Ignacio drifts up and down the coast from book to book. I know the highways I used to get there don't actually go there, or they're the longest, most circuitous routes. If I hadn't learned the roads first hand driving my daughter up and down the coast to the University of California at Santa Cruz, I might still be utterly ignorant.

So, for the sake of continuity, I've put a pin in the map for my little fictional town. It coincides with a place that strategically and visually resembles the town I imagined. (Sorry Cayucos, but you're just irresistible!)

Also, a great big thank you to LE Franks, Morticia Knight,

Belinda McBride, and Sue Brown for being my partners in Writerly Shenanigans. For all you do to help foster an environment of commerce, cooperation, enthusiasm, and community, I love you all!

ALSO BY Z.A. MAXFIELD

Novels

Crossing Borders

Drawn Together

Family Unit

ePistols At Dawn

Gasp!

The Pharaoh's Concubine

Rhapsody For Piano And Ghost

The Long Way Home

Home the Hard Way

The St. Nacho's Series

St. Nacho's

Physical Therapy

Jacob's Ladder

The Book Of Daniel

Men of St. Nacho's Series

A Much Younger Man

A Flighty Fake Boyfriend

The Brothers Grime

Grime and Punishment

Grime Doesn't Pay

Partners in Grime

The Deep Series

Deep Desire

Deep Deception

Deep Deliverance

The Bluewater Bay Novels

Hell on Wheels

All Wheel Drive

The My Cowboy Series

My Cowboy Heart

My Heartache Cowboy

My Cowboy Homecoming

My Cowboy Promises

My Cowboy Freedom

Honky Tonk Hellion

The Stirring Series

Stirring Up Trouble

All Stirred Up

Novellas

Lights! Camera! Cupid!

Blue Fire

Fugitive Color

Through the Years

Holiday Stories

I Heard Him Exclaim

Lost And Found

Secret Light

What Child Is This?

ABOUT THE AUTHOR

Z. A. Maxfield is a fifth generation native of Los Angeles, although she now lives in the Inland Empire.

She started writing in 2006 on a dare from her children and never looked back. Pathologically disorganized, and perennially optimistic, she writes as much as she can, reads as much as she dares, and enjoys her time with family and friends.

If anyone asks her how a wife and mother of four manages to find time for a writing career, she'll answer, "It's amazing what you can do if you give up housework."

Look for ZAM on Social Media!